The Spotted Pony Casino Mystery

This series is set in and around a fictional casino on The Confederated Tribes of the Umatilla Reservation in NE Oregon. The reservation is real. I have researched, and while I've made up people and where they live, I will try to stay true to the life people live on the reservation.

The casino is modeled a little bit after the real Wildhorse Casino at the reservation. But I changed some things around. The operations of the casino in my series are all my own common sense, not a complete knowledge of how any casino is run.

Poker Face

Spotted Pony Casino Mystery
Book 1

Paty Jager
Windtree Press

This is a work of fiction, Names, characters, places, and incidents either are the product of the author's imagination or are used fictitiously, and any resemblance to actual persons living or dead, business establishments, events, or locales, is entirely coincidental.

PUBLISHING HISTORY
Published in the United States of America
ISBN 978-1-952447-81-5

Special Thanks:

To Kola Shippentower-Thompson for enlightening me about how a casino works and answering my questions about The Confederated Tribes of the Umatilla Reservation.

I'd also like to thank my group of beta readers, line editor, and proof reader. Without your input, this would not be a quality book. Thank you!

Chapter One

Dela Alvaro stood in front of a single wide mobile home older than herself. She was thankful Mimi Shumack, an elder on the Umatilla Reservation, was happy to help her look for a place to rent, but this wasn't a place Dela could settle into. The single wide trailers along this street were less than twelve feet apart. Not only would her neighbors hear when she had a bad dream or cursed her missing leg, she'd be able to hear everything that they did. Judging from the overflowing bags of cans on the one side and cardboard window coverings on the other side, the nights around here could be pretty noisy.

Not that she was home much during the night since she'd taken over as the Head of Security at the Spotted Pony Casino.

"No. This is not going to work." She headed toward her compact car as a jacked-up Ford truck came barreling down the road into the small community of mobile homes.

Something brown and gray darted into the road.

The thump, yelp, and screech of brakes were instantaneous.

Dela jogged out to the road. A large dog lay on its side, whining, as a male in his teens hopped out of the truck.

"I didn't see him! Damn dog ran in front of me!" the teenager yelled.

Dela knelt on her bad knee and studied the dog. His back leg had several compound fractures. He was bleeding a lot. "Get me something I can wrap around his leg to stop the bleeding."

The teenager ran to his truck and came back with a t-shirt. It had the logo of the local Nixyaawii Community School.

She ripped it in half and put a tourniquet on the leg. The dog whimpered and raised its head up as if to protest.

"Shhh. I'm here to help you. Just hold on long enough I can get you to a vet."

"I'm not paying no vet bill for a dog that ran out in front of me," the teenager said.

Dela glared at him. "You wouldn't have hit him if you hadn't been going so fast."

The teenager cast a glance down the road and back to her.

"Take a photo of him. While I take him to the vet, I want you to find out who he belongs to."

While the young driver had his phone out, she gave him her phone number. "Call me when you find the owner." She nodded toward her car. "Go open the back door so I can set him in."

Dela slid her arms under the dog, keeping her face away from his head, and using all the muscles in her good leg and what was left of her other leg, pushed to her feet. The dog clamped onto her upper arm. She felt the pressure of his teeth and hoped he didn't break her skin.

"He bit you!" the young man said, staring at the dog's bared teeth.

"He's in pain. Sometimes it helps to have something to bite down on." She knew how this animal felt. She'd clenched her teeth down on her dog tags as the medic tended to her wounds when her Jeep and fellow MPs had encountered a IED on a routine trip to check the perimeter of their compound at Camp Banzai.

She bent at the waist, setting the dog down in her back seat. As soon as the dog's leg had something stable underneath, it released her arm.

"Good boy." She straightened and closed the door. "Find out who he belongs to and let me know."

The teenager nodded, staring at the bloody spots on her shirt where the dog had bit her.

Dela could tell the wounds weren't severe. Her arm still ached and there would more than likely be a bruise but she didn't blame the dog. She'd been in his situation. She slid into the driver's seat and backed out of the mobile home parking space. A high school friend was now a veterinarian. She had a practice on the edge of the rez close to Pendleton.

Driving quickly, but carefully, Dela pulled into the parking lot ten minutes later. Rather than cause the dog anymore pain, she strode into the building.

The receptionist, her friend's son, looked up and smiled. "Dela, what are you doing here?"

"I have a dog in my car. He was hit. I'm pretty sure his left rear leg is toast."

He jumped up. "I'll get mom."

She nodded, staring at the photos and posters of cats and dogs for sale and to give away on the poster board.

Dr. Molly Taylor walked out of the backroom a syringe in her hand. "Where's this dog?"

"In the back seat of my car." Her heart thudded at the sight of the syringe. She pointed at it. "You're not putting him down, are you?"

"This is a sedative. We'll knock him out, get him in here, and take a look at the damage. Then we'll discuss putting him down versus fixing him." She patted Dela's shoulder. "I won't put him down unless there isn't any other option."

Dela thought of how the dog had trusted her. He had to have come from a good home. Someone would be missing him. She walked out to the car and opened the back door. The dog looked at her as Molly grasped his front leg and injected the sedative.

"We'll give him a few minutes to let that take effect." Molly motioned to her son. "Travis, keep an eye on him."

"Come back inside and tell me what you know about the dog." Molly looped her arm with Dela's and led her into the small building that smelled like animal and antiseptic.

As Molly poured them both a cup of coffee, Dela relayed the animal darting in front of the pickup and not knowing who the animal belonged to.

"There are a lot of strays around here." Molly sipped her coffee. "If you don't find the owner and have them agree to pay for an operation, I'll have to put him down."

Dela's gaze landed on her friend. "If I don't find who owns him, I'll pay for whatever you need to do."

"Are you sure? If I have to set his leg in several places it will be an extensive surgery."

Her mind went to the moment she'd been stabilized. She'd looked down at the bloody bone sticking out from her leg mid-way down her shin. She'd started to shake and the medic yelled she was going into shock. Later waking up in the hospital, her lower leg wrapped up, she'd realized she was alive. Something that few could say after their Jeep ran over an IED.

"Dela?" Molly's soft voice entered her memory. "Are you okay?"

She snapped out of the memory. "Yeah. Fine. If the leg can't be repaired, remove it. I've seen lots of three-legged dogs. Grandfather Thunder has had Three-leg for years."

Molly grinned. "I was hoping you'd say that. I'll get the dog now and you can go about looking for a place to stay." As they walked out to the car, Molly asked, "What's wrong with living with your mom?"

"She gets worried if I don't come home when she thinks I should. She is overprotective. I was in the army for seventeen years. Most of that time I was in a foreign country we were at war with. You'd think she'd realize I can take care of myself."

"Take it from me. Mothers never stop worrying." She walked up to the car and put a hand on the dog. "He's sedated. Let's get him in the operating room and take some x-rays. I'll give you a call when I know anything."

Dela patted the dog on the head. "I'll let you know what I find out as well."

Driving back toward Mission, she wished she had gotten the teenager's name and phone number. There was only one way to find him. She headed back to the area where the dog had been hit. The teenager had to have been going home or picking up someone.

♠ ♣ ♥ ♦

Frustration at not finding the young man and running late to get back to work nearly caused Dela to hit Grandfather Thunder. He stood on the side of the road a mile from his home. She'd been splitting up her shift at the casino. Going in from seven to two at night and then following up with a couple hours from nine to eleven or some days noon, depending on if the security guard schedule needed changed or security issues came up.

She slammed on the brakes and backed up to where the eighty-something Umatilla elder stood beside the road.

"Are you going home?" he asked.

"Yes. Can you give an old man a lift?" His infectious smile and nod, made her smile back.

"Yes, I can give you a lift. What are you doing so far from home?" He no longer drove, but would on occasion walk to Mission Market to purchase a cold drink and chat with anyone who would stop and talk.

"I thought I was feeling well enough to go to the market, but my bones are telling me different." He walked around to the passenger side of the car and eased down onto the seat.

When the door was closed, Dela continued on.

"Why were you driving so fast?" he asked.

"My mind was off somewhere else." She told him about the dog and how she should have taken down the teenager's phone number because she couldn't find him and he hadn't called her to let her know who owned the dog.

"Where did this happen?" Grandfather shifted in his seat to watch her.

Dela told him the area.

"Describe the dog to me."

She glanced at him. How would he know a dog over in that area of the reservation when he didn't travel any farther than the Mission Market and the casino?

"He is about forty pounds. His head is shaped like a German Shepard but his body is fuller. Mid-length brown and gray fur."

"I'm not seeing what he looks like. Do you have a photo?" Grandfather Thunder asked.

Pulling into the old man's driveway, Dela pulled out her phone. "I'll have Dr. Taylor send me a photo and I'll show it to you before I go to work."

"Good. Good. Thank you." He opened the car door and pulled himself up using the handle by the windshield.

"You're welcome. Talk to you before I leave." She and her mother had been neighbors to Silas Thunder before Dela was born and her mother started teaching at the community school. Silas was the only grandfather she'd ever known and he wasn't blood related. Her father died before he and her mother married. Dela was growing inside her mother when she applied for teaching jobs at schools all over the state. Even though it was 1986, her single mother with an illegitimate child found it hard to find a school that would employ her.

Her mom had heard Indian reservations needed teachers. She started applying, and this one, Confederated Tribes of the Umatilla, accepted her without questions. They treated Dela, a Latina Swedish mix, like she was one of them.

She texted Molly asking her to send a photo of the dog, and then drove the forty feet over to her mother's driveway.

"Where have you been?" Debra Bolden asked as Dela walked up to the porch.

"I told you I was looking at a place that Mimi Shumack told me about." She brushed by her mom and into the house. Her phone dinged. A picture of the dog appeared in the comments.

"Whose dog is that? Why is it hooked up to all those tubes?" Her mom peered over her shoulder.

"A kid hit it by the house I was looking at. I took it to Molly." She knew how the animal felt. Lying in a sterile environment, not knowing what was happening. She'd been wheeled into surgery three years ago after the doctor had told her, they'd try to save her leg, but no guarantees.

"Dela, you can't have a dog like that. He's too big. He'll knock you down." Her mom pointed to the phone.

"He's not my dog. Grandfather Thunder is helping me find his owner." She dropped her purse on the couch, wishing she could plop down and watch a movie. That wasn't happening. Not until Monday or Tuesday, her days off.

"I need to get ready for work." She headed toward the hall and her bedroom.

"Don't you need to rest before you go in? Surely, they can do without you for a few hours more?" Mom hurried down the hall behind her.

"Mom, right now things are up in the air whether the Board of Trustees will keep me on as head of security or give it to someone else. I have to work and keep things running smoothly if I want to keep it." She faced her mom and wrapped her arms around her. "I'm not your little girl anymore. I know when I'm at my limit. I had to in Iraq and Syria. I'm fine. I won't work more than I can handle. If I do, I'll be no good at my job." She released the woman who had taught her to be confident and work hard.

"I wish you weren't looking for a place to live. I like having you around." Her mom had told her the same thing before she left to look at the mobile home.

"I know. But I've been out on my own as many years as I've lived at home. I love you, but I need my space." She stepped into her room and closed the door. If only the rest of her life could be dealt with by closing a door.

Chapter Two

Rubbing the back of her neck, Dela walked into the security room of the Spotted Pony Casino. Instead of going home at two a.m., as she'd been doing since the head of the casino's security was arrested for aiding a human trafficking ring, she'd ended up spending all night due to a glitch in a bank of slot machines. After the cashier noticed a machine had paid out more than it took in three times, she'd called Dela.

Not wanting to leave the premises until the technician checked out what had caused the glitch, Dela had grabbed a couple hours of rest in a small room off the security suite.

The ear bud connected to her shoulder mic buzzed and Kay James, one of the surveillance members, voice said, "Something odd is happening on the tenth floor."

"What do you see?" she asked, heading toward the door.

"Kara is standing just outside the door of the

supply room on the tenth floor. She looks like she's seen something awful. And there is red streaked on the bottom of the wad of sheets in her arms."

Dela's gut twisted. That didn't sound good. "I'll grab Kenny and head up there. Keep an eye on things." She hurried across the casino as quickly as her swollen lower limb would allow her to travel. She'd been warned too many hours on her feet would inflame the still tender nub where her leg was amputated.

Shoving the pain and irritation to the back of her mind, she glanced toward the entrance and found Kenny. She motioned to the big Umatilla man who had moved into her second in command since she'd become the head of security.

He fell in step with her. "What's up?"

Her phone buzzed. Housekeeping. "Dela," she answered.

"Kara says there is a body in the laundry chute on ten." Mrs. Young's voice faltered as she relayed the message.

"I'm on my way." She punched the up button on the elevator, ticking off the seconds until the doors opened.

"Did I hear her say a body in the laundry chute?" Kenny asked, following her onto the elevator.

"That's what she said. From what Kay said, I have a feeling that's what we'll find."

The elevator doors opened. They made a right and a left.

Kara still stood outside the supply room.

"Give me those." Dela grabbed the sheets, avoiding getting any blood on her gold colored polo shirt and navy slacks. She set them on the housekeeping cart inside the door and walked over to the laundry chute door. The metal panel stood open. She eased her head close enough to see the bottoms of a pair of shoes, small hands, the top of a head and bloody sheets around the body. From the crew cut and loafers she'd say male, but these days, one couldn't be too sure.

Dela called housekeeping. "Make sure no one on the eleventh and twelfth floor put laundry in the chute."

"I already called up," Mrs. Young said.

"Good. Thanks. And call the tribals. We have a homicide." Dela sighed. "Have someone meet them out front and bring them up the employee elevator, please." She didn't need this just as she was trying to convince the casino Board of Trustees she was the right person to replace their discredited head of security. When Godfrey Friday was convicted as an accessory to a human trafficking ring, the board told Dela she had six months to prove she deserved the job. In the meantime, they would either be looking to hire someone to be the head or to take over as the second in command, what she had been to Godfrey.

"Do we pull him out?" Kenny asked.

"No. We need to leave him there until the police arrive." She turned to Kara. "Do you want to continue working until they arrive and take your statement, or do you want to go to the breakroom and wait?"

"Can I just…just stand here?" The woman's face had drained of color.

Dela had to remember she was one of a handful of women from the rez who had gone off to war and had seen death up close before. Especially violent death.

"Sure. Do you want Kenny to get you a chair?" As the words came out, Kenny was already headed out of the room to find one.

She hollered after him. "See if you can get a flashlight brought up." She wanted to know if this was an employee or a guest. A flashlight would be needed to see the man's face in the dark chute.

While she waited, Dela walked back over to Kara. "Did you see anything when you came up and grabbed your cart?"

The woman, nearly ten years younger than Dela shook her head. "I came in as usual, turned the light on, loaded my cart, and headed out to clean rooms. I came back to toss the trash and shove the bedding down the chute…" Her lip quivered. "When the bedding wouldn't go down, I tried shoving it. That's when I smelled something funny and pulled the sheets out. I looked in and…" She stifled a small cry. "I think I shoved him in farther."

Dela patted the woman's shoulder. "That's okay. He didn't feel anything."

Kara stared at her open-mouthed before snapping it shut and saying, "How can you say such a thing. A man is dead."

"You didn't make him any deader by shoving on him."

Kara's body made that involuntary jerk of something being rejected in the stomach.

Dela spun her into the room and leaned her over the large sink used to fill buckets.

Her friend lost what was left of her breakfast into the sink.

Dela turned on the faucet washing it down the drain. She grabbed a wash cloth off a shelf and handed it to her friend. "Use this."

"What's wrong with her?" Kenny asked, handing Dela a flashlight.

"Shock caught up with her. Help her out to the chair." Dela walked over to the chute, turned on the beam of the flashlight, and shined it down into the hole.

There was no way to see his face with the body folded in half and wedged into the chute. All she could tell was his general build. He was a smaller framed man. His shoe looked about the same length as her size eight.

She pulled out her phone and dialed their head of surveillance.

"Hey, what's up?" Marty Casper asked.

"Pull up the video footage from the hall outside of the supply room on the tenth floor from midnight until this morning when Kara is standing in front of the door looking terrified. I want to know how a body was put in the laundry chute and no one on duty saw it."

"I'll get right on it."

The line went silent. She glanced at her watch. It had been about ten minutes since Mrs. Young called the tribal police. The idea of a homicide on the reservation should get them moving faster. Especially one at the Confederated Tribes of the Umatilla's largest employee and money-making enterprise.

Since the Casino opened, half of the tribal members had been employed at the casino. Not only did it supply jobs, the profits were used to build the community, adding new businesses, cultural buildings, and improving roads and schools.

The casino had helped the Confederated Tribes of Umatilla progress with the times and live a better life.

"How long do you think it will take the police?"

Kenny asked, breaking into Dela's thoughts.

"I would think they'd be showing up any time. Why don't you get a list of the people staying on this floor last night? If they are still around, I'd like to find out if they heard or saw anything." Dela had participated in murder investigations as part of the military police during her years in the Army. She'd planned to make it a career and retire after thirty years. However, an IED had shortened her career plans. Months of recovery and rehab had her cooped up on base until her discharge papers came through. From there she came back home to live with her mom.

Dela walked out of the supply room to check on Kara. "How are you doing?"

"Better. Am I going to get paid for sitting here? If not, I need to get back to work."

"You're fine. You'll get paid. I'll make sure payroll doesn't dock you." While she didn't have any authority over in payroll, she did know the person who cut the checks, and she'd make sure no one docked Kara's pay.

The service elevator dinged, the door whooshed open, and Detective Dick stepped out followed by a tribal officer who was the reservation coroner. Dick wasn't the detective's name. It was what Dela and a couple others called him. His real name was Detective Richard Jones. But he always talked down to the Umatilla people as if because he was white and a detective, he was superior.

"How do you know this is a homicide?" he asked, walking up to Dela, his eyes on Kara.

The five-eight, bald headed man in his fifties had only one thing going for him, he was one of the few white officers on the tribal police who didn't carry around an extra forty or more pounds.

"I doubt he accidentally fell ass first into the laundry chute. And no one, even someone wanting to end their life, would jam themselves in there as a way to commit suicide. Not to mention the blood." Dela led him into the supply room and pointed to the chute.

Dick stuck his head in the opening and peered down. "Got a light?"

Dela handed him her flashlight.

He shone the light down for several minutes before pulling his head out and waving to the hole. "Get several photos, then we'll pull him out."

Dick stepped back and the tribal officer held a camera in the opening, clicking and flashing light down the hole. The officer pulled his camera out of the opening, set it on a stack of sheets on the rack, and grabbed an arm and a leg.

The officer pulled and tugged, but the body wasn't coming loose.

"Let me do this." Dick shoved the officer, who was shorter than him, out of the way and grabbed into the chute, pulling on the victim's feet.

Kenny returned with the list of guests still at the casino.

"Would you help Detective D-Jones pull the body out?"

The security guard's eyes sparkled at her near slip of the tongue. He walked over, grabbed a hand and foot, and motioned for the detective to do the same. After back-and-forth tugging, the body popped out of the opening. They laid him down face up.

"That's Tristan Pomroy from accounting."

Chapter Three

Dela grabbed her ringing cell phone as the tribal coroner handed Detective Dick his observations. Glancing at the name she sighed. Her mom.

"Hi Mom. Not a good time to talk," she answered.

"Sorry. I was worried because you didn't come home last night." The reproach in her mother's voice made Dela's eyes roll. This was why she was looking for a place to move into. On the reservation, but far enough from her mom that she didn't know her every move.

"We had an emergency. I don't know when I'll be home. Don't worry about me."

"You can't keep putting in these long hours," her mother said.

"We'll talk about this later." Dela hung up on her mom and spied Kara, Kenny, and Detective Dick all watching her.

"That's not good to hang up on your mom like that," Kenny said.

She glanced at Kara, hoping for a little help.

"He's right," Kara said. "You should respect your elders."

Dela wanted to say, I'm not Native like you two and I do respect her, but she doesn't respect I'm thirty-seven and can take care of myself. But she didn't say a word. Not with Detective Dick giving her a smug smile as if he thought her mother calling her at work was funny. After dismissing Kara, she asked Dick, "Where's the body going?"

"Waiting for the wagon to pick it up and take it to Clackamas. The State Medical Examiner."

She nodded. That would be the best facility to check it out. She wondered at the lack of blood in the room. When the body had been unfolded it was apparent Tristan had been stabbed in the neck. Blood covered his neck and right shoulder. The carotid artery had been severed, given the amount of blood on everything. Yet, there was no sign of blood anywhere in the room. It was as if the body had been folded and shoved in the chute then the wound inflicted. No mess, no fuss, just getting the job done. Which didn't make any sense at all. How would you fold a man in half without him fighting you?

Footsteps in the hallway drew all of their gazes toward the door.

FBI Special Agent Quinn Pierce stepped into the already full room. He stood by the door studying the body before he raised his gaze and locked on her. "What happened?"

Detective Dick held out his hand. "Special Agent Pierce, you must have got the call."

Quinn shook hands with the tribal detective but his

gaze remained on her.

"One of the casino employees was stabbed and shoved in the laundry chute," she said, ignoring the glare Dick shot her way.

"Which area did he work in?" Quinn asked.

"Accounting. Tristan Pomroy." She glanced at the body. She didn't know him well. He had a wife and child, she thought.

Quinn pulled out a notepad and wrote. He shifted his attention on the detective. "Was the coroner able to give a time of death?"

"The best he could say given the shape of the body, sometime after midnight."

Dela's phone buzzed. She glanced at the number. Marty. She walked by the body and the two men out into the hall. "What did you find?"

"Someone turned off the camera from midnight until two."

"Double frickin' shit!" she swore under her breath. "Why didn't someone see that?"

"I'll check into who was watching that camera and get back to you." The line went silent.

She muttered the same words again.

"What's wrong?" Quinn asked, stepping out of the room.

"Someone turned off the camera in this area from midnight to two this morning." She didn't like the idea they had another criminal working for the casino. With eight hundred employees there was always a good chance someone who worked here could be approached to do something illegal for monetary gain. But she didn't like the thought. She knew most of the employees. It came with being head of security.

"That means it was most likely someone who works in the surveillance department." He stared into her eyes. "You ready to take on something like this so soon after the last problem?"

"I have to be, if I want to keep my job." She shook off her dread and gave him her best business face. "Did you learn anything of value from Detective D-Jones."

Quinn chuckled. "You really need to use his real name in your head before he realizes what you think of him."

"Oh, he knows." She flashed a smug smile.

"Take me down to accounting. I want to talk to the people our victim worked with."

She glanced at the supply room. "One second." She walked back in and nodded for Kenny to come to her.

When he stood close, she whispered, "Once the detective leaves, start interviewing all the guests on this floor. But don't leave until the body is gone and the detective leaves."

Kenny nodded and went back over to stand guard over the body.

Dela joined Quinn out in the hallway. "Are you going to interview the guests?"

"I figure you have that handled. Less rumors if your staff does that."

"Thank you. The less hotel guests know about this the better." She walked over to the employee elevator and punched the down button.

"How you holding up?" Quinn asked.

Her gaze shot to his face. He looked like he really wanted to know. She didn't want to like the man. He'd let a rapist go free in Iraq. One that was her prisoner. A man who had spit on her when she'd arrested him for raping a young Iraqi woman. She'd harbored a dislike of, then Lieutenant Quinn Pierce, for many years. When he ended up the Special Agent in charge of the FBI Field Station in Pendleton, Oregon, she'd thought the gods were against her. Now, staring into his eyes, she realized he might be on her side. He'd proven it a month ago when Mimi Shumack's son, an Oregon State Trooper, had shoved himself into an investigation to find Sherry Dale a missing Umatilla woman. Quinn had followed Trooper Hawke's leads and together, the three of them, had found Sherry and brought down a human trafficking ring.

The elevator doors opened. Dela stepped in. Quinn followed. She punched the button for the bottom floor.

"Why did you stay?"

He faced her. "You mean in Pendleton?"

"Yeah. After bringing down that trafficking ring, I'm sure you could have had your choice of assignments. Why here?"

He shrugged. "I like the laid-back environment and helping the Umatilla people." His gaze drifted from her face down her body and back up. "And I like working with you."

Her chest hitched for a second. She knew better then to let his words influence her feelings about him. He had worked intelligence. You couldn't believe a word intelligence officers said.

The elevator hit the end of the cable, sprung up a little, and settled. The doors opened and she hurried out. Crossing through the breakroom, she fielded questions about the laundry chute and moved as quickly as she could without limping into the hall near the accounting office.

She opened the door and asked the secretary to call the compliance officer and whoever worked with Tristan Pomroy to the front. Dela and Quinn stood inside the door as two people walked into the front office.

Her phone rang. Molly. "I'll be right back," she said to Quinn and the others, before stepping out into the hallway.

"Hi. How's the dog?" she asked, wanting to get the conversation over quickly to get back to work.

"Hello to you. Grandfather Thunder called and said he found the owner, but they don't want anything to do with the dog. They can't afford to pay his bills or feed him. What do you want me to do?"

"Can you save the leg?" she asked as Quinn poked his head out.

His eyes widened.

"Just a minute," she told Molly. "I'll only be a couple of minutes. Can you wait to ask questions until I get back in there?"

He nodded and disappeared.

"No. The leg was smashed. I can amputate this morning. He'll need to stay here about a week to keep him sedated so he doesn't move around too much, but then you'll have to take him off my hands."

She sighed. "I'm still at work from last night, and I don't see getting over to your clinic until tomorrow. Is that soon enough to settle up and find out what I need for his recovery?"

"That's fine. See you tomorrow." Molly ended the call.

She wanted to sit down and figure out how she could bring a dog her mother thought was too large into her home and help it with rehab when she had a job that required so much of her attention. Especially now, after finding a body in the laundry chute.

Dela reentered the office.

The compliance officer was the first to speak. "Does this have to do with Tristan not showing up for work today?" She was an older Umatilla member. Brenda started when the casino first opened. She had moved from the gift shop to this position.

Dela took the lead knowing the casino employees would look more favorably on her asking questions than the outsider FBI agent.

"Yes. Can you tell me when you each saw him last?" Out of the corner of her eye, she watched Quinn pull out a notepad.

Brenda started. "He left here his usual time last night. Shortly after six."

The secretary nodded.

"Did he say anything about where he was going?" Dela asked.

"He left his usual time. I figured he was going home. What happened?" Brenda let her gaze pass over to Quinn and back to Dela.

"Someone killed him last night and dumped his body on the tenth floor." Dela watched each person. While they looked shocked, they didn't appear overly disturbed by the announcement. "Anyone know why he would have been back here last night?"

The two women shook their heads. The only male, Luis Page, looked thoughtful. He was in his early thirties, the last hire in this department.

Dela zeroed in on him. "Did Tristan tell you about coming back here last night?"

He shook his head. "No, he didn't say anything about coming back to the casino. But he'd been antsy all week. When I asked him about it, he said he was coming into some money." He shrugged. "Maybe he came back to gamble and get rich?"

The women twittered then stopped when she and Quinn stared at them.

"What would be funny about Tristan getting rich from gambling?" Dela asked.

Nicole, the secretary and the only non-Indian in the room besides Dela and Quinn, glanced at the other accounting employees and said, "When one of us talked about spending time on the floor gambling, Tristan would tell us it was bad for the casino to see the people in charge of the funds gambling. It could make others think we were using the casino money to gamble."

Dela studied each one. "He accused you of using the money you counted to gamble?" She knew the surveillance team would have notified her if any of these employees were shoving money into the machines or playing at the gaming tables. They had attended concerts and social gatherings, but they weren't habitual gamblers. They kept track of that in security and surveillance.

"Not so much as accusing as just a warning to not do it," Nicole said.

The others bobbed their heads.

"Okay. Then," she studied Luis. "What more can you tell me about his being 'antsy' all week?"

The man shrugged. "He seemed to be having trouble focusing on his ledgers. I caught him tabbing out of something on the internet when I walked by to get some coffee."

Dela pounced on that. "Show me his computer."

The women parted. She and Quinn followed Luis into the rooms behind the secretary's desk. He opened a door to a room with two computers.

"That one is Tristan's." He pointed to the one closest to the door.

Quinn slid in the chair behind the desk and started tapping keys. "It's locked." He glanced over at Luis. "Do you know his login?"

"No. We don't know each other's logins. Better security that way." Luis shrugged, again.

"What did he talk about other than work?" Dela asked.

"He was always watching True Crime shows. He'd come in all excited about something he saw on the TV. Tell me how some woman killed her husband slowly with a poison and then would have gotten off if she hadn't done something dumb." He shrugged. "I didn't listen all that much to what he said. I prefer video games and movies over True Crime."

Quinn started unplugging the computer. "I'll take this back to the field office and see if I can get a tech to get into it."

"Ummm. No." Dela stepped over and took control of the computer. "That has numbers and clients on it that doesn't go outside of this casino. I'll take it to Wallace in I.T. to give it a try."

"I'm only doing my job." Quinn crossed his arms, looking so much like the lieutenant who released a rapist that she scowled.

"I'm doing my job. Protecting the casino's interests. We'll take care of this in house. I'll give you copies of the websites he searched that didn't relate to his work." She wasn't about to give up the computer as easily as she had the prisoner. Then she was outranked. Here they were equal. The F.B.I. might be higher ranking than her status as head of security, but he couldn't take the computer unless he got a subpoena.

"If you think of anything else, you know where to find me," she said to Luis as she packed the computer out of the office.

Quinn was on her heels, opening the doors. When they stepped out of the office area, he held out his hands.

"Let me carry that for you."

She peered into his eyes. "I want it to go to security, not out to your vehicle."

"Yes, ma'am. This is your turf. I won't do anything to undermine your job." He grasped the computer.

She didn't want to give it up, but at the same time, her stub burned and ached from being shoved in the prosthesis for more hours than normal. Relinquishing the modem, she said, "This doesn't mean I believe you won't undermine me if it benefits you."

"I'll keep that in mind." He grinned at her, walking alongside of her over to the door that led to the I.T. offices.

He stopped one step back from the door and blocked her opening it. "What was that call about saving a leg?" His gaze dropped to her feet. "I thought you were limping but I didn't know it was that bad."

She wasn't about to tell him she wasn't a whole woman. He might think she couldn't do her job, like so many others. "I found a dog that had been hit by a car yesterday. I took it to the vet. She can't save it's leg."

"Oh. That makes more sense. Glad to hear you

aren't having problems." He moved away from the door and she opened it.

The way her leg felt right now she was going to have a hard time not limping in front of him. She didn't want him to know she hadn't come out of the army unscathed.

Chapter Four

"What did you bring me?" Wallace asked when they walked into the I.T. room. It had computers running the casino and pieces of slot machines strewn about work benches.

"This is Tristan Pomroy's computer."

"I heard what happened. Sorry to hear about it." Wallace wasn't your typical computer geek. He also didn't look like someone who would have deep emotions. The large Umatilla man had a round face that rarely had a smile. Talking to him, he seemed to have a motherboard in his head. He could answer any question that had to do with computers or anything electronic.

"Yeah. Not a good thing for the casino." Dela nodded to the computer, Quinn placed on the desk in front of Wallace. "Luis said Tristan had been looking something up online one day this week and hid it when Luis questioned him. Think you can get in and see what his browsing history has to tell us?" Dela took a seat, giving her stub a break by propping her foot on a box.

"I can try. It depends on how hard he wanted to keep people out of his computer as to how soon I can get in." He glanced up at Quinn and back at her. "You should probably follow another lead while I do this."

Her phone buzzed. Marty's name flashed on the screen.

"What have you found?" she answered.

"I've pulled video together from views of the guest and service elevators starting at midnight. I think you'll want to come take a look."

"We'll be right there." She smiled at Wallace and stood, wishing she could have remained in that position for a while longer. "Marty is providing us with entertainment. Give me a call when you get it open."

"Will do."

When they stepped out into the casino to walk over to surveillance, Quinn asked, "What has Marty found?"

"He's pulled up the footage on the guest and service elevators."

"I'm impressed." Quinn waited as Dela tapped her ID card on the lock box and the door to surveillance opened.

They crossed through the large room filled with walls of monitors and into Marty's office.

"I have the feeds for both elevators synchronized," Marty said when the entered.

Dela pulled out a chair and propped her foot on a box, Marty kept under his table just for this purpose.

"Good thinking about the service elevator," Quinn said, pulling a chair up on the other side of Marty.

On two monitors the service and guest elevators appeared.

Dela noticed that Marty also had the live feed from outside the supply room on floor ten rolling on another monitor. The only problem with each one watching a monitor, they didn't have control over fast forwarding the video.

Dela kept her gaze on the guest elevator. Couples, groups, and singles entered the elevator. At a quarter to one the victim punched the elevator button, getting on with a middle-aged couple. "There. Can you see if he goes to the tenth floor?"

Marty directed his attention to the keyboard. "All I can do is pull up all the cameras at elevators on every floor at this time." Six small frames appeared on two monitors above Dela.

She studied the small frames and pointed. "There that one. What floor is it?"

"Ten." Marty made the image enlarge. The victim disappeared from that camera. "He walked down the hall where the camera was disabled from midnight to two."

"At least the time frame is definitely between one and two," Quinn said. "I saw several employees get on the service elevator between midnight and one. Can you see where they all got off?"

Marty began his magic on the keyboard and up popped all the service elevators on each floor in small frames on two monitors.

Dela studied the frames. Two busboys took food up to rooms. A concierge delivered towels on another floor. A maintenance man got off on the eighth floor. "Why was he on the eighth floor? I didn't hear of any mechanical problems."

Marty made the frame larger. "That's Van

Branson."

Dela shoved to her feet, even though she was enjoying the break of sitting down. "I'll go check the logs for last night and see what he went up there to repair."

"What would someone from accounting have to do with someone from maintenance?" Marty asked.

"Probably nothing. But I didn't hear of any trouble on that floor last night." Dela walked to the door. Quinn appeared in front of her to open the door.

She scowled at him and walked through slowly to hide any limp.

On the way through the main room, she asked, "Everything look normal?"

"Except the activity on the tenth floor," Kay said. "Kenny has been going door to door."

"That's what I asked him to do." She didn't understand why that would raise a flag.

"He's being tailed by Detective Jones. Who seems to get people upset from their expressions."

"Double frickin' shit," she muttered and picked up her pace. Her anger overrode her desire to not let Quinn see her disability.

He stayed with her step for step. "You want me to go get rid of Detective Jones while you check on the maintenance records?"

She stopped, glared at him, and opened her mouth.

He raised a hand. "Don't swear at me. I'm only expediting things by us splitting up. It has nothing to do with Detective Jones not listening to you or the fact you've been up all night."

"Like hell it doesn't. You wouldn't have brought it up if it didn't matter." She swore under her breath and continued to the elevator. She punched the up button so hard her finger hurt, but she didn't say a word. In her head she was reaming out both the detective and the special agent.

Quinn stepped in as she pressed the door close button and then 10.

"Dela, I'm not here to undermine you. I'm here to help you catch a killer. I have more resources at my disposal than you or the tribal police."

"Then go to your office and dig up all the background you can on our victim, not follow me around like you think I can't do my job. During my time in the army, I worked several homicides. I know what I'm doing."

"I didn't say you didn't." Air whooshed out of him and he rubbed a hand over his handsome face. "Can you just work this case with me without busting my balls for something I did seven years ago?"

The elevator dinged and the doors opened. She stepped out. "Are you going to override my decisions?"

"Only if you make a bad one." He stared her in the eyes as they stood in the hallway.

"I won't, so there shouldn't be a problem." She headed down the hall and found the unlikely duo of Kenny and Detective Dick walking toward them.

She stopped in front of the detective. "We are capable of gathering information and not worrying the guests, Detective Jones."

"I have a job to do," he said, glaring back at her.

"No," she waved between her and Quinn, "we have a job to do. I need to keep this as low key as possible to avoid guests leaving, and Special Agent Quinn has the resources to help us discover who did this faster than the tribal police. I will need your help though in piecing together where the victim went when he left here after work and came back at one P.M."

Detective Dick studied her. "You think you can handle a homicide?"

"I helped find Sherry Dale and Meela Skylark as well as discovered my boss was helping a human trafficking ring that was going on under the nose of the tribal police, so yes, I think I can handle this investigation."

The detective's face grew red and he huffed.

"We can deal with this, Detective," Quinn said. He nodded toward the elevators and followed the tribal detective onto the conveyance.

Dela faced Kenny. "Did you learn anything?"

"The couple staying at the end of the hall thought they heard the door to the fire stairs open and close around one-fifteen." Kenny said.

"The stairs! We looked at the elevators. I need to go down to maintenance and ask about a problem on floor eight."

"I've finished questioning the people who were here last night. Want me to come with you?" Kenny asked.

She shrugged. "You're better company than Special Agent Pierce." *But not nearly as good to look at*. She shocked herself with the thought. There had been a time, before Quinn had taken away her prisoner, when she'd thought the two of them could be friends, possibly with benefits, but not anymore. He just made her mad when she talked to him.

Entering the service elevator with Kenny, she asked, "What do you know about Van Branson, one of the maintenance people?"

"He started here about nine months ago. Does a good job according to Clarence. Why?"

"He's the maintenance person who made a call on the eighth floor about the time Tristan was killed on the tenth." She stepped out when the elevator doors opened. Her leg throbbed, but she chose to ignore it and placed her foot as easily as she could, putting more weight on the good leg.

"You need to sit down for a while," Kenny said.

"After I talk to Van. I can sit while I drive to talk to Tristan's wife."

Kenny shook his head. "You can't keep working and not resting. You'll be no good to anyone and make mistakes which will leave us without you as the boss."

She stopped and stared at him. "All of you would like me to be the boss?"

He grinned. "You are so wrapped up in helping everyone, you don't see how much they all think of you. Yes, we all want you for our head of security."

The thought her peers wanted her to take over this job permanently boosted her spirits. "Thank you. That means a lot."

They walked into the large room that smelled of grease, paint thinner, and strong coffee. There were various gadgets and pieces of décor being worked on around the area. She walked by the half a dozen men and two women working on the items on her way to the room where the head of maintenance kept the building maintained and scheduled the workers.

"Dela and Kenny, what are you two doing back here?" Albert Simple, an Umatilla man in his fifties, asked. Like Brenda in accounting, the man had started as a maintenance man when the casino first opened and was now in charge of that area of the casino.

"We were wondering why Van Branson went up to the eighth-floor last night around one?" Dela asked.

Albert flipped back a page on a logbook on his desk. "Says room eight-thirty-four had a plugged toilet." He studied them both. "You've never come in and asked about a maintenance call before."

"We had a man killed on the tenth floor around the same time. We were checking the elevator footage and saw the two events happened close together." Dela glanced over her shoulder. "When will Van be coming in to work today? I'd like to ask him if he saw or heard anything."

"He works the night shift. He won't be in until eleven." The man smiled. "Glad to hear you are just asking him questions and not suspecting him. Van's a good worker. Keeps to himself, but he is knowledgeable in everything."

"Thanks Albert." Dela smiled at the man and headed back through the workroom. When they were out in the hallway she said, "You go up and see about the plugged toilet in eight-thirty-four. I'll round up the special agent and go talk to Mrs. Pomroy."

Chapter Five

Dela kept telling herself the only reason she'd asked Quinn to come along to talk to the wife was so he would drive and she could rest her leg. After realizing she'd been staring at the man who hadn't said a word since they'd left the casino, she averted her gaze and clenched her hands to keep from rubbing her missing leg that ached. They'd told her in the hospital it would be years and possibly her lifetime that her body would think her leg was still there. Right now, it felt like her leg from her knee down was on fire.

"You haven't said a word other than drive you to see the wife. What's up?" Quinn glanced her direction as he eased off the freeway and down into Pendleton.

She didn't say anything, afraid his kindness would make her lips loosen and tell him more than she wanted him to know.

"Are you still mad that I'm shoving my way into your investigation? You know the reservation is federal land, which means Federal Bureau of Investigation will be involved."

She didn't want him to pull the card he should be the one in charge, so she cleared her throat and said, "I haven't had a full eight hours of sleep since Tuesday. I really don't want to argue about anything. I just want to sit here and get ready to question Mrs. Pomroy. Did you happen to dig up anything about her?"

"Didn't realize you were working two people's shift. When will they make the decision you are head of security?"

She stared at him. "What makes you think they aren't looking for a head of security?"

He laughed. "You don't play the martyr well. You are more than qualified for the job and you know it. They would be idiots to not make you head of security."

His compliment meant a lot, but she wasn't going to let him know. "The Board of Trustee's words to me were: We will be looking for either a replacement for you or a replacement for Godfrey. If you prove you deserve head of security in the next six months, it's yours." She held up her hands. "And now I have a homicide on my hands which could cause bad publicity for the casino."

"We'll figure it out and not cause the casino any bad publicity." He pulled into a driveway of one of the homes in a newer subdivision in town.

She stared at the house. If only she could find something like this on the reservation. There were some new homes but they were, again, too close to one another for her comfort. She sighed. "What do I need to know before we go in?"

"Paula Pomroy has been married to Tristan for five years. They have a small child, a son, and she works part time at a store downtown."

"Then she may not be here?"

"This is her day off." Quinn opened his door and slid out.

Dela heaved a sigh, opened her door, and stood. She hoped her tiredness didn't keep her from asking the correct questions.

Her phone beeped. A text message.

The dog came through surgery like a champ. Will fill you in when I see you.

Thanks.

She smiled. The dog had made it. Her mood brightened and she walked up to the front door with Quinn, feeling a bit more optimistic.

Quinn pushed the doorbell and they waited.

A baby cried then went silent.

Quinn glanced at her then pushed the doorbell again.

The door opened.

"I'm here, you woke the baby." A woman in her thirties, brown hair, about five-five and a hundred and thirty pounds glared at them.

"Mrs. Tristan Pomroy?" Quinn asked, holding up his badge.

The woman stared at his badge then at Dela.

She didn't have a badge. Instead, she held out her hand. "I'm Dela Alvaro with the casino security. May we come in and talk with you?"

"S-sure." The woman backed up allowing them to enter the house.

Dela led the way into a living room that still

smelled of wood and new paint. The furniture appeared as new as the house. There was no way to avoid what they'd come to tell the woman.

"Have a seat, Mrs. Pomroy," Quinn said.

The woman glanced from one to the other then sat down in a chair. Dela took the couch and Quinn sat beside her.

"I'm sorry to tell you that your husband, Tristan, was found murdered this morning." Dela started to reach out to pat the woman's hand.

Paula Pomroy recoiled. "I told him working on that reservation wasn't good. Who did it? Was it one of them?"

"Them who?" Quinn asked as casually as if they were talking about the weather.

Dela's anger started to build. The woman was talking about the people she'd grown up around and respected like family.

"You know. The Indians. He said there were some really lazy ones and some sneaky ones that he worked with. Tristan must have seen something he shouldn't and they killed him." The woman believed what she was saying.

"I can guarantee you that he wasn't killed by a co-worker," Dela said, barely restraining the anger from her words.

The woman peered into her eyes. "You're one of them so you would say that."

"Do you mean a co-worker or an Umatilla Tribe member?" she asked coolly.

"Both."

Quinn put a hand on Dela's arm stopping her next words. "Ms. Alvaro is the head of security at the casino.

However, she is not a tribal member. Meaning, you are wrong about her. She is here to find out who killed your husband. How has he been acting lately?"

"Excited. Like he had a secret he wanted to tell but didn't want to ruin the surprise." She sniffed and pulled two tissues out of a box sitting on the table next to her chair.

"Any idea what the secret was?" Quinn asked.

"It could have been anything. We have an anniversary coming up." Her eyes teared up. "Had an anniversary."

"Did he get excited about things often?" Dela asked, not wanting Quinn to do all the questioning.

"At least once a month when he'd think he'd seen someone wanted in a crime." The woman blew her nose.

"What was an accountant doing thinking he'd seen a criminal?" Quinn asked.

"He liked to watch the real crime shows and movies. He was always thinking he saw someone in a store that looked like a person on a wanted poster." She rolled her eyes. "At least he didn't go out drinking and watch football all day long."

"What day did he start acting excited?" Dela asked. If they could pinpoint what show he'd watched, maybe he had found a real criminal hiding here in Pendleton, Oregon. Had he reached out to the person first, and they killed him to remain anonymous?

"I don't know. Last week sometime? He said we'd be able to spend our anniversary where we wanted to go for our honeymoon."

"Where was that?" Dela asked.

"The Caribbean. I've always wanted to go there."

"Did your husband have an office here at home?" Quinn asked.

"Yes. Well, it's more of a den. I didn't like watching the crime shows." Mrs. Pomroy stood and led them out of the living room and back to the entry where she opened a door to a man cave.

The room was the same size as the living room but one wall held bookcases. In the middle of the bookcases hung a large flat screen television. A recliner was directly in front of the tv against the opposite wall. A small desk with a laptop set against the wall opposite the door.

"May we see if we can discover what shows your husband watched?" Quinn asked.

Dela liked how friendly he'd been to the woman.

Mrs. Pomroy nodded. With her consent, they didn't need to get a warrant which could get this brought up in the news.

While Quinn messed with the television remote, Dela scanned the books in the book cases. Most were about true crime and murder investigations. Some dealt with forensics. She moved to the desk and found printed out pages from several websites with information about wanted criminals. In a drawer was a list of four names. One name was Jeff Twigg, a dealer at the casino. The other three she didn't know but took a photo of the paper.

"What did you find?" Quinn asked, his breath hot on her neck.

She held up the paper. "The top name is a dealer at the Spotted Pony."

Shoving the papers around, she said. "He was definitely into ratting out criminals. He has printouts on several here."

"I think I've figured out which crime shows he watched the most. I'll get a tech to watch the episodes from the first of last week and see what pops up." Quinn touched her arm. "Ready to go?"

Dela pulled out a drawer in the desk. A ledger caught her eye. "You wouldn't think he'd be this old school." She pulled the book out and scanned the list of numbers and letters. "What do you think this is? I know it's not his income from work. And he doesn't show paying any bills from it."

"Let's ask the wife." Quinn plucked the book from her and walked out of the room.

Dela only fumed for a second before following him. The nerve of the man taking over the evidence she'd found. If it had been up to him, they would have walked out of the room and never found the book.

She entered the living room as Quinn held the book out to the woman.

"Do you know what the information in here means?" he asked.

The woman's eyes widened as if she recognized the book.

"No, I have no idea what this is. Where did you find it?" She studied the page.

"It was in the drawer of the desk," Dela said, walking farther into the room. "The expression on your face when Special Agent Pierce showed it to you, proves you know what it is."

The woman shook her head. "No. I haven't a clue what it is. Maybe household expenses? Tristan kept track of all our money."

Dela drew the book out of the woman's grasp and

took a photo of the page before returning it to the woman. "If you can think of anything else that may help us catch your husband's killer, please give me or Special Agent Pierce a call." She wiggled her fingers for Quinn to hand her one of his business cards. On the back she wrote her name and cell number.

"Yes, call either of us at any time if you think of something." Quinn snatched the card from Dela and handed it to Mrs. Pomroy.

They walked out of the house and slid into the car.

"I take it head of security at a casino doesn't get a perk of a business card?" Quinn asked, a grin on his face as he started the car and backed out of the driveway.

"I'm not head of security, yet. And no, we don't really have anyone who we normally ask to call us." Dela flipped back and forth between the photos she took. "I think our mild-mannered true crime enthusiast was blackmailing."

"Why do you say that?" Quinn asked, driving them out of the subdivision.

"The letters on the ledger page match the initials of the people on the list." She glanced over at him.

"Or, being as he deals with money, maybe he gave out loans?"

Dela peered out the window. "Where are we going?"

"I'm hungry. Thought we'd grab lunch." Quinn was driving through a neighborhood with older homes.

"As far as I know, there isn't a restaurant in this area." She tromped on her panic with a dose of reassurance her gut was rarely wrong about a person. While she still held Quinn responsible for an injustice, she knew he would never hurt her. That he might dig into her thoughts and find out things she hadn't told anyone… that's what worried her.

"I'm not abducting you. It will be quieter and you can put your foot up at my place. And I can make phone calls without someone eavesdropping."

Quiet did sound good. But his place… That she wasn't too sure of.

Until he pulled up to an 1800s two-story home with a turret front.

"This house is gorgeous!" She sat in the car staring at the home. It needed some TLC but the bones of it looked like a storybook house.

She hadn't realized how long she'd been ogling the house until the door opened and Quinn offered her a hand. Dela slapped his hand away and shoved out of the car. "Are you buying or renting?" She noticed a ladder up against the side of the house.

"Bought it. I figured might as well put my money into an investment and live here while I'm fixing it up." The pride in his voice told her he loved the house.

"That's what I'm hoping."

"You're looking for a house? Where do you live now?" He unlocked the front door, and they stepped into a large entryway. Off to one side was a room that had to be the parlor. The other side had a sheet up across the doorway.

"What's through there?" she asked, pointing.

"I'm working on that room at the moment. The turret windows were leaking and the floor needs replaced. It's a mess."

She stepped around him and swept the sheet to the side. "Oh! This would be my favorite room." The turret windows looked out into an overrun yard and flowerbeds. She took a step inside the room, wary of the flooring that had been pulled up. "So this is what you do when you aren't FBIing."

Quinn chuckled. "Yeah, I like fixing up houses."

"I think you picked a good one here to keep you busy." She glanced up at him. The wishful smile and far-off gaze had her wondering what he was thinking about.

Her stomach grumbled. "Where's that lunch you promised me?"

"In the kitchen." He held the sheet back and she stepped through, waiting for Quinn to lead the way to the kitchen.

The room was at the back of the house. The counters hit Quinn mid-thigh.

"It looks like you need to remodel the kitchen," Dela said, taking a seat at the round wood table with four matching chairs. She shifted her body to place her right leg on the chair next to her.

"Yeah, whoever this house was built for must have had a short wife." He opened the fridge and pulled out a pitcher of orange juice. "This okay?"

"Yeah."

He poured two glasses and left the pitcher in the middle of the table. "I can whip up a salad or I have sandwich stuff." He peered at her from over the refrigerator door.

"Sandwich fixings are easier. I'm not here to be impressed." Though she was impressed by the house he had purchased and was renovating and the fact he had salad and sandwich ingredients that were fresh enough to serve to a guest.

He placed bread, meat, cheese, and condiments on the table. Then he set the head of lettuce on the table. "If you want some in your sandwich." He pulled his phone out of his suit pocket. "I need to make this call. Help yourself."

Dela nodded, reaching for the bread. But her ears were focused on the conversation.

"Special Agent Tucker, this is Pierce in Pendleton."

She spread mustard on her sandwich and picked up the turkey.

"Yes, I should have asked for your help in the human trafficking ring. But in all fairness, it was running through Seattle and not Portland."

She grinned. Sounded like he was getting reamed for not letting his Portland counterparts in on the action.

"What I need is a technician to take a look at the true crime shows that ran the first of last week and send me the names and photos of the suspects in those shows."

She layered the turkey, added a slice of cheese, and then a leaf of lettuce.

"Because we have a homicide on the reservation and the victim was a true crime buff."
Frustration seeped into his voice.

Dela winced as she moved her leg and pain shot all the way down to non-existent toes.

"Yes, we are looking at other angles. This is just one."

Picking up her sandwich, she caught a glimpse in the kitchen window above the sink as Quinn walked back into the room. He looked as worn out as she felt.

He took off his suit coat, hung it on the back of a

chair across the table from her, and sat down. He rolled up his shirt sleeves.

"The agent in Portland thinks you're crazy?" She smiled and bit into her sandwich.

"Doesn't know how I could have brought down a trafficking ring when I think a man was killed for watching true crime shows." He gave her half a grin and started making a sandwich.

Her phone rang. She pulled it out of her pocket. Mom.

"Hi, Mom," she answered with more enthusiasm than she felt.

"You need to come home and get some sleep. You were at that casino all night. How can you heal if you don't rest?"

Quinn's eyebrows rose.

"Mom. I'll be home when I can. We had a homicide at the casino. As head of security, it is my duty to help solve it. You may not see me for a few days. I'm going to stay in a room at the casino so I can grab sleep when I have an hour or two."

"What about clothes and food? And Silas asked me about the dog. He thinks he's found the owner and wants to talk to you."

"I'll give him a call when I get the chance. Molly told me about the dog. I'll swing by and get some clothes in a couple hours. I want to check in with Molly, too. Don't worry. I'm a grown woman."

"A bullheaded woman who doesn't realize your body is compromised."

Dela closed her eyes and counted to ten. "Mom. You are the only one who believes that. Good-bye."

Hitting the end button gave her satisfaction. Then

guilt. She knew her mom only wanted what was best for her. However, mom didn't have to live with the realization that if she allowed people to treat her differently, she could end up as helpless as they treated her.

Quinn cleared his throat.

She peered across the table at him.

"Mom problems?" he asked.

"More like life problems. I am trying to find a place to move to so my mom doesn't know what I'm doing every single minute of every day. It's suffocating after being on my own for so long." She bit into her sandwich and chewed.

"There are half a dozen places like this in town." He cut the sandwich he'd made in half crosswise.

"That's the problem. I want to be on the rez. Closer to the casino, and it's my home. It's where I grew up and where I want to be." She shrugged.

His eyes narrowed. "I thought you weren't Native American."

"I'm not, but I wish I were. It's what I grew up around and feel comfortable with." She swallowed juice. "There aren't very many houses for sale or rentals that aren't five feet away from another one. I like my space."

He nodded. "Besides the architecture, that's what I liked about this place. The neighbors aren't butted right up to my eaves."

"I could probably live with my neighbors the distance yours are. But nothing closer. I don't like to know their business and I don't like them knowing mine."

He stared at her and laughed. "And you think

you'll get that living on the reservation?"

She laughed. "Yeah, I know."

"Do you really plan to stay at the casino until we figure out who killed the victim?" He bit into his sandwich and studied her.

"Yeah. It's easier than running back and forth to my mom's house if I can crash for a couple of hours." She finished the sandwich and pulled out her phone. "Do you mind stopping at the vet clinic in Riverside and then my mom's on our way back to the casino?"

"I think we can take the time. We're waiting on forensics and information anyway." He started cleaning up the table.

Dela dialed Grandfather Thunder.

"Hello?" he answered.

"Hi, it's Dela. Mom said you found the owners of the dog."

"Yeah, I did. Otis Deerstalker. He said he hasn't been able to keep the dog home since he got it. Doesn't want to pay the vet bill and doesn't want the dog back."

"I see." She felt bad for the dog. "Did he say how old the dog is or what its name is?"

"Yeah, he thinks he's about eight months and his name is Eats a Lot."

Eight months and Eats a Lot? That meant it was going to get a lot bigger. "Any idea what kind of dog?"

"He just said a mutt. What you going to do?" Grandfather Thunder asked.

"The dog has had his leg amputated. I'm paying the bill, so I guess he's my dog now." She wasn't sure how she felt about having to take care of a dog when she was still trying to find a home for herself. But she felt a kinship to the animal.

"It's how it should be. I've been asking around about a place for you to live." Grandfather Thunder sounded pleased with himself.

"How did you know I was looking?" She thought it was only her mother and now Molly and Quinn who knew she was looking for a place.

"Your mother told me. Well, she complained to me that you wanted to move out." He chuckled. "I told her, how were you supposed to catch a man if you lived at home with her."

"Grandfather!" she exclaimed. "That is not the reason—"

He cut her off. "It is what made your mother more accepting of the idea."

"Thank you for that and the information about the dog. I have to get back to work."

"I heard. You had a body at the hotel."

She didn't even ask how he knew. "Yes. Thank you." She ended the call and found Quinn watching her. "What?"

"You don't have a house but you have a dog?" He slid his arms into his suit jacket.

"It's a long story."

"Which you can tell me on the way to Riverside. Why are we stopping there?"

"To see the vet and my dog, Eats a Lot."

Chapter Six

"I'll make phone calls while you check on the dog," Quinn said as he parked at the vet clinic.

"I won't be long." She slid out and walked up the ramp into the small building. The sounds of a dog whining and a printer printing filled her ears as she opened the door. The smell of antiseptic and fear stopped her forward motion. Until she'd served in Iraq and Syria, she hadn't believed an emotion could have a scent. It did. And it was one she would never forget and always triggered a need to protect herself.

"Dela. Mom said you'd be coming by."

The friendly voice reminded her she wasn't in a dangerous situation. With a shake, she focused on Travis.

He watched her from behind the counter and the keyboard he was typing on.

"I wanted an update on the dog. Well, Eats a Lot."

"Seriously? You named him that?" Travis stood.

"I didn't. It's what his previous owners called him." The wide grin and mischief in the young man's eyes were contagious. She grinned back at him. "What do you think I should call a pony-sized dog?"

"King Kong. Goliath. Godzilla."

"Funny. He's too cuddly looking to be any of those names."

"How about Teddy Bear?" Travis motioned to the backroom. "Do you want to see him?"

She followed the young man back into a room with half a dozen cages. The largest one on the floor held her dog.

He whimpered. Dela knelt in front of the cage and put her fingers through one of the squares.

His tail thumped and he licked her fingers. Her chest expanded with pride that she'd helped this animal.

"I see you and the dog have bonded already," Molly said from behind her.

Using the cage, Dela shoved to her feet. "According to Grandfather Thunder, he is now my dog. The owner doesn't want him. His name is Eats a Lot and he's only eight months old."

"I figured he wasn't a year old yet. He's going to grow some more. Are you ready to handle a dog the size of a horse?" Molly led her over to a counter where there was a file laid out.

"I think he'll train easily. He'll have to realize we are both disabled and act accordingly." Dela had had a good feeling about the animal ever since it looked at her after she'd put him in her car.

"We'll be keeping him for a week. That way he stays down, and we can clean and bandage the stub. I left about eight inches on the leg. This type of amputation causes less trauma to the bone."

Dela nodded. She knew all about leg amputations. "Thank you for taking such good care of him. Is there anything he needs that you can't provide?"

"It would help if you could bring in some food and maybe a chew toy?"

"I can do that. I'll try to bring it in tomorrow."

"We heard about the body at the casino," Molly said.

Dela stared at her. "How does this get around so quickly?"

Molly laughed. "Because a relative of nearly everyone on the rez works at the casino."

"Maybe you can find out if anyone had a problem with Tristan Pomroy who worked in accounting." Dela said it as a joke but the look on her friend's face said she would ask around.

"Are you ready?" Quinn walked into the room with Travis a step behind him.

Molly's face lit up. "Dela, where have you been keeping this guy?"

Embarrassed by her friend's outright ogling, she said. "Dr. Molly Taylor meet FBI Special Agent Quinn Peirce. We're working the homicide together."

"Lucky you." Molly held out her hand. "Pleased to meet you Special Agent."

Quinn grinned. "The pleasure is mine. Where's this dog that isn't Dela's dog, but is her dog?"

Molly laughed and pointed to Eats a Lot's cage.

Quinn studied the animal and then stared at Dela. "That's not a dog, it's a horse. Do you think you can handle him?"

Tired of everyone telling her that the dog was too

big for her, Dela glared at him. "I'm getting tired of people telling me about the limits they think I have. He's perfect for me. Let's get going."

She stomped to the door, mostly on the good foot, and faced the room. "Molly, I'll be back tomorrow with the food and settle the bill." A thought came to her. "Otis said he couldn't keep the dog home. Is he fixed?"

Molly winked. "He is now. And I gave him a microchip in case he takes off after you get him home."

"Thanks." She nodded toward the door, staring at Quinn. "I thought you were in a hurry?" Dela continued out through the reception area and to the car, where she slid into the passenger side and waited for Quinn.

He slid in behind the steering wheel and started the vehicle. "I didn't mean you couldn't handle the dog. It's going to be a big animal to feed and keep under control for anyone. I thought it was going to be a lap dog."

"Don't mention the size of the dog to my mom. All she saw was a picture and told me I shouldn't keep him."

"I don't know where you live." He backed out of the clinic parking area and faced Mission Road.

"Turn left and keep going until I tell you to turn." She leaned her head back on the seat to rest.

"Don't fall asleep. I don't know where I'm going," Quinn said.

"I'm not. I'm just resting my eyes. Tell me when we pass Mission Market." She dropped into oblivion.

"Dela, I just passed the market."

Quinn's words confused her. They were sitting on a rock on a mountain. Their backpacks were beside them. Why would he be talking about the market?

Her body swayed.

"Wake up. Hey. You told me to tell you when we passed the market."

She shook awake, even though her eyes didn't want to stay open. "Take the third road to the left and follow it to the end." She dropped off again.

♠ ♣ ♥ ♦

A car door slammed and her body shook.

"Dela? Dela, wake up," Quinn's voice filtered through her slumber.

"Oh no! What happened? Is she hurt?"

Her mother's raised voice, snapped Dela's eyelids open. Mom stood in the open car door, leaning over her.

"Dela, honey, are you hurt?" Mom picked up one of her hands and patted it.

"Mrs. Alvaro—"

"It's Ms. Bolden. Who are you?" her mom asked.

"Special Agent Quinn Pierce. I'm working with your daughter on the homicide at the casino."

Dela drew in a deep breath and sat up. It had been several years since she'd been so tired she'd fallen that deep asleep in a blink of an eye. "I'm fine. I'm here to get some clothes and get back to the casino."

She stood, wobbled a moment, and had both her mom and Quinn grabbing for her. She shoved away their hands and walked toward the house.

"Is she always this surly when she wakes up?" Quinn asked.

Dela wanted to flip him off but just kept walking. Her mother hadn't seen the hardened soldier side of her and Dela didn't plan on revealing it to the woman who gave her a life.

She left her mother and Quinn conversing in the living room while she found a duffel bag and tossed in a pair of pajamas, toiletries, a couple sets of clothes, liner liners, liners, socks, a prosthetic sleeve, and her running foot into the bag. She didn't plan on staying there too long. If they were lucky the leads from Pomroy's computer would help them find his killer. Unless it was a random killing, which she doubted.

Entering the living room, she found Quinn looking through a photo album. Dela crossed the room and tore it from his grasp. "What are you doing looking at that?"

"Learning more about you." He grinned. "You looked cute in pigtails. You should try them out as an adult."

"In your fantasies. Let's go."

Mom entered the room with glasses of iced tea and cookies.

"This isn't a social visit, Mom. We have a killer to catch." Dela stood by the door, holding her duffle bag as the other two grabbed glasses of tea and leaned back in their respective chairs.

"Sit down. I'm sure you could wake up a bit more before we get back to the casino," Quinn said, between sipping his iced tea and nibbling on an oatmeal cookie.

Sighing, she set the duffel bag by the door and sank onto the other chair. Her mom smiled and handed her a glass of tea.

"Have you found a place to move to yet?" her mom asked.

Dela started to roll her eyes and though better of it. The action would only make her look the age her mother treated her. "No. I haven't had time since we found a body at the casino."

"You know you don't have to move out. I enjoy your company." Mom glanced at Quinn. "I bet if you could live with your mom, you would."

He choked on a bite of cookie.

Dela grinned behind her drink. "Yeah, Quinn, would you live with your mom if you could?"

His blue-gray eyes turned the coldest she'd ever seen. "I would not live with my mother. But then she wasn't much of a mother."

Dela found this information about his past interesting. She'd have to see if she could round up information about Special Agent Quinn Pierce.

"I'm ready to go if you are." Dela downed the rest of her drink and picked up three cookies as she stood.

Her mom remained sitting, watching Quinn.

He stood and strode to the door, picking up the duffel bag. "It was nice meeting you," he said before continuing out the door.

"I like him," Mom said, finally standing and walking to the door with her.

"He's good to have on your side, I guess. I'll call you when I'm coming home. I can't promise when that will be."

"I know. You want the head of security job and finding the killer could get it for you. But I worry. It's my job." Tears glistened in her eyes.

"I know. Even if it frustrates me, it's nice to know someone cares." She gave her mom a one-armed hug and headed out to the vehicle.

Quinn sat behind the wheel, his sunglasses on, and face forward.

Dela slid in, buckled up, and waited until he had the vehicle headed toward the casino to say anything.

"We all have things in our past we are running from. Don't let it make you lose track of who you really are."

He glanced over at her. "It's something I tell few people."

"Then my mom and I are honored you told us. It won't be repeated by either of us." She pulled out her phone and called Marty. "We're on our way back. Anything new pop up?"

"Kenny said no one in eight-thirty-four called for a maintenance man. I've pulled the video of the stairway for our time frame and guess what?"

"Those cameras weren't working either." This was starting to irritate her. Who turned off the cameras?

"Correct."

"Who on the staff watched those cameras last night?"

Chapter Seven

At two in the afternoon, Dela couldn't stand on her prosthesis any longer and her eyes wouldn't stay open. She retired to a second-floor room at the end of the hall. As soon as she entered the room, she took off the layers that held her prosthesis on and cushioned the end of her leg. Her stub was red, swollen, and aching. She had been warned that wearing the fake leg for long periods of time could result in tenderness. This was the longest she'd not rested the stub since wearing the prosthesis eighteen months ago.

Using the furniture, she made her way to the bathroom, ran a bath of lukewarm water, and undressed, lowering her body into the water. She wished she'd thought to grab some Epsom salts to add to the bath. She'd have to grab some from the gift shop before she came back up next time.

She leaned her head back against the tub as she swirled her stump around in the cooling water.

The list of people she needed to talk to on the night shift was growing. Jeff Twigg, the Blackjack dealer, Verna Pyle, the surveillance member watching the monitor for the missing camera footage, and she'd learned one of the other names in the victim's book was a local who frequented the casino, Luke Saxton. And they, she and Quinn, planned to visit with Van Branson.

The water had grown cold. She shivered and grasped the handicap bar. Using both arms and one leg, she raised her body and swung the shorter leg over the edge of the tub, then her good leg and sat on the edge as she dried off. The eighteen months she'd spent in rehab had been not only to make sure her leg had healed but to teach her new ways to go about things she'd always taken for granted.

Before the IED, she'd had her sights on twenty years in the army, and after the army, a job with either the local or state police, and a loving husband and children. Now all she saw in her future was head of security for the casino until they made her retire. And if she didn't get out of mom's house, living with her mom until she passed. Not an inviting future to look forward to.

Once she was dried off, she slipped into a camisole and her underwear and hopped to the bed, using the furniture. At home she used crutches to get around without her prosthesis. Dela hadn't wanted to carry them into the casino. She never let anyone see her weaknesses.

Slipping between the covers, she set her watch for four hours. By then Quinn should have pulled up backgrounds on the people they planned to question tonight.

♠ ♣ ♥ ♦

Dela walked into the surveillance offices at 7 PM. Her stomach was rumbling, but she wanted to see if Quinn and Marty had learned anything new.

She stepped into the backroom, and Quinn glanced up. "You look better."

"Thanks, I didn't know I had to look good to do my job." She walked over to a chair.

"Don't sit. I'm hungry. I'll fill you in over dinner." Quinn rose, gathering up a file that had been spread across the table in front of him.

"Okay." She faced Marty. "Will all your night shift be here tonight?"

"No one has called in sick."

"Good. Go get something to eat and take a break. We'll start the questioning with Jeff when we finish dinner, then Van when he comes to work, and finally Verna. Can you think of anyone else?"

"No. I think those are the only people we know of who work here." Marty leaned back in his chair and stretched his arms up to the ceiling.

"Quinn and I will pull Jeff away from his table after we eat. I'll just close it until we finish talking to him."

Quinn stood at the door waiting. She walked over and out the door he'd opened for her.

Several heads turned and watched them cross through the room. She didn't care. The surveillance staff on duty knew they were trying to figure out who killed Tristan.

On the casino floor, she spotted the security staff working the floor. They were either in a specified spot watching or mingling through the crowd, looking for potential trouble. She and Godfrey had trained every member of the staff. Dela was proud of the quality of people they had working for them.

"You want the buffet or the dining room?" Quinn asked.

"Actually, I'd prefer the grill." She didn't like the buffet. Walking along trying to balance a plate as she reached under the sneeze guards to grab food wasn't how she like to get her meal when dining out. The fancy food they made at the Stallion Restaurant didn't fill her.

"The grill it is."

They crossed the casino floor dodging people and slot machines. At the entrance to the Pony Bar and Grill, the hostess on duty smiled at Dela. "A table or booth?"

The tables were high, and while she liked sitting up high, they weren't a good idea.

"Booth please."

"We have one in the back of the room. It's quieter there." The hostess smiled at Quinn and led them to a booth in the corner. "Cherry will be right over with water and menus."

Dela nodded at the woman and stayed seated at the edge of the booth while Quinn slid all the way in on his side. She reached over for the file and pulled it in front of her. "Did anything pop out at you about any of the people we're going to talk to?"

Cherry arrived with two glasses of water, two menus, and a bubbly personality. "Hi! Can I get you anything to drink besides water?"

Quinn ordered iced tea. Dela asked for coffee. She would need to be fully awake when questioning the people tonight.

"I'll be right back with your drinks and get your order," Cherry said, before spinning around and bouncing back to the kitchen.

"I wish I had her energy," Dela muttered and opened the file.

"You could have slept longer," Quinn said.

She glanced up. He watched her with a softness in his gray-blue eyes that unnerved her. Dela dropped her gaze to the file. "This isn't very much on Branson. He practically didn't exist before three years ago." She glanced up. "That's suspicious."

"That's what I thought."

Cherry returned with the drinks. "What would you like from the grill?"

Dela ordered a hamburger, thick fries, and a salad. Quinn went for a club sandwich and fries.

"Those will be out in a jiffy." Cherry smiled at them both and flounced away.

"As far as I can tell, Jeff and our victim didn't have anything in common other than they both work here." Quinn sipped his tea.

"And this Luke Saxton. Did you find anything that connects him to Tristan?" Dela read through the sheet on him.

"No. The staff on duty tonight have orders to keep an eye on him if he comes in." Quinn set his glass down and peered at Dela. "I don't know how long this can stay quiet. Everyone at the casino knows there was a murder here last night. And from what we heard as we were out and about, so does everyone on the reservation. When do you think you'll get a call from the board?"

"Either tonight or tomorrow morning for sure. That's why I want to talk to as many people as we can tonight and see if we can piece anything together." She leaned back as Cherry arrived with their food.

"Do you need anything else? More drinks? Ketchup? Ranch?"

"We're good. Thanks." Dela picked up a fry and savored the saltiness.

"Okay. Enjoy!"

"She is way too perky," Quinn said, when the woman was out of hearing.

Dela chuckled. "Glad it wasn't just me."

They dug into their food, saying little until the last fry and crumb of bread were gone.

Dela was reading the information Quinn dug up on Verna, one of the surveillance staff. "This looks like what we have on file on Verna. I don't understand why she didn't notice the cameras out on ten last night."

"That's why we pull her in and talk to her. Find out why she was negligent." Quinn shoved his plate to the center of the table. "What's the plan?"

"We start with Jeff, move on to Verna, and when Van arrives, we talk to him. In the meantime, let's visit with the guards and see if they noticed Tristan hanging around the casino after his day was done. There has to be a reason he has Jeff and Luke's names in his book next to dollar amounts." That thought had been in her head when her phone woke her. The victim had to hang out at the casino after his work hours to have run into the two men on his list that they had identified.

"That makes sense. We could have Marty check the floor footage from a week prior to the victim's death and see if he was around here." Quinn downed the last of his iced tea.

Dela knew one person besides the guards who would know if Tristan frequented the casino in the evenings. She grinned. Actually, two people who were very observant.

"What are you smiling about?" Quinn asked right before Cherry swooped in and picked up their plates.

"Would either of you like some dessert? We have a delicious brownie tower tonight."

Dela didn't quite hide her desire for the dessert.

"We'll take one tower and two forks," Quinn said. When Cherry left, he asked, "What is a brownie tower? I could tell by the way your eyes lit up it must be pretty good."

"It's a chocolate brownie, blondie, and chocolate chip cookie bar stacked up with vanilla ice cream in between layers and caramel drizzled over the top." Her mouth watered thinking about it. A lot of calories when she wouldn't have time to jog for several days. However, the sugar might give her some short spurt energy.

"I'm not much of a chocolate eater, but the blondie and caramel sauce sounds good." Quinn leaned back as Cherry placed the tower of bar cookies in the middle of the table.

"Enjoy!" she said, placing the ticket at the end of the table.

Dela snagged the ticket.

"Hey, I invited you to dinner. Besides, I can call it an expense." He plucked the paper from her hand and tucked it into an inside pocket of his suit.

She glared at him but cut a corner off the brownie and popped it into her mouth. There was nothing better to drown any fears, doubts, or apprehensions than chocolate.

Quinn worked on the blondie. "You were interrupted when you were going to tell me what you were smiling about." He raised an eyebrow and peered at her with a bite on his fork.

"We happen to have two casino employees who know or see nearly everyone who comes into the casino. If it hadn't been such a struggle for people their age to have received a college education, they would probably be scholars right now rather than working here."

"And who are these two you're talking about?"

"Rosie, at the coffee shop. She's never met a male she didn't like." Dela loved how the woman made men uncomfortable by her forwardness. Dela could never be that forward. She could be bossy and knew how to motivate men and women, but the outright flirting Rosie did was something Dela enjoyed to watch and not participate in.

"I see. And this makes her scholarly how?" Quinn's forehead under his light brown crew cut was furrowed.

"She can remember every face and name that goes with the face. Also, just about word for word what someone tells her."

"And the other person?" Quinn asked, pulling another bite from the blondie and swirling it in the sauce.

"Arthur, the night valet. He sees everything and remembers everyone. He's better than surveillance cameras." She scooped up a bite of chocolate chip cookie and slipped it in her mouth.

"Trooper Hawke was impressed with him when we were working the human trafficking case. He always went to the valet to ask questions." He picked at the blondie.

"Hawke understood where the people were who knew what was going on. He's a good trooper. He should be a detective. I wonder why he hasn't been promoted?" She pondered that. She would have loved to have visited with the Oregon State Trooper after he'd brought home two of their missing women and helped take down a human trafficking ring. But he and his friend, Dani Singer, an ex-air force pilot, left as soon as they'd finished eating spaghetti with Dela and his mom after Meela Skylark was returned home. While his mom, Mimi Shumack, had been calling her once a week with suggestions on places she could rent, she hadn't thought to ask when her son would be back.

"He could easily be FBI material if he wasn't in his fifties. But I also agree, they are missing out not making him a detective." Quinn shoved the rest of the dessert over in front of her. "Finish that up, and I'll go pay the bill."

She nodded, trying not to let him see how happy it made her to finish off the tower of goodness.

Cherry swept by. "Would you like more coffee?" she asked, as she filled Dela's cup.

"Actually, could you put this in a to-go cup? I need to get back to work."

"Sure. I bet you are really busy since a body was found in the laundry chute." The woman said it a bit too loud for Dela's liking.

"Keep your voice down. This isn't gossip to be spreading," she said in a voice just above a whisper.

"Oh. Right. Sorry." The young woman didn't act as if she'd been reprimanded as she hurried away from the booth.

It made Dela wonder if the waitress had been telling everyone she served about the body. That was all she needed, customers of the casino thinking they could be the next fatality.

Quinn sat back down on his side of the booth. This time he didn't slide over and his foot hit her fake foot, jarring her leg.

Dela tried to hide a wince.

"All that chocolate getting to you?" he asked, studying her.

"Yeah, I think it was too much. I haven't eaten a lot of sweets lately." She swung her legs to the end of the booth to stand.

Cherry arrived with the to-go cup. "I just filled a cup. Have a good night."

Dela took the cup from the waitress and stood, using the table to help her push to her feet. A glance at Quinn caught him with his brow furrowed again. She didn't know what he was thinking about, but she wanted to get busy questioning people. "Come on. Let's go talk to Jeff."

Chapter Eight

Before walking over to the Black Jack table Jeff Twigg manned, Dela made a detour over to the entrance and Arthur. The night valet was in his sixties. His two long braids were laced with gray and draped down the front of his snap western shirt.

"Dela, you've been putting in too many hours since Godfrey left us." Arthur greeted her.

"That I have and they aren't going to get any shorter with the body found on the tenth floor this morning."

He nodded. "Hello Special Agent Pierce. Didn't think I'd be seeing you so soon."

"Me either," Quinn responded.

"Can you tell us if Tristan Pomroy spent any time on the casino floor after work?" Dela asked, knowing that Arthur had a keen eye and memory.

"He did. But he wasn't gambling. He'd wander around the gaming tables and sit at slot machines near the tables. But I don't think I ever saw him put a dime in a slot." Arthur rubbed a hand across the back of his neck. "He was always watching people. He had a little book he carried with him that he would write things down in."

Dela glanced at Quinn. They hadn't found a small book with the body, at his desk, or at his home. She wondered if it could have fallen down the laundry chute. Another place to check out this evening. "Thank you, Arthur. If you can think of anything else, let me know." Dela turned to head to the gaming area.

"His wife was here last night."

She spun back around. "You know his wife by sight?"

"The two of them came here a couple times for concerts and to have dinner in the Stallion once." Arthur nodded. "But she came in by herself around eleven. I hadn't seen Tristan all night. I was surprised to see her alone."

"Thank you." Quinn grasped Dela's elbow, leading her away from the entrance. "It seems the wife forgot to tell us she was here last night."

"I wonder why? Maybe because she had something to do with her husband's death?" Dela wanted to confront the woman with their information but they had other suspects right here that needed to be questioned.

"We'll catch up to her in the morning," Quinn said.

Dela nodded and walked up to the Black Jack table. "Finish this hand and then this table will be closed for thirty minutes," Dela said to Jeff, the dealer.

He nodded but his hands shook as he called out the cards and dealt to the players who asked for another card. When the hand was over, he paid the winners, scooped in the loser's money, and tossed a cloth over the table, putting a sign, "Be back in 15" on top.

Quinn walked over next to the man. "Let's take a little walk to the security offices."

"I don't understand why you want to talk to me," Jeff said, walking between them. His forehead glistened with perspiration.

"We just have a few questions we'd like answered," Dela said as Quinn held the door for them both to enter.

They walked through the main office, where Tammie Rhoda sat monitoring employees coming and going, and into the smaller interview room.

Dela found the photos of Tristan's ledger and the list of names on her phone and showed them to Jeff. "We were wondering why your name and initials, with money next to them, were in a book belonging to Tristan Pomroy who was killed last night."

Jeff's hands were clasped on the table in front of him. He stared at his hands, not even glancing at her phone. "I don't know. He would come in at night and watch us dealers. It made all of us a bit jumpy when he was around. We thought he was watching us for you."

"No. I just learned of this behavior tonight." Dela could tell he was holding something back.

"What did he have on you?" Quinn asked.

The dealer's head snapped up as he stared at Quinn. "He didn't have anything."

"I'm not so sure. Your name. Your initials. Money. He had something and was blackmailing you. That's a pretty good motive to kill him." Quinn leaned back in his chair.

Dela wasn't feeling so calm. This was her mess,

but Quinn had more experience interrogating suspects. It was what he'd specialized in for the marines and now the federal government.

"We have him watching you, putting your name in his little book…"

The perspiration on the man's head was dripping down the sides of his face. He swiped at it with a hand.

"You know about the little book. The one he kept all his blackmail information in." Quinn leaned closer. "Information that was worth killing him for."

"I didn't kill him. I'm glad he's dead, but I didn't kill him. I worked all last night. I only took my usual break at nine and that was it. You can ask Brie. She filled in for me last night. She only filled in the one time." Jeff was offering up his alibi, but not confessing to anything.

Dela had to find out if he was a crooked dealer. That was the only thing she could think Tristan would have on the man. If he was, he needed to be fired. She pulled out her phone and texted Marty.

I need as much footage as you can get where I can see Jeff Twigg dealing. Also, any footage of Tristan Pomroy hanging around the gaming tables and his wife arriving last night around eleven.

Ok.

"Finish tonight. If I discover you've been shorting the house, there is no need for you to come back to work tomorrow." She stood.

Quinn stood, but he had a puzzled expression.

Jeff nodded and sprinted out of the room.

"You think Pomroy noticed he was shorting the house?"

"That's the only thing I can think of that Tristan

would notice watching Jeff work his table." Dela sighed. "I hate how when you dig up one bad thing there seem to be roots that have spread throughout the building."

"Like the human trafficking ring we broke up," he said, holding the door for her.

"Yeah." She straightened her back and walked over to the door that entered the bowels of the casino. What could Jeff have been doing that caused Tristan to blackmail him? And the others. Who could they be and why? As these thoughts flit through her mind, she navigated the hallway leading to I.T., the laundry, maintenance, and breakroom.

"You think someone found the book in the laundry chute?" Quinn asked.

"We can hope." She entered the large room with four huge commercial washers and dryers. A small crew was on duty through the night washing bedding and towels that didn't get finished during the day. To make sure there would be enough for housekeeping in the morning.

"Dela, what brings you back here?" Crystal, an Umatilla woman in her forties, asked. Her gaze landed on Quinn and she smiled bigger. "And who is your handsome friend?"

"Crystal, this is Special Agent Pierce with the FBI. We're investigating the death on ten last night." Dela wasn't going to let Quinn use his charms on the woman. Not when she and Crystal had always had a good relationship. In school and out.

"That was terrible. See these stacks of dirty sheets? We're still working on what should have been done during the day." She waved to the piles of sheets and towels still in need of laundering.

"Did anyone happen to come across a book in the sheets that came out of the chute for floor ten?" Dela wandered over to the large rolling metal basket below one of the chute openings.

"It would have been this chute here." Crystal walked over to the basket under the opening to Dela's right. "We have four floors per chute. This is the nine, ten, eleven, and twelve."

Quinn stepped by Dela and started moving and shaking each sheet and towel in that basket before he tossed it into the closest basket. He went all the way to the bottom.

"Nothing." He scanned the area. "Do you have a lost and found where items are put that might end up down here with the bedding?"

"Everything we find goes to security. I don't think anything was handed in today." She marched over to the small office and opened a book. "Nothing has been turned in since Sunday."

Dela pulled out her phone and put it to notes. "Can you give me the names of the people who worked in here today?"

Crystal nodded to the door. "I don't know for sure who was here today. You'll have to ask personnel."

"Everyone that is in here right now worked last night?" Quinn asked.

The woman glanced around the room. "Yeah. We're the same crew minus Mattie. She called in. Her cousin is sick and she couldn't come to work."

Dela glanced at Quinn. "Did you see or hear anything unusual last night?" she asked the laundry supervisor.

"No. the baskets were half empty, as usual, we finished washing the bedding and towels, ironed and folded the sheets, and loaded up the carts for each floor. Same as we do every night." Crystal glanced over at a worker. "Stella, put that phone away and get to work." She mumbled. "I don't know why you can't make it mandatory that cell phones have to stay in their lockers."

Dealers had to leave their phones in their lockers. It might be a good idea to ask the same of all the employees. "I'll check on that."

"Thanks!" Crystal said.

"Let's talk to Stella first." Quinn verbalized her thoughts.

Dela nodded.

They walked over to the woman who appeared to be nineteen or twenty. Her short hair had a red section. It could be a symbol of a family member who was missing or had been murdered. Red, the color for strength, had become the symbol of the MMIP- Missing and Murdered Indigenous People movement across the U.S. at all reservations. Too many women, children, and even some men, had become victims of murder, human trafficking, and hate crimes with the local authorities not taking their disappearances as serious as they should. The vast wilderness of some of the reservations and the lack of family in urban cities also made it hard to find people who went missing.

"Stella," Dela started. "Did you see or hear anything different last night when you were at work?"

The young woman looked up from her phone. "Is this about the man who was shoved into the laundry chute? How big was he? How did he fit?"

When her gaze drifted back to her phone, Quinn snatched it out of her hand. "This is an FBI investigation. We need your full attention and cooperation."

Stella glared at him but shifted her attention to Dela. "Not really. I mean, all the laundry from the chutes had already been dropped down when we came on duty. We fill a basket with a washer load from one of the large baskets, roll it over to a washing machine, shove it in, start the machine, and go back to folding until the load needs transferred to the dryer then we go grab another load for a washer."

"Do you each have an assigned chute or washer?" Dela asked.

"Not really, we just come in and start working on one of the large baskets, but usually stay with the same one all night." She nodded to the large industrial ironing system that resembled a large pasta rolling machine. "Only Crystal, Jeri, and Eve are allowed to iron the sheets."

"Which chute were you taking the dirty linen from?" Quinn asked.

"Number two."

"Who had number four?" Dela asked.

"Mattie." She glanced around. "I guess she took tonight off."

"Thank you," Dela said, and Quinn handed the woman's phone back to her.

"I don't think we need to speak with anyone else, do you?" Quinn said quietly, as they both started walking for the door.

"Nope. I have a feeling the book fell on top of the laundry and Mattie picked it up, possibly knew some of the names and took it home with her."

"That's my thought, too." Quinn held the door open. "Personnel to find her address?"

Dela nodded, wondering if the woman was stupid enough to contact the people in Tristan's book, considering that the book was probably why he was killed.

Chapter Nine

Glancing to her right while exiting the personnel office, Dela caught sight of the maintenance sign. "We need to check on Van Branson's plugged toilet last night since the person in the room said he didn't call maintenance."

"Let's go." Quinn led the way to the door of the maintenance department.

Albert, the head of maintenance, wasn't on duty. At night only four people were available to take care of problems that arose. One was Clarence White who had helped them put sensors on the doors when they were catching a human trafficker.

"Dela, surprised to see you here. Have you had any sleep since becoming head of security?" Clarence asked.

Dela smiled at the man. He was the uncle to her best friend in high school. A young Umatilla woman who had been a victim of rape and murder. A crime that

Dela beat herself up every day believing she could have prevented.

"Not much since Tristan Pomroy was shoved in the laundry chute last night." She studied the two men behind Clarence. Both watched with interest. Neither were the man they wanted to speak with. "Is Van Branson here tonight?"

Clarence nodded. "Just got a call about one of the doors at the cinema plex sticking. He went to have a look at it."

She walked out of earshot of the other two, motioning Clarence to follow her. When he did and leaned close, she asked, "What can you tell me about Van?"

The man's eyes widened. "You think he killed Tristan?"

"We're ruling him out. The occupant of the room he was supposedly called to said they didn't have a plugged toilet last night."

Clarence narrowed his eyes. "I took that call myself. They said, this is room eight-thirty-four. The toilet is plugged."

Dela glanced at Quinn. She would believe Clarence if he said he saw the Queen of England walking down the street.

"Thank you. That means the person in the room is lying. Why?" Dela pulled out her phone and dialed Kenny.

"Hey, what's up," he answered.

"Can you remember exactly what the man in room eight-thirty-four said when you asked him about the maintenance man coming to his room?"

"He said he didn't call about a plugged toilet."

"Did you get his name?" Dela wanted to have Quinn do a check on the occupant.

"Just a minute."

She heard paper flipping.

"Ronald Edmond. A salesman from Portland."

"Thank you. Get some sleep. I'll need you fresh in the morning."

"Same for you, boss."

She ended the call and faced Quinn. "Can you run a check on Ronald Edmond, a salesman from Portland?"

Quinn stared at her. "That name sounds familiar."

"Then check it out. I'm going to see what Van has to say about last night." She headed toward the door.

"You're not going alone." Quinn was on her heels.

"He's not going to do anything. The area where he's working has several cameras."

"There were cameras on the tenth floor last night, too." Quinn responded as they stepped out of the offices and into the lobby area.

That was true. However, if Van had been the one to kill Tristan, he had thought ahead and found a way to turn the cameras off. This would be an unexpected encounter with her right now.

A tall, wide shouldered man with a full beard and shaggy dark hair to the collar of his casino shirt, carried a tool box as he walked toward them.

"Van Branson?" Dela asked.

"Yeah? Why?"

"I'm Dela Alvaro, head of security, and this is FBI Special Agent Quinn Peirce. We're checking on everyone who was moving about last night during the time frame of the murder on the tenth floor."

The man had looked worried when they first approached him. Now he stood slack hipped and smiled. "I heard about that when I came on shift. When did it happen?"

"About the same time you went up to the eighth floor for a plugged toilet," Quinn said.

Van glowered. "Yeah, that bogus call. I knocked on the door and some woman said she didn't know what I was talking about. The toilet wasn't plugged."

"Then what did you do?" Dela asked.

His eyes widened and what she could see of his face grew red. "I figured the guys in the maintenance room thought I was unclogging a pipe, so I went to the stairs and had a smoke."

Dela knew more than Van who used the stairwell for smoking even though it was against policy.

"Did you see or hear anyone on the stairs while you were smoking?" Quinn asked.

"I thought I heard a door above me open and close. I didn't hear any footsteps though."

"Were you still on the eighth floor?" Dela asked.

"No, I'd walked down a couple floors. When I finished smoking, I walked the rest of the way down to the first floor."

"You didn't hear anything other than the one door opening and closing above you?" Dela didn't understand why he would only hear one door. That meant someone had been on the stairs when Van came out to the stairs and went in or came out and didn't use the stairs, just hid. Neither one made sense.

"That was it," Van said.

"What were you working on down here?" Quinn asked.

Van waved his hand toward the cinema plex. "The second door going into theater two was sticking. I sprayed it with some lubricant and swung it back and forth a few times. It was definitely sticking in the hinges."

Dela studied the man. So far, he'd appeared unfazed by their questions and seemed truthful in his answers. "Where did you live before moving here?"

His head whipped around and he stared at her. "I've lived in Oregon my whole life."

"Then why isn't there a record of you before three years ago?" Dela studied him, watching for tics to show he was lying.

"I was born at The Big Muddy Ranch in Antelope. I didn't get a social security number or legal driver's license until three years ago."

"How could you go without a social security card or license that long?" Quinn asked.

Dela nodded her head. "It does seem like you would have encountered a time before now that you needed one. I believe it was one of the things the Rajneeshees wanted—more voters and would have made sure you were a citizen."

He shook his head. "I was only a child when I lived at Big Muddy. I had no reason to be legal to vote. Then they dispersed and my mother moved to a commune. I had odd jobs that paid cash, mostly, and never had a need for a social security number until I decided to find full time work." He shrugged. "As for a driver's license, I'm an adult and as long as you don't break the rules you don't get pulled over."

"But you need a license to register your vehicle," Quinn said.

The man's face reddened. "Not if you pay cash and there is already a license on the vehicle."

Dela studied him. He'd learned all the ways to get around being counted by the government. She wondered if these were things taught at the Rajneesh compound. Stepping aside, she said, "Come tell me if you think of anything that might help us."

"I will." Van walked around her headed to the casino floor.

"He knows all the ways to get around the government." Quinn stared at the man. "You didn't ask him if he knew the victim."

"His name wasn't on the list or his initials in the ledger. But I wonder why someone asked for a maintenance man and then said there was nothing wrong. That feels more out of place than him having a smoke in the stairwell." She pivoted and her fake foot stuck. She swayed, falling against Quinn.

He grabbed her. "Let's call it a night. You go to that room you're staying in, and I'll go make some inquiries."

She shoved against him, righting herself. "I'm not tired. My stupid—" She stopped. When she realized she'd be considered handicapped the rest of her life, she'd promised herself she would never use having one leg as an excuse for anything. "I need to talk to Verna. Then I can call it a night."

"Call Marty and have him send her out to the Deli. You wanted to talk to Rosie anyway."

She liked the idea of giving her aching stub a rest and talking to Rosie while they waited for Verna.

At the deli, Rosie greeted them both. "Dela, you keep showing up with handsome men and I may have to start arm wrestling you for them." The woman was as wide as she was tall and her jolly personality was as warming as the sun.

Dela shot a glance at Quinn. She wished she hadn't told him about Rosie ahead of time.

"Pleased to meet you, Rosie. Dela was telling me what a great judge of character you are." Quinn smiled and his one dimple deepened.

"Oh, I like this one Dela, don't let him get away." Rosie patted her hand. "Coffee?"

"Actually, if you have a few minutes Special Agent Pierce and I would like to ask you some questions."

Rosie leaned over the counter and asked quietly, "Is this about Tristan?"

"Yes."

"Harvey, I'm taking a break," Rosie called into the small kitchen behind the counter. She filled a drink cup and led them to a table in the back of the seating area. She settled onto a chair and waited for them to sit.

"What can you tell us about Tristan?" Dela started.

"He liked true crime. Every time he'd come in here for lunch, he'd tell me about some show he'd been watching."

"Did he ever have lunch with anyone?" she asked.

"Once in a while Luis would join him, but not very often. Most of the time Tristan would sit back here in this area either looking at his phone or a little book." Rosie slurped her soda.

"Did anyone stop by and talk to him when he sat here?" Quinn asked.

Rosie shook her head, then stopped. "Yeah, last week. A guy kind of dressed like you." She nodded at Quinn. "They were deep in conversation, then Tristan shook his head, and the man said, 'We'll see about that,' and left.'"

Dela shot a glance at Quinn. He didn't look like the woman had divulged anything interesting. "Can you remember the day? Or as close as you can?"

"I believe it was Thursday. Tristan had the soup. We always have split pea on Thursdays and it's his favorite." Rosie smiled. "Does any of this help?"

"Yes, Rosie. You are the reason I love my job." Dela meant it. Loyal employees made her job so much easier.

"And you are why we all love our jobs. I hope that board is smart enough to make you head of security." Rosie patted her arm.

"Thank you. It means a lot to hear that." Dela pulled out her phone and texted Marty.

Send Verna to the deli, please. And pull up video in the deli for last Thursday from 11 am to 2 pm.

K.

"I'll get us coffee while we wait," Quinn said, standing and following Rosie back to the counter.

Dela nodded. Her mind was working through what they knew. She wondered who the man was in the suit.

Quinn returned with the coffee, placing one in front of her. "I like Rosie."

She smiled. "Me too. She always brightens my mood and while you can learn a lot from her, she would never tell anyone but me what she sees and hears here."

"I am also impressed with how loyal everyone at this casino is to you. Makes me think you aren't that hardnosed, tight-assed M.P. sergeant I met in Iraq."

She narrowed her eyes. "I believe in justice for everyone, but especially women who have been wronged. My prisoner deserved to be prosecuted for what he did to Amaris. Her family wouldn't take her back and I couldn't get her a visa to the U.S. Last I heard she was begging on the streets and most likely was assaulted again or killed. No one deserves to be treated that way." The plight of the Iraqi women burned in her soul as much as the plight of the American Indigenous people.

"How many times do I have to apologize for doing my job? Zaid had information that saved a whole platoon. I had to put that over the woman getting justice." He stared into her eyes. "Even if the case had gone to court, do you think she would have been treated any differently?"

Dela shifted her gaze to the table. She knew deep down, saving her own country's people was what she had signed on for when she joined the army. But Amaris had needed someone to champion her.

Verna arrived. Her hands were clenched in front of her and her gaze darted back and forth from Dela to Quinn and back to Dela.

"Have a seat, Verna," Dela said, motioning to the seat between she and Quinn.

Chapter Ten

The woman sat with her hands clenched in her lap.

"Do you know why we wanted to talk to you?" Dela asked the surveillance member.

"Marty mentioned something about the feed I watched last night." Verna Pyles hadn't been hired as just a surveillance monitor. She'd been hired because of her technology skills with the hope of using her as Marty's backup. But she had to learn all the ins and outs of the surveillance and the casino before they would start her helping Marty.

"Yes. Tenth floor surveillance cameras near the storage room were blank. Why didn't you notice?" Dela asked.

The woman, in her thirties, ducked her head. "I did notice, but I wanted to impress Marty. I tried to get them back up by myself. I thought I'd accomplished it when it came back on."

Dela stared at the woman. "You were hired to learn

about surveillance and how it worked with our security so when you are ready for promotion you will understand how we all work together. What is the protocol for when a monitor goes blank?"

Verna mumbled, "Call Marty and ask another person to try and bring up the camera on their monitor."

Della sighed loudly. "You didn't follow protocol. I'll have to report this to Marty and Human Resources. It will be up to them to discuss whether you continue as you are or leave."

She hadn't thought the woman's expression could get any sadder, but tears welled in her eyes and her chin dropped to her chest.

"When you were trying to get the monitor back up and running did you noticed anything about the system?" Quinn asked.

Verna raised her head and shoved her glasses up the bridge of her nose. "It responded as if there wasn't any power to the camera."

Dela knew where he was going with this. It wouldn't take security personnel or a computer person to take out a camera if the person knew how to cut power to the camera.

"Thank you, Verna. Go back to work." Dela waited for the woman to walk out of the deli before standing. Her stump burned like fire when she put pressure on it.

"We have all we need tonight, go to your room and sleep," Quinn said, putting a hand on her elbow.

"I need to tell Marty what we found out and go over the tapes of Jeff dealing. Not to mention the video of Paula's arrival and the man who met Tristan right here." She put weight on her prosthesis and hissed.

"What's wrong?' Quinn asked, moving to block

her way.

"Nothing that would concern you. I will go to my room. Can you tell Marty I'll be in surveillance early in the morning to check out the tapes?" Her leg needed to be soaked and rested.

"Yes. Get some rest so you're ready to tackle this tomorrow." Quinn peered into her eyes. "You and I both saw what happens when people are sleep deprived. If you want to keep this job, you need to rest."

That was the phrase that made her forget trying to be super woman. She did want this job. "Fine. But call me if you learn anything that I need to know. And tell Marty to do the same." She slowly walked over to the guest elevators. He followed, making it hard to for her to hide the pain shooting up what remained of her leg.

"I'm giving you lead on this investigation. I'd hate to get someone in here that I can't work with." He grinned and headed across the casino floor. As much as she hated to say he was right, Dela knew she wouldn't be any good to anyone, including finding the killer, unless she rested her leg and got some sleep.

♠ ♣ ♥ ♦

Being at the casino, Dela rose early, showered, put on her prosthesis, and dressed. She started to cross the gaming floor when her stomach growled. The twenty-four-hour coffee shop was the best place to get a cup of coffee and something to eat at 5:30 in the morning.

She sat sipping her coffee after finishing the last bite of toast when her phone buzzed. A glance at the name and her lips started to curve into a grin, but she stilled them.

"What are you doing up so early?" she answered.

"I'm at the casino. I have something to show you,"

Quinn said.

"I'm in the coffee shop having breakfast." She sipped her coffee as the FBI Special Agent walked into the establishment.

As soon as he sat, the waitress arrived with a cup of coffee. He ordered breakfast. When the waitress walked away, he slid a folder toward her. "This is what happens when we sleep. These reports were on my computer when I woke this morning." Quinn picked up his cup of coffee.

Dela opened the file. On top was a list of how many times Tristan Pomroy called the FBI stating he had found someone on their most wanted list. "Wow, he was really trying to make money by finding people on your list." She scanned. "But it doesn't appear that any of his accusations held up."

"They didn't. And the next page are the shows he might have watched that caused him to be antsy."

She flipped the page and found a list of shows and the mug shots of the people that were wanted. The second from the bottom looked familiar. It was the eyes, but she couldn't place him. Dela tapped a finger on him. "Does he look familiar to you?"

Quinn grinned. "I had the same reaction. He's wanted for an armed robbery in California. Two bank tellers ended up dead, and they didn't catch any of the people involved in the crime."

Dela pulled the page out of the folder. The next page was a full dossier on Paula Pomroy. It read pretty much as she'd figured. "She stands to gain more from her husband's death than when he was alive."

"That's a hefty life insurance claim on him. It's through the casino insurance group. Thought I'd let you make that call." Quinn leaned back as the waitress arrived with his breakfast. "Thanks."

She smiled, refilled their coffee cups, and sashayed away.

Dela raised her coffee cup to her mouth to hide the smile watching Quinn's disinterest in the woman's outward flirting. She figured he got it all the time being single and good looking.

"Any other reasons she might want her husband gone?" She scanned the rest of the page.

"Like a lover? Not that the team could come up with. But we haven't been following her." Quinn raised a forkful of food to his mouth.

"We need to talk to her neighbors." Dela shoved her finished plate to the end of the table.

She flipped the page and saw a report on Mattie Collier. The report was short. She was eighteen, dropped out of school two years earlier, and lived with a cousin in Pendleton. "We need to check on Mattie. See if she found the book."

Quinn nodded as he ate.

Dela moved to the next page and found information on the dealer, Jeff Twigg. "Interesting." Reading down the page and flipping to the next, it appeared the dealer had been living larger than he should as an Indian Casino dealer. Until three months ago. At which time the large sums of money going into his bank ceased.

"Did you get a warrant for Tristan's bank records?"

Quinn nodded, finished chewing, and said, "I have them in my car. We can go get the records when the bank opens."

"Good. That will give me enough time to go over

the videos I had Marty pull yesterday." She shoved to the end of the bench to stand.

"Not going to keep me company while I eat?" Quinn asked.

She peered into his eyes. Was that hurt she saw? "You served me lunch yesterday. I guess the least I can do is sit here."

His eyes lit up.

"And I also need a favor. On the way to Pendleton, I need dropped off at my mom's to get my car."

"I can drop you off on the way back. Save two of us driving to the same place." He studied her more intently than this conversation needed.

"I need to go by the vet clinic after the bank and didn't want you to have to waste your time on something personal." And she preferred not having him chauffer her around. She liked it too much.

"It makes more sense to leave here via the freeway, go to the bank, and come back through town and by the clinic to go fetch your car." He'd finished eating while she'd been trying to find a way out of riding with him. Quinn tossed money on the table and moved to slide out of the booth.

She stood and stepped away from the table. "I guess I lost that battle."

He stared at her. "You think that was a battle?"

A nervous giggle bubbled in her throat. She swallowed. "Only in my head." She strode as quickly as her fake foot would allow out of the café, across the quiet gaming floor, and to the surveillance offices door. Her leg was feeling better this morning after being off of it a good six hours. She tapped her ID on the lock and the door swung open. Four sets of eyes peered at her entrance. "Anything new happen overnight?" she asked, walking to the backroom where Marty did his wizardry with the videos.

"Nothing like the night before," Russ said, stretching his arms and returning his attention to his monitors.

"That's good." Dela continued into the backroom with Quinn on her heels.

She found a note on the keyboard. Marty had instructed her where to find the footage she wanted to see. Because the idea of a dealer being dirty bothered her, she started with the camera aimed at Jeff's table.

"We're starting with the dealer?" Quinn asked.

"Unless you want me to start one of the other videos up for you?" She glanced sideways at him but didn't move to allow him to look at anything other than what she was looking at.

He leaned back, stretched his long legs out under the table, and watched.

Dela did the same thing, only propping her fake foot up on the box kept under the table just for her. As she watched, she noticed a pattern. Leaning forward, she rewound and then started the video again.

"Watch when that brunette walks up to the table and hands her money over." Dela pointed to the woman at the right who handed Jeff what looked like two fifties. He then stacked up chips and slid them over to her. She messed with the chips during the first hand— stacking and unstacking them. "See there? She has two less chips." She tapped keys, rewinding and then zooming in on the stack as it is slid across to her. "See that? He has two one-hundred-dollar chips under that stack."

Keeping the video zoomed in, the brunette played with the stack of chips and then deftly slid the two hundred-dollar chips into her purse.

"Double frickin' shit! He *is* stealing from the casino!" Dela slapped a hand down on the table, making Quinn jump.

She yanked her phone out of her pocket and hit Kenny's number. It rang, but her second in command didn't answer. He wasn't due in until later in the day. After the beep, she said, "Kenny on your way into work today, grab Jeff Twigg. He's been stealing from the casino." She ended the call and moved on to the next video.

"You sure after last night he hasn't left town?" Quinn asked. "I can have Shaffer or the Pendleton Police go by Twigg's house and pick him up."

"We'll deal with this in house, unless he ran." Dela knew the Board of Trustees liked to deal with the problems at the casino before handing anyone over to the tribal or local police.

She found the footage of Paula Pomroy entering the casino. The monitor flashed from camera to camera as the woman went into the gift shop, then over to the elevators. A couple entered the elevator with her and the doors closed. The footage blipped and the next shot showed the victim's wife getting out of the elevator on eight. Paula studied the signage and turned left. She hung whatever she'd purchased in the gift shop on a door and walked back to the elevator.

The video caught up with her as she exited the elevator and made her way across to the Sports Bar. In the bar she sat in a corner, drinking and watching the door. Dela fast-forwarded and thirty minutes later a man walked in, kissed her cheek, moved a chair next to her, and sat down. Dela backed up the video, stopped at a good view of the man's face, and tapped the printer to life.

"Did you see the number on the room she visited?" Quinn asked.

"Yeah, eight-thirty-four." She rose, plucked the frame from the printer, and said, "This must be Ronald Edmond. Think it's a coincidence?"

"No. All the more reason to have a talk with Mrs. Pomroy." Quinn pushed to his feet.

Dela reached for one more flash drive. "Let's see who Tristan met with at the deli first."

Quinn dropped back into the chair.

She shoved the flash drive into the USB drive and clicked to start it. A view of the deli came up on the monitor. Dela fast-forwarded until Tristan entered the deli and sat down. They watched him sip his soup, look at things on his phone, and write in the little book they needed to ask Mattie about. As he finished off his soup, shoving the empty bowl to the center of the small table, a man walked in. Unfortunately, his back was to the camera as he walked up, sat down, and then began a discussion with Tristan. The accountant became agitated.

"Whoever that is, said something Pomroy didn't like." Quinn leaned closer.

"He has to face the camera when he leaves," Dela said, willing the man to get up and leave.

He did stand. With a parting shot that angered Tristan even more, the man spun and headed out of the deli. It was the same guy who met Paula in the sports bar.

Dela fell back against the back of her chair. "Do you think he told Tristan he was having an affair with his wife?"

"No. It was something else. He would have looked devastated not angry," Quinn said, quietly as if musing to himself.

"You have experience with losing a wife?" she asked, making a joke. A glance at his face and she wished she'd kept the thought to herself.

"As a matter of fact, yeah." He slapped his hand on his legs and stood. "Come on. Let's go have a talk with Mrs. Pomroy after we gather her husband's bank records."

Dela turned off the monitors and followed Quinn through the next room and across the casino floor. She didn't say anything, waiting to see if he brought it up.

Chapter Eleven

Quinn's phone rang as they parked at the bank. He answered the call.

"Detective Jones, what a surprise." He rolled his eyes and Dela chuckled. "Yes, we are following multiple leads." He listened. "Really? I would have thought your office would have come up with the murder weapon by now." Quinn grinned. "Oh, forensics hasn't told you the murder weapon. That could be because they haven't sent out a report yet. No, I haven't received one." He nodded. "Yes, when I get the report, I will let you know what they concluded could be the murder weapon." He pressed end and slid the phone back in his pocket.

"I do believe your favorite tribal detective was trying to see if I, or should I say we, he did mention you, know more than he does."

Dela narrowed her eyes. "I'm sure we do. He hasn't been interviewing anyone that I know of."

"He said, he'd talked to people at the casino. The ones who would talk to him, but until he knows the weapon, he can't really send out men to look for it."

Dela made a noise deep in her throat. "That's a lie. Anything that had blood on it could be the murder weapon." She thought a moment. "You know, it would have made sense for the murderer to shove it into the chute along with the body."

"But that would have been something the laundry room would have notified you about. A bloody weapon mixed in with the sheets."

"True. It has to be somewhere on the tenth floor if not in the supply room." She pulled out her phone and dialed security.

"Spotted Pony Casino Security, this is Marie," answered the guard in the office.

"Marie, send two guards on floor security to the housekeeping supply room on ten to see if they can find the weapon from yesterday's murder."

"Didn't you search it yesterday?" she asked.

"No. I figured Detective Dick would. I have a feeling he didn't."

The woman laughed. "That sounds about right. I'll send Bruce and Ross."

"Good choice." She thought a second. "Have them check the stairway as well. I should be back by noon. Let Kenny know when you see him."

"Will do."

Dela ended the call and noticed Quinn watching her.

"That's why everyone likes you," he said.

Narrowing her eyes, she asked, "Why?"

"Because you don't order them around, you treat

them like equals. I would have thought after so many years in the army you would have been ordering everyone around. Like you do me."

If he hadn't said the last sentence with a smile on his face, she would have laid into him about he needed to learn to follow orders. Instead, it started a small flicker of happiness in her chest. "Thanks, I think. The army taught me that you get more help when you treat everyone equal. Well, except the major and generals. They don't like that."

He laughed.

She liked the deep sound.

He finished and opened his door. "Do you really think the weapon is still in the hotel?"

"Not really. It would make more sense for whoever killed him to take it with them."

"I agreed." They walked up to the bank and entered.

The bank manager was more than willing to help once Quinn handed him the warrant for Tristan and Paula Pomroy's bank records. With the photocopied pages in her hand, Dela settled into the passenger seat of Quinn's car.

"There isn't any out of the ordinary deposits or withdraws." She glanced over at Quinn. "If he was blackmailing people, he must have been keeping it away from his wife."

Quinn started the car. "Still want to go ask her about her trip to the casino the night her husband was murdered?"

Dela shook her head. "Let's go talk to Mattie first. The little black book might have the information we need."

"Where does she live?"

She picked up the folder Quinn brought with him that morning and read the address out loud. Shoving the bank statements into the folder, Dela studied the photo of the man the FBI wanted. Why did he look familiar? He was bald, no facial hair, and had wrinkles at the back of his neck. Granted it was a rendering from witnesses but the eyes…

The car stopped in front of a smaller home on the edge of town. A dented older compact car sat in the driveway.

"Do you think she's here?" Quinn asked as they exited.

"I hope so. If she is nosing around about what she found in the book, she could be in trouble." Dela walked up to the porch, climbed the two steps, and knocked on the door.

There wasn't a sound from inside.

Quinn glanced around. "No one's home."

Dela glanced at the window to the right of the door. The lace curtain jiggled. "Why would the curtain move?"

"Mattie, this is Dela. Answer the door," she called out.

Quinn walked over to look through the window.

A flash of white and red appeared in the window.

Quinn jumped back.

A white fluffy cat with what looked like blood on its fur sat on the windowsill staring at them.

Dela tried the door knob. It turned.

She didn't carry a weapon but her hand automatically went to where she had carried her Sig M11. Quinn's breath was warm on her neck as he squeezed by her and shoved the door open all the way. He stepped in front of her with his Glock raised.

"FBI," he announced and began a room-by-room search.

Dela noted the knocked over furniture and sliced cushions. Someone was looking for something.

"Dela!" Quinn called.

She followed the sound of his voice and stopped inside a bedroom door. The white cat sat beside Mattie. The young woman's eyes were open, staring up at the dingy ceiling.

"Double frickin' shit." They should have questioned her last night. Dela knelt next to the body as Quinn called it in.

She'd seen similar bodies in Iraq. Mattie had been tortured. "She must have hid the book or gave it to someone. But why let herself be tortured if she knew where it was?" Dela glanced up at Quinn.

He stared down at the body, remorse showing in his eyes. "Whoever wanted the book would have killed her as soon as she told him. Damn!" He spun away and exited the bedroom.

It appeared he was feeling just as guilty for this woman's death as Dela. She stood and followed him into the living room. "Do you think the person found the book?"

"We won't know until forensics goes through here. I called in the state police team."

Dela pulled on the latex gloves Quinn handed her. She righted a photo. It was of Mattie and another young woman. "I wonder where her roommate is."

Quinn pulled out his phone. "Shaffer, find out where Mattie Collier's cousin works. We're at the house they rented. The cousin isn't here." He listened. "Go over there and bring her to the house. We have some questions for her." He shoved his phone into the inside pocket of his jacket. "Shaffer is going to bring her over here."

"You think that's a good thing?" Dela asked, picking her way through the mess, keeping her gaze locked on the floor. There had to be something in this house that would tell them who had been here.

"I think seeing her cousin dead might scare her into telling us everything she knows." Quinn was shaking magazines by the spine and looking into everything that had an opening.

"Or she could go into shock." Dela had seen many hardened soldiers go into shock after witnessing a buddy get killed.

"We'll only have her see the body if she stonewalls us."

"I don't understand. Who even knew she had the book? I mean, we only found out yesterday it even existed. How could anyone else have determined she had it?" Dela straightened and headed to the bedroom. "Maybe her phone will show who she called."

In the bedroom, she wandered around looking for a phone or a purse. She found one empty purse on the floor of the closet in the pile of clothes. From the mess, it was pretty clear the killer hadn't found what they were after. She wondered if the cousin's room had been torn up as well. She stepped across the hall and opened that door. The room was a mess. She felt sorry for the cousin and their family. Grief was something she'd learned about growing up as well as in the military. She had lost one friend in grade school to cancer and then her other friend in high school to violence. But her "rez family" had helped her through and continued to help her as she learned how to manage a job and living with one foot.

She closed the door on that bedroom as a short man in a suit stepped into the house with a young woman. Her facial features and the photo of the two young women revealed it was Mattie's cousin. She walked down the hall to them.

"Oh my god! What happened to our house?" The young woman shrieked and started to drop to her knees.

The man who had to be FBI Special Agent Shaffer, grabbed her arm and kept her on her feet. "Don't touch. This is a crime scene."

"I'll say! Who the hell would want to vandalize our place?" Her head snapped up from staring at the floor and her gaze landed on Dela. "Where's Mattie? Was she here?"

"I'm sorry to say, yes, Mattie was here. She-she's no longer with us." Dela never liked telling anyone they had lost a loved one. She knew the sorrow and guilt that came with a death. Especially one, you could have stopped.

The young woman's face scrunched up and tears ran down her cheeks. "No! Not Mattie. She was taking classes to get her G.E.D."

"Miss Sommers, can you tell us what your cousin was doing when you left for work?" Quinn asked, righting a slashed cushion and motioning for her to take a seat.

Dela wandered into the kitchen and came back out with a glass of water. She handed it to the woman and sat on the edge of the chair next to the couch without bothering to replace the cushion.

Miss Sommers swallowed several gulps of water. "I can't believe. Oh God! What am I going to tell her parents? My parents?" She started crying.

Reaching out, Dela touched the young woman's knee. "We need to know all you can tell us about why Mattie didn't go to work last night and anything she said or did after coming home from work Friday morning."

She nodded, gulped more water, and stared at Dela. "She was excited when she came home Friday morning. She said something about not having to work at the casino anymore. When I asked her if she got fired, she said no. But didn't say anything more. I went to work and I figured she went to bed. That was what usually happened with us working different shifts."

Dela nodded. "When you came home? Was she awake?"

"Yeah. She said she'd found a way to get to California and see if she could get a modeling gig." The cousin shook her head. "I kept telling her she was too short to model, but she had it in her head that she could get a job, if she could just get there."

"How did she plan to get to California?" Quinn asked.

Dela shifted her gaze to him, and Shaffer, standing behind him taking notes. She returned her gaze to the young woman.

"I don't know. She wouldn't tell me. But she said she was meeting with someone who would pay her lots of money for something she'd found." Miss Sommers studied each of them. "Is that what got her killed? Whatever it was she found?"

"We think so. Did she show you a little book?" Dela asked.

The woman shook her head. "No. But she had something shaped like that in her back pocket when she left the house last night."

"Were you up when she returned?" Quinn asked.

"Yeah. She was only gone about an hour. She wanted to party. I told her I couldn't, I had to work."

"Would she have called anyone else to party with her?" Dela asked.

"I don't think she did. When I went to bed, she was sitting in her room looking up the route to L.A."

"Did you notice the book after she'd returned?" Dela glanced at Quinn. He'd been ready to ask the same question.

"I don't remember seeing it. But I wasn't looking for it."

"Close your eyes and tell me what you saw in Mattie's room when you looked in on her before going to bed." Dela leaned forward. "Put yourself in the door, take a deep breath, and scan the room."

Miss Sommers did as she was asked. Closing her eyes, her head slowly rotated to first one side, "Her suitcase was sitting on the small dresser. Clothes piled in it." Her nose pointed straight in front of her. "Mattie lay on her bed, her laptop in front of her. No shoes on." Slowly, her head turned to the right. "Her piggy bank was sitting on top of money. She must have pulled it all out."

"Do you see the little book anywhere?" Dela asked in a soft voice.

The woman shook her head. "No. It's not in her back pocket anymore. Not on the dresser or the desk."

That meant her cousin must have stashed it somewhere else. They were going to have to figure out where she'd gone when she left the house with the book in her pocket. Dela sighed. That was not going to be an easy thing to do.

"Thank you."

Commotion on the porch announced the arrival of a forensic team and a county deputy.

Quinn took over, explaining what to look for and sent the deputy and a medical examiner into Mattie's bedroom. "Thank you for talking with us," he said to Miss Sommers. "Do you have some place you can stay? It's going to take some time to go through all of this."

"Can I get some clothes from my room and take Snowball?" she asked.

Dela nodded toward the white cat the forensic team was taking bloody hair samples from. "Do you mean the cat?"

"Yes." The young woman's eyes flicked away from the bloody animal.

"Dela will escort you to your room. Once the techs get a sample of her fur, you may take the cat," Quinn said, making eye contact with Dela.

She nodded and followed the woman down the hall. Luckily the two men in her cousin's room, prevented Miss Sommers from seeing her tortured cousin.

Chapter Twelve

Leaving the forensic team and the deputy at the house, Dela and Quinn headed to speak to Paula Pomroy. Dela found it telling that Quinn ordered Shaffer to take Miss Sommers back to work to get her car and then wanted him to canvass the Pomroy neighborhood and ask about the Pomroys' relationship and the wife's movements the last couple of days.

"Even though you and Shaffer are both special agents, are you higher up than he is?" she asked.

Quinn stared at her as he put the car in park. "Why are you asking this?"

She shrugged. "You seem to order him around, but he is the same level as you."

"We are equals. However, I was given the lead on this investigation. That makes me ask him to gather information."

She chuckled. "Oh, that is you asking? It sounded more like orders to me."

"When instructing someone to do specific tasks, it might sound like orders."

He opened his door. "Car is in the garage. She should be home."

Dela had noticed the open garage door when they pulled up. The garage had everything neatly boxed and stacked. Except for a small box on the top of two stacked totes. It stuck two inches out beyond the edge of the tote.

They walked up to the door and Quinn rang the doorbell.

Paula arrived with the toddler on her hip. "You again." She left the door open and spun around.

They followed her into the living room. It looked the same as before, except for the playpen set up in front of the large window. Sun streamed across the structure. Dela wished she could lay down among the blankets and stuffed animals and take a nap.

"Mrs. Pomroy—"

"Paula, please," she interrupted Quinn.

"Paula, what were you doing at the casino the night your husband was killed?"

The woman's eyes widened then narrowed. "Friends were passing through. I purchased a gift for them at the gift shop. When they didn't answer my knock, I left it on the door handle and waited for their return in the sports bar."

"Did your husband know you were visiting friends at the casino? Is that why he returned that night?"

Her face flushed. "I didn't know he wasn't home watching our son. That was where I'd left him. Here, with little Alfie." She walked over and sat the child in the middle of the playpen. She handed him several small toys and walked back over to them.

Dela opened up the folder and pulled out the photo of Ronald Edmond. "This is the man you met in the sports bar. He's also the man who called down to maintenance about a plugged toilet." She handed the photo to Paula.

She glanced at it and handed it back. "Yeah, that's my friend."

"What's his name?" Quinn asked.

"Ronnie. We met in the bar so I could help him come up with a good anniversary gift for my friend, his wife." She sat down on the couch. "I don't understand what my visiting with a friend would have to do with my husband's death."

"That's what we are trying to figure out as well," Dela said, taking a seat on the couch an arm's length away from the woman. "That night was the only night casino personnel remember seeing you at the casino without your husband. A night when it was clear that he was in the hotel."

"I didn't know he was there. Like I said, I thought he was, here, at home with Alfie."

"But that's not what you told us when we arrived here Thursday. You made it sound as if you were home all night." Quinn took a seat on a chair.

"Why are you treating me as if I'm the one who killed my husband? Why would I? I don't want to raise Alfie by myself. I'm going to have to put him in preschool while I work."

Dela glanced over at Quinn. Did the woman not know she would be wealthy by her husband's death or like before was she playing them? Thinking they didn't know she was about to get a lot of money.

"I think if you don't go out and purchase expensive things, you'll find the insurance money will keep a roof over your head and food in your mouths," Quinn said.

"Insurance? What insurance?" Her eyes were wide and her mouth slightly open as if surprised.

"You didn't know he took out a quarter-of-a-million life insurance policy?" Dela asked.

The woman shook her head. "No. I had no idea." She focused on Quinn. "I'm going to get that much?"

"If you aren't guilty of his death." The tone Quinn used had Dela fighting her lips from curving into a smile. It suggested the woman had killed her husband.

"I didn't kill him. I can't help it my friends came into town the same night." Paula shifted her attention to Dela. "You work for the casino. How do I go about getting my insurance money?"

Her husband's death hadn't been fully investigated and she was ready to grab the money. "You'll have to talk to the personnel department to find out that information. I'm here to discover what happened to your husband."

"Then go talk to his friends at work." The woman's hand waved like she was swatting at a fly.

"Who were his friends at work?" Dela asked.

"He said he talked to the guy who he shared his office with, a woman at the deli. Rose, I think it was. And lately he'd been talking to someone else, but he didn't mention them by name. I think whoever it was worked with you." She pointed at Dela.

"Security or surveillance?" That could solve how the cameras were turned off at the right time on the correct floor. Had someone watching the monitors discovered what Tristan had been up to and wanted in on it? "Man or woman?"

"I don't know. He kept it all secretive. Just like he did every time he thought he'd found someone on a wanted poster. He'd get excited then get secretive until he realized he'd been wrong. Then he'd hide out in his den for days before he'd be back to himself again."

"Do you remember seeing a small book your husband carried?" Quinn asked.

"His surveillance book? He kept all his sightings and information on the wanted people he called the FBI about."

"That's all he kept in the book?" Dela asked.

The woman stared at her. "What do you think was in the book?"

"We don't know. However, the book has disappeared since your husband's death and another person, who we believe had possession of the book, is now dead as well." Quinn put the information out there in a monotone, non-committal way.

Dela wished she could stay so disconnected to the two lives that had been taken too early.

"Someone else has been murdered! Who?"

"We aren't at liberty to say at the moment. You're sure the only information your husband kept in that book had to do with wanted people?" Quinn persisted.

"That's what he always told me when I'd see him looking or writing in it."

"He's called the FBI enough times that his book should have been full and in need of another one if he was keeping surveillance on people he suspected." Quinn stared at the woman.

Dela wondered about that. If he had been keeping surveillance, why had he been watching Jeff? Had he spent time walking around the casino studying the people who came there looking for wanted people? How had they not known this about him? Maybe they needed to speak with Luis again. The sums of money that stopped showing up in Jeff's bank account looked like blackmail. But wouldn't someone who was wanted by the FBI keep a lower profile than a dealer? And, who was the woman he had helping him skim money from the casino? There were too many questions.

Quinn stood, drawing Dela's mind from the thoughts whirling around. She stood, not realizing he'd finished his questioning.

"We'll be in touch if we have any more questions," he said to Paula, and headed to the front door.

Dela followed behind. She turned at the door and peered into Paula's eyes. "Did you really think your husband was here watching his son when you met up with Ronald Edmond?"

Paula's eyes widened. "Who is Ronald Edmond?"

"The man you called Ronnie and met with in the sports bar." Dela studied her closely. The woman appeared stunned to know that was the man's last name.

"Oh, that's right. I always just think of him as Ronnie. My friend still goes by her maiden name."

The comment came so quick it sounded authentic, but Dela wondered.

Out in the car, Quinn faced her as she settled into the passenger side. "How much of what she told us do you think is the truth?"

"Maybe fifty percent. That woman is good at lying." Dela wasn't ready to rule her out as a person of interest in her husband's death.

"That's what I was thinking. I don't buy that he

used the one small book to keep surveillance on people. She knows what's in the book."

"But does she want it enough to kill another person? And what was that about not knowing Ronald Edmond's last name? How is that possible if they are working together?" Dela didn't like any of it. Least of all that there was a security guard or surveillance member who knew more than they were saying.

♠ ♣ ♥ ♦

After stopping at a store for Dela to pick up two bags of dog food and a couple of dog toys, they parked in front of Molly's vet clinic.

"I'll get Travis to come out and help you with those bags," Dela said, exiting the car quickly to get a conversation with Molly without Quinn present. She didn't wait for a response, just hurried into the building.

Travis glanced up from the desk.

"Can you go help Special Agent Peirce bring in both bags of dog food?" She carried the bag with dog toys.

"Sure. He's helping you out a lot lately." The young man grinned. "Mom is in the back cleaning a dog's teeth."

Dela walked through the waiting room and into the first exam room.

"Hey, good to see you. Give me a minute. I have to finish this." She nodded to the room with the cages. "You can go in and scratch Eats a Lot while you wait."

Dela nodded and continued to the room where the dog lay in the large cage. "Hi, Eats a Lot. Remember me?"

His big fluffy tail moved up and down, thumping the blanket under him.

"I brought you something to do." She pulled out a squeaky chew toy, pulled the tags off of it, and opened the door, placing it in front of him.

His big brown eyes peered at her, ignoring the toy. She put a hand on the wide space between his ears. He was a large dog and would only get larger. Could she take care of him? Now she was allowing her mother's and Quinn's doubts to enter her head.

She continued to stare into his eyes and worked her hand down to scratch his neck. Her fingers curled into his thick fur. He kind of reminded her of a wolf. His long snout and coloring were kind of wolfish. But his floppy ears and brown kind eyes, showed he was a lover, not a fighter. He was a survivor, just like her.

"I don't know where you'll come to when you get out of here, but if I can make it happen, it will be at our own place." She scratched him and stared into his eyes. "We have to change your name. Is that why you ran away? You didn't like the name."

Footsteps behind her ended her conversation with the dog.

"He's healing nicely. He will be ready to leave here by the end of next week." Molly held out an arm to help her stand.

Dela let few people help her, but her friend had been one of the first to let her know she didn't think for one minute that Dela was any weaker than she'd been before losing her foot. She glanced around to make sure Quinn wasn't watching and used the offered arm to grasp and pull herself to her feet.

"Thank you."

"I'm always here for you. Just like you have always been here for me."

She knew Molly didn't mean literally. However, while she'd been in the army, she and Molly had stayed in touch and it had been Dela's letters to Molly that had given her friend strength to leave an abusive relationship and head off to college to become a veterinarian. Even with a small child in tow.

"I doubt this dog will eat two bags of dog food while he's here, even if his name is Eats a Lot," Quinn said, entering the room.

Dela glared at Quinn. "Molly and Travis also take in strays and find homes for them."

"Then why don't you have them find a home for that brute and you take a smaller dog if you want one?" His gaze was on the dog, studying Quinn from the cage.

His comment didn't help her attitude. "Because this dog came into my life for a reason. I will keep him."

The scowl on Quinn's face said he didn't understand. But Molly and Travis's smiles confirmed what she'd come to see. The dog had been run over in front of her for a reason. Only the powers that be knew why.

"I need to settle my bill and then we have to get my car." Dela walked out to the reception area. The others followed her.

While Travis printed out the sheets summarizing the costs, Dela watched Quinn looking at his phone. She wondered if the forensics report had come in yet on their first body.

Her phone rang. Mom. She sighed heavily and answered.

"Hello, Mom."

"How are you?" she asked.

"I'm fine. I'll be coming by in the next thirty minutes to pick up some more clothes and my car."

"I'll have lunch ready for you. Is Quinn coming with you? I want to make sure I have enough iced tea made."

Dela glanced at Quinn. "He will be bringing me but I don't know if he'll be able to stay."

"Stay for what?" Quinn asked, walking over next to her.

"Lunch."

"I can always make time to eat," he said.

The shit-eating grin on his face made her wince. He was only accepting the invitation to dig into her past and irritate her.

"I guess he'll be staying for lunch." Maybe she could come up with a reason to load up her car and leave. But then she didn't know what her mom would tell Quinn. If she stayed, she could manipulate the conversation.

"Good. See you then!"

Dela ended the call and glared at him. "You made my mom's day." She took the papers Travis held out to her, and walked out of the building.

Chapter Thirteen

Lunch wasn't as bad as Dela had anticipated. Her mom didn't bring up embarrassing things and Quinn, while being inquisitive, didn't ask questions that she didn't want answered.

Once he had left, with her agreeing to meet at the casino to see what Marty had come up with, she hugged her mom. "Thank you for lunch. It was what I needed."

Her mom's eyes glistened with tears. "You and any of your friends are always welcome here. I don't care if you are thirty-eight or sixty-eight, you will always be my little girl."

She eased out of her mom's arms and picked up the bag she'd used to hold the crutches she'd taken apart so no one would know she needed them. Other items in the bag were Epsom salt, more liners and socks for her socket, and more slacks and polo work shirts.

"I hope you find out who killed your employee soon," Mom said, as she opened the door.

"Me, too." Dela walked out to her car and tossed the bag into the passenger seat. Turning the key, her phone rang. Bernie Moon, the chairman of the Board of Trustees.

"Hello, Bernie," she answered more cheerful than she felt.

"Dela, good to hear you are in such good spirits. Does this mean you have found the person who wronged our casino?"

She backed out of the driveway and headed toward the casino. "No. We haven't found out who killed a casino employee. I am working with the FBI and the tribal police. We have leads, and I hope to have this cleared up by the end of the weekend." She crossed her fingers. They'd be lucky if they cleared up both murders in that amount of time.

"I see. I can keep it out of the CUJ, they know how important the casino is to our economy. But the editor at the East Oregonian always wants to spread things before he has the truth." Bernie's voice held disappointment.

"I'm sure you can easily talk the editor into holding off until we have more information." The Confederated Umatilla Journal, a newspaper run by Umatilla members, wouldn't write anything harmful to the casino. However, the editor at the Pendleton newspaper always wanted to dig up more gossip than truth.

"I had hoped you would have good news for me to relay to both papers."

Ah, here was his way of making her feel like she might not have Head of Security much longer.

"We are following two possible leads." She pulled into the casino parking lot. "I really need to go. Special

Agent Pierce is waiting for me so we can go over the forensic report and see if we can put either of our suspects at the scene." She was blowing smoke. Quinn had said he had the forensic report, but whether they could learn enough from it to go after anyone was still up in the air.

"Do keep me informed of your investigation."

"I will call you as soon as we know enough for you to contact the media." She ended the call and carried her bag into the casino. Walking up to the registration desk that wasn't as busy at this time of day, she handed the bag over to Faith Whitebird. They had attended school together. While Dela went off to join the army, Faith married and now had two teenaged children. "When you get a chance, could you run this up to the room I'm staying in?"

Faith smiled. "I can do it when I get off work. Is that soon enough?"

"That works. I need to catch up to Special Agent Pierce. He has some new information."

Her friend leaned across the counter and whispered, "I hope you and he are talking about more than the murder. He's cute."

Dela shook her head. "Always the matchmaker. We aren't a good match. Too much bad past."

"Oooo, that means your next night off you have to come to my place and tell me and Molly all about your past with the handsome FBI agent." Faith wiggled her eyebrows.

Dela laughed. "Have you learned anything about my life in the army?"

"No." She studied Dela. "Was your life in the army so bad you don't want to share it?"

She shrugged. "It was a different life. One I enjoyed while I lived it, but one I don't care to revisit."

"Fair enough." She winked. "But you still have to come hang out with the girls your next night off."

"I'll try." She walked across the casino floor, smiling. She'd only been back at the reservation a year and had taken back up with several of her friends from school. It had been awkward at first. She didn't know how they would accept her considering her injury and having been gone for so long. Having grown up a part of the community, she shouldn't have worried.

Dela entered the security offices. She walked up to the podium, a small office, where Kay was on duty keeping things running. Could it have been one of the day security guards who were friends with Tristan? Wouldn't that person have come forward after his death if they were?

Kay said, "Bruce and Ross didn't find anything that looked like a weapon on the tenth floor. They also went the length of the stairway and didn't find anything other than cigarette butts." She scrunched up her face.

"Thanks. Anything happening I need to know about?"

"Kenny hasn't come in yet."

"I'd asked him to do something for me before he came in." Dela headed back to the door, "I'm headed over to surveillance if you need me."

She walked the distance from the security offices to the surveillance offices and held her ID card up to the hidden door. It opened and she crossed the large monitor room and entered Marty's office.

Marty and Quinn were watching a video up on the monitor. "What is this of?" she asked, taking a seat on the other side of Marty.

"Footage of Pomroy every time he came to the casino after his work hours." Marty held out a bag of popcorn. "Want some?"

She grabbed a handful. "Anything interesting so far?"

"He was watching Jeff and the other tables, but mostly Jeff's table. And he seemed to be studying a local who comes in often."

"Find more footage on that man. Kenny hasn't arrived yet with Jeff." Dela stood, pulled out her phone, and scrolled through her contacts for her second in command.

"Hey," Kenny answered.

"Do you have Jeff?" Dela asked.

"Can't find him. I've been looking everywhere. I think pulling him in last night scared him." Kenny blew out a breath. "We might need to get some help on this."

She glanced at Quinn. "I know who to contact. Come on in to work." She ended the call and shifted her attention to Quinn and Marty. "He can't find Jeff. Looks like he's running."

Marty stopped the video and dug through papers on his desk. "Here's information on Jeff. You might want to get the local police to look for him."

Quinn grabbed the papers from her hands. "I'll get my guys on it."

"Good. I really don't want to hand this over to the city or state police. Bernie called. He doesn't want bad publicity in the local papers."

Marty groaned. "I suppose if you don't solve this fast, you will be demoted."

"Something like that." Dela studied the paused

video. "Did you put together footage of the hall outside of room eight-thirty-four on Thursday night?"

"Yeah, you can watch it on the right monitor." Marty tapped the keyboard and the monitor in front of her chair came to life. She sat back down and propped her foot back up.

Quinn walked over to a corner of the room and pulled out his phone. She turned her attention to the monitor. The time stamp showed Paula leaving her gift on the door at 11:26 pm. She disappeared from sight. Around 12:30 am she and Ronald Edmond entered the room, taking her gift bag with them. Who was the woman that Van said told him there wasn't a plugged toilet? Was it Paula? A busboy arrived with a cart. Ronald let him in. The person left five minutes later, without the dishes that were on the cart. She fast forwarded to 1 am. Van walked down the hallway, knocked on the door, and Paula talked to him. He looked upset, but walked away. As he'd said, he walked toward the stairs.

A few minutes later, Paula exited the room wearing a robe. She didn't go to the elevator, she walked toward the stairs.

"Look at this," Dela said, pointing to the monitor.

Quinn stood behind her, staring at the image. "What?"

She rewound the footage.

"Mrs. Pomroy took the stairs in our time frame of the murder." Quinn's tone was thoughtful.

"Let's see when she comes back." Dela fast forwarded. The woman never returned to the room. "She must have had the robe on over her clothes to keep them from getting bloody." Dela thought back. "I wonder if there was a bloody robe in the chute with the body?"

"I'll ask forensics." Quinn wandered to the corner to make his call.

She wondered what was on the forensic report he'd received during lunch. They needed to either find the small black book or get into Tristan's computer.

"We need to go see if Wallace has had any luck with Tristan's computer. We need to know what he was up to." She glanced up at the monitor. "I think he had help from someone in either security or surveillance."

Marty stopped sliding his chair back. "We have a breach, again?"

She sighed. "I hope not, but Paula Pomroy said one of Tristan's friends worked in security. That could mean either security or surveillance given the camera on ten was compromised." She studied him. "You need to keep watching video of Tristan Pomroy the nights he came back to the casino. We want to know the people he focused on the most. We already know he was on to Jeff Twigg skimming money from his table. I want to know what else he found." She glanced at Quinn who was still on the phone. "We believe Tristan was killed because he was blackmailing people and one of them didn't want to pay anymore."

Marty whistled. "Who would have thought he had the guts to do that."

"He was more complex than any of us imagined," Dela said, sitting back down to rewind and watch the video aimed at the hall of room 834.

Quinn walked over. "I have two people searching Twigg's house, seeing if we can determine where he went."

Dela nodded. She fast forwarded after Paula left the room. Around 5 am Ronald entered the room. "What the…?" She rewound and fast forwarded again. "Either there was another breach in the video or Ronald Edmond left the room hidden in the cart the busboy brought up."

Quinn pulled a chair up beside her and watched the film. "You're right in your assumption. It doesn't show him leaving, and yet, there he is going inside the room."

"Not to pull you from that, but did you know Tristan was studying this guy?" Marty pointed to a still shot.

"If that's Luke Saxton, yes, we did know."

"Did you know it was probably because I've watched this guy lift wallets from women's open purses?"

Anger and frustration shot heat through Dela's body. How had this man's actions not been noticed by her security? "How obvious is it?"

"He sits next to a woman with an open purse. He talks to her a bit, then plays the machine. When someone comes along and talks to the woman, he reaches in, takes the wallet and walks away. But he comes back in a few minutes and drops the wallet back in the purse." Marty kept the video running.

"That's why no one reports having their wallet stolen. They probably figure they gambled more money than they thought." Dela leaned back in the chair.

"Here's the thing." Marty fast forwarded the video. Over in a corner Tristan stood talking to the man.

"Bingo!" Quinn said. "That proves Pomroy was blackmailing the people in his book."

"No wonder Jeff ran when I confronted him last

night." Dela stood. "He couldn't have killed Tristan, the cameras had him working the hours when the murder happened."

"We're going to have a talk with Luke Saxton. Can you pull up more footage of Tristan? We need to find out who in security or surveillance he had mess with the camera on ten."

Marty heaved a sigh. "I know this murder is top priority. I could really use Verna's help."

Dela shook her head. "Sorry, I don't trust her. She is the one that didn't follow protocol when she noted the cameras weren't working the night of the murder." She walked over to the door, hand on the knob, waiting for Quinn.

As they left the surveillance area, Quinn asked, "I thought you wanted to ask about a bloody robe?"

"Was it in the forensic report?" she asked, holding the door open.

"No."

"We need to know when Paula left the casino." Dela grasped her mic. "Marty, do you copy?"

"Yo."

"Also go through footage of the entrances after one-thirty. I want to know when Paula Pomroy left the casino."

"I'll get on it."

"Thanks." She released the mic as they walked across the casino floor, dodging the colorful slot machines and the growing number of players. The smoke from cigarettes hung head high and higher, the scent fading when she walked by a person doused in cologne.

"I don't think word has gotten out about the

problem the other night," Quinn said as they walked up to the security door to pass through into the bowels of the casino's operations.

"Or people are curious and have come to see if they can learn more." Since losing her friend in high school, Dela had become a cynic. She knew it about herself, but didn't care. Seeing the worst in people never had her being disappointed in anyone.

Quinn snorted.

"What is that for?"

"Always looking for the silver lining, I see." His sarcasm wasn't lost on her.

"It's a good way to never get hurt."

They stopped outside of the laundry. Quinn stared at her. "Someday you'll have to tell me about the people who have hurt you."

She shook her head. "We will never become that close of friends." Pushing the door open she walked into the hot, humid laundry room. There were three times the number of staff as at night.

Dela walked over to the supervisor's room. Ester Sanchez sat at the desk her head bent over a schedule. "Ester?"

The Hispanic woman was in her sixties. She pressed her palms to her chest. "Dela, you give me a heart attack. I don't hear anything over the noise of this place."

"I'm sorry. We have a question for you regarding the morning the body was found on ten."

The woman's lips pursed and she made the sign of the cross. "That was a terrible morning. Bloody sheets and towels. They had to soak before we could put them in the washers."

"Did there happen to be a robe with the bedding?" The video of Paula sneaking to the stairs in a robe, might be enough to have Quinn pick her up for questioning, but she didn't know if it was enough to actually arrest her for her husband's murder.

Ester nodded. "There were three robes that had blood on them."

Dela glanced at Quinn. If there were three, they could have just been in the chute under the body and soaked up the blood before his heart stopped pumping. Which drew her to the fact, she didn't know what the forensic report had said.

"Thank you." She led Quinn back out to the gaming floor. "Let's grab a cup of coffee and you fill me in on the forensic report."

He nodded and led the way to the coffee shop.

Dela liked his choice. There would be less traffic in the coffee shop than at the deli.

When they were seated, Quinn pulled out his phone, messed with it, and placed it in front of her on the table. He'd pulled up the forensic report.

She scanned the obvious information- name, gender, race. A puncture in the carotid artery on the right side of the neck. It was described as a round hole with jagged edges. Perhaps a round tool with a serrated edge caused the wound. No other injuries were reported.

Sipping her coffee, she stared at the report. "Right side of the neck. If the killer was facing him, they would have been left-handed."

Quinn nodded. "But if he was attacked from behind, it would be a right-handed person."

"You had to go and ruin our first good clue." She

glared at him and sipped more coffee. "What would cause a wound with jagged edges?"

"Something with a serrated edge." Quinn raised his cup to his lips and she caught a glimpse of mischief in his eyes.

"Stop mocking my comments." She focused her gaze on the report. "He didn't weigh as much as me. I bet a woman could have doubled him over and shoved him down the chute."

"When you looked in the chute was there a robe or anything on top of him?" Quinn asked.

"No." She caught on to what he was saying. "Damn. That means Paula didn't stab him, put him in the chute, and then toss the bloody robe in on top of him." She stared into her coffee. "There had to be a lot of blood. Did forensics find any sign of blood on the floor or wall around the chute?" The room had looked spotless when they'd entered.

"It had been cleaned but there were still traces. It was the victim's blood." Quinn nodded. "I don't know how the killer managed to get out of the room without blood on them. And it's strange that Edmond secretly left room eight-thirty-four and then Paula wore a robe to walk up or down the stairs."

"We really need to know more about good ole, Ronnie," Dela said.

"I'll see if Shaffer has written up his report on talking to the Pomroy neighbors and if anything more came up about Edmond." He pulled his phone across the table. He slid his finger across the screen, and tapped on it.

As he talked, Dela watched the people walking into the coffee shop and the people wandering around outside the door. Who could Mattie have talked to about the book besides her cousin? Had she called Paula about the book? So many questions and so few answers.

Quinn ended his call. "Shaffer got the name and address of Mattie Collier's boyfriend. He also sent subpoenas for Mattie, Paula, Edmond, and Tristan's phone records."

"Why did he subpoena Ronald's phone records?" She understood the others.

"Because according to the neighbors, he's been hanging around the Pomroy residence a lot the last month." Quinn finished off his coffee. "And now I know why his name was familiar. He's a bounty hunter out of Portland."

Dela stared at Quinn. "Bounty hunter? I didn't think that occupation still existed."

"They usually work for bail bondsmen. Bringing in fugitives who jump bail." He stood. "We're going to have a talk with Edmond."

"Is he still in the hotel?" She stood and followed him out of the coffee shop.

"There's only one way to find out." Quinn walked over to the registration desk.

Chapter Fourteen

Dela grimaced when Faith smiled sweetly at Quinn.

"Special Agent, what can I do for you?" she asked.

He motioned for Dela to tell her friend.

"Faith, can you tell us if Mr. Edmond, in eight-thirty-four, is still registered?" Dela asked, ignoring her friend's gaze jumping back and forth between her and Quinn.

"Let me see." Faith finally dropped her gaze to the keyboard and tapped. She smiled and shifted her gaze from the keyboard to Quinn. "Yes. He is still registered to that room."

"Thank you," Quinn said, putting a hand on Dela's back, moving her toward the elevators.

She swatted at his hand. The warmth from it disappeared. In the elevator, she faced him. "Please don't put your hands on me while I'm working."

His right eyebrow arched. "Does that mean you're

open to me putting my hands on you outside of work?"

Heat blasted her face. "No! I meant, don't give my matchmaking friend anymore kindling."

"That's why her eyes were bouncing back and forth. I thought maybe she had an eye disorder."

Dela restrained the laugh that bubbled in her throat. Wait until she told Faith, Quinn thought she had an eye problem. "Yes. Ever since I moved back, she has been trying to hook me up with men. I'm not interested."

"In men?" Both his eyebrows raised.

"No! Quit messing with what I'm saying. I don't have time for a relationship. You've seen how many hours a day I spend here. I'm not even sure I should have a dog, I'm away from home so much." The elevator stopped and they stepped out.

Neither one talked as they walked down the hall to room 834. Quinn raised his hand and knocked on the door.

The door opened. Mr. Edmond stood in the opening, holding a cell phone to his ear. "I'll call you back." He stepped back, shoving his phone in his suit pocket. "I gave all my answers to your security man and a tribal detective."

They both entered the room. Quinn closed the door behind them, and Dela walked over to the desk. The two queen beds in the room were both rumpled as if they had both been used.

"Can you explain what Mrs. Pomroy was doing in this room the night her husband was killed?" Dela asked.

The man raised his hands as a goofy smile spread across his face. "We met in the bar. She didn't say she was married. How was I supposed to know her husband was getting killed while we were, you know?"

She shook her head. "No, I don't know. Why did she leave this room with a robe on and go to the stairs?"

He stared at her. "What are you talking about?"

"And why did the camera not show you leaving this room but it shows you returning early in the morning?" Quinn crossed his arms, his gaze leveled on the man.

Dela was delighted to see the bounty hunter squirming. Not literally, but perspiration beaded his forehead and his eyelid twitched.

"Who are you here to collect a bounty on?" Quinn asked.

"No one. I just came for some fun. You know R and R after working hard." Ronald relaxed a little.

Dela wondered if he was really here for relaxation and now found himself caught up in a murder investigation. "What are you doing holed up here in your room?"

Ronald stared at her before opening his mouth. "I was asking about any possible fugitives in the area. Thought since I'm stuck here until your police say I can go, I might as well try to drum up some business."

She didn't buy that. "Who said you were stuck here?"

"Detective Jones, I think it was. With the tribal police."

Dela and Quinn exchanged a glance. Why would he tell Ronald to stay here? They hadn't even considered him a part of the equation until now.

"Why did he tell you to hang around? Did you have information about the murder?" Quinn asked.

"Nope. But when he heard I was a bounty hunter

he said my help might be needed."

Dela couldn't stop her eyes from rolling. Leave it to Detective Dick to think someone as unqualified as a bounty hunter could help him find a killer.

"At least he did something right," Quinn said. "You are now a person of interest in this murder since you were messing around with the victim's wife on the night of his death and you have been hanging around his home for the last month." Quinn walked toward the door. "If you leave town let myself or the tribal police know where you are."

Dela walked out the door Quinn opened.

"What gives you authority to tell me what to do?" Ronald spat back.

Quinn flashed his badge. "The Federal Bureau of Investigation."

The bounty hunter's eyes widen. It was evident, he thought he'd been dealing with casino security.

Out in the hall, Dela faced Quinn. "He either helped Paula or was used by her to give her an alibi."

"We need to find out where they each were when Mattie was killed." Quinn punched the button on the elevator.

"We could go back in and ask him," Dela said, making an about face.

"Let's see what Marty can find on video of his actions this morning first. I'd rather catch him up in a lie than have him tell me some story."

She spun back to the elevator and they entered.

As the elevator descended, Dela's phone buzzed. She slid her finger across the screen.

"Hey, I think I found something."

"We'll be right there." Dela ended the call and

smiled at Quinn. "Wallace found something."

♠ ♣ ♥ ♦

In the technology department, Dela and Quinn took seats on either side of Wallace.

"I made it into Tristan's computer. There were the usual forms, spreadsheets, and documents that are necessary for his job. But he also had three encrypted files." He handed Dela and Quinn a paper. "This appears to be a bank account in the Cayman Islands."

"A country that doesn't disclose your information," Quinn said.

"This is way more than his wages," Dela said. She glanced at Quinn. "Do you think Paula knows about this?"

"We'll have to ask when we see her later." Quinn's gaze landed on the papers in Wallace's hands. "What else did you find?"

"A list of transactions that match the dates of the deposits in that account." He handed them each a page. "Two of the initials line up with what we know so far. J.T.- Jeff Twiggs, and L.S. – Luke Saxton. There's also a R.E. and V.B. As far as I can tell, no money had been received from the V.B."

Dela stared at the page. "Do you think R.E. is Ronald Edmond?"

"If so, that gives us even more reason to want to look into his whereabouts at the time of the death." Quinn rattled his pages. "Do you think the V. B. is Van Branson?"

"It could be. He was also in the vicinity at the time of the murder. All we have is his word he was smoking on the stairway. And he would have knowledge about how to cut power to the camera."

"That's what I was thinking." Quinn swung his gaze to Wallace. "What else do you have there?"

"Correspondence between Tristan and someone in the FBI about a man who is wanted for armed robbery in California." He handed that over.

"This is the same information your agent came up with," Dela said, seeing the sketch and reading the name of the wanted man, Vladimer Chernoff. "Do you think Tristan really found this man?"

Quinn shrugged. "It's a possibility. But what would he be doing here in the Pendleton area?"

"Blending in? You'd think with a name like that he'd have an accent." Dela's stub was throbbing. She walked over and sat down, propping the prosthetic foot on the box under the table. "Was there anything else on the computer?"

"He'd been looking into plane tickets to the Cayman Islands," Wallace said.

"Tickets? As in for two people?" Quinn asked.

"Tickets as in researching prices. I'm not sure if it was for one or two." Wallace sat down at his desk. "That's all I found on the computer."

"It's enough to give us several good suspects," Dela said. "Let's go see what Marty found."

Quinn followed her out of the tech department, down the hall, out through security, and along the edge of the casino floor to the surveillance rooms. She gained access to the rooms with her ID card and they walked through the main room and over to Marty's office.

Marty glanced up when they entered. "Paula Pomroy left the casino at three a.m."

"Can we see?" Dela asked.

The monitor came alive with the front entrance of the casino. Walking toward the camera was Paula. Dressed the same as when she'd walked in. Her hair wasn't as neat, but her clothing didn't appear to have any blood on it.

"We never did see what she purchased in the gift shop," Dela muttered.

Quinn studied the footage. "Let's go ask."

"We can't unless she paid with a credit card. Teresa, the woman who works the gift shop nights, hasn't come into work yet." Dela studied the video. "Did you get a chance to pull up more of Tristan visiting the casino?"

Marty nodded. "I went back another week."

Quinn's phone rang. He answered and moved to a corner of the room.

"Roll the video," Dela said.

She watched Tristan wander around the casino a couple of times when Quinn broke into her concentration.

"Don't get comfortable. Guess who Mattie's boyfriend is?"

Dela glanced back at him. "One of our suspects?"

"Luke Saxton. I think we need to visit him."

Dela pushed to her feet. "I think so, too." She motioned to the monitor. "Keep watching and see who he actually talks to."

Marty nodded.

Her leg throbbed as they walked out of surveillance and across the casino floor. Her only solace was knowing she could rest her leg as Quinn drove. "Where are we headed?"

"Saxton's work," Quinn said, as they exited the

building.

"Where does he work?"

"For a construction company."

"He would have access to a serrated tool." She slid into the passenger seat of Quinn's SUV. "Did you ever hear how Mattie was killed?"

"Stabbing in the neck." Quinn glanced over at her. "Too soon to know if it's the same weapon as killed Pomroy."

Chapter Fifteen

The construction site was in Tutuilla, a neighborhood on the reservation south of the interstate. Dela hadn't driven through this area since she'd returned home. It had more houses with small acreage than she remembered all nestled inside of farm ground. She liked the mix of agriculture and manageable parcels of land with horses and other farm animals.

A one-story home on a corner lot had a For Sale sign. The house sat in the middle of what looked like an acre of land. The neighbors were far enough away, she wouldn't feel like they were watching her every move. She'd saved up most of her pay from the army. She had a good feeling about this place. Dela pulled out her phone and put the number for the realtor in her contacts.

"What are you doing?" Quinn asked.

"Thinking about my future." She studied the place in her side mirror. She could put up solid fencing and

Eats a Lot—she really needed to come up with a better name—could run around all day long outside with a large dog house to stay out of the weather. The more she thought about it, she wanted that house. And it was only three miles from work. Closer than her mom's place.

Ahead she spotted a new house being built. "You're sure he's here? If he found out about, or killed, Mattie he could be on the run."

"His roommate told Shaffer he was at work." Quinn parked the SUV out of the way of the crane being used to lift rafters on the house.

They stepped out of the vehicle and a short pot-bellied man with a hard hat walked up to them. "No Lookie Lous. We haven't had an accident in the thirty years I've been doing this."

Quinn flashed his badge. "We need to talk to Luke Saxton."

The man stared at the badge before hollering, "Luke, people to see you."

When Luke walked up, the foreman walked away.

"I need the money, what's this about?" The man was in his twenties, tall, slender, brown hair and brown eyes. Dirt, sawdust, and grease clung to his boots, jeans, and long-sleeved shirt.

Quinn showed his badge. "We need to talk to you about Mattie Collier."

Luke's eyes widened. "Mattie? What's wrong with Mattie?"

Dela's chest squeezed. He didn't know she was dead.

"Did you see her last night?" Quinn asked.

Luke took two steps toward him. "What happened?

Where's Mattie?"

Dela stepped between the two. She hated telling soldiers one of their friends hadn't made it. She knew the gut-wrenching loss. "Mattie was killed this morning at her place."

Luke shook his head. He grabbed the hard hat and flung it at the ground. "No! You're lyin'."

"I'm afraid not. We need to know when was the last time you saw her and what she talked about." Dela grasped the young man's arm and led him over to a pile of lumber. She forced him to sit.

Quinn returned with a bottle of water.

That's when she spotted the foreman standing ten feet away and the rest of the crew staring at them.

"I told her to just throw that fuckin' book away." He wiped at the tears trickling down his face.

"The book that Tristan Pomroy kept all his blackmail information in?" Quinn asked.

Luke's head snapped up, starring at Quinn. "You know about the book?"

"And that your name was in it."

"I didn't kill him, but I was happy to see the book when Mattie showed it to me. He'd been taking every cent I made that didn't pay for my rent and food."

"Because you had been stealing money from purses at the casino," Dela said, reminding him he wasn't any better than the man who'd blackmailed him.

"I didn't take that much. It was an adrenaline rush better than gambling. I hated that Mattie worked nights and we couldn't go out or spend time together because of our schedules. I'd wait around and she'd come see me on her breaks until I had to go home and get some sleep." His eyes narrowed. "Who killed her?"

"That's what we hope you can help us with. Her place was torn up. Did she happen to say what she was going to do with the book? Who she planned to call?" Quinn had pulled out a small notepad and pen.

"Not really. When I didn't want the book, she said she'd get us enough money to go to California." He shrugged. "I didn't care where we went as long as she took me with her."

"She didn't mention who she thought would pay for the book?" Dela had a hard time believing the young woman didn't tell her boyfriend her plans.

"She said something about maybe the wife would like to know her husband had money stashed somewhere." His gaze hopped between them. "Do you think she did it?"

"That's our next stop. Any idea where Mattie might have hid the book?" Dela asked.

He shook his head then stopped. "You might check her car. A couple times she made a comment about she could run drugs. Her car had a secret compartment. I just laughed. I knew she wouldn't do that. Her mom is a crackhead."

Quinn and Dela exchanged a glance.

"Thank you, and I'm sorry for your loss," Dela said, before she and Quinn walked back to the SUV.

"The car or Paula Pomroy's?" Dela asked.

"Let's talk to Paula."

Quinn started the vehicle and drove toward the interstate. They passed the house with the For Sale sign. It would be perfect. As Quinn accelerated onto the interstate, Dela pulled out her phone.

She dialed the realtor's number.

"Cathryn Wright, realty," a woman's voice

answered.

"Hi. My name is Dela Alvaro and I'm interested in the house in Tutuilla." She rattled off the number of the home and the road it was on.

"That house has been on the market a while. The seller wants to get it off their hands."

The woman's statement sent tendrils of happiness squirrelling around in Dela's chest. If it was affordable enough, she could get a fence put up right away. She asked questions as the woman told her the price and how it had all the appliances and a dining room table that went with it. "Is there a chance I could take a look inside later today or tomorrow morning?"

"Of course. I can meet you there in twenty minutes."

Dismay struck. She would have loved to turn around and meet the realtor. However, catching a killer was more important than her looking at a house. "That's not going to work. I guess we should make it tomorrow morning. Nine o'clock?"

"It is Sunday."

"Oh, I'm sorry! I work at the casino and forget what day of the week it is."

"I can come but could you make it more like noon or one?"

"One, then." Dela hoped she wasn't running off to talk to a suspect then and waste the woman's time.

"I'll be there."

She ended the call as Quinn left the interstate.

"You're going to look at the house out where we just were?" he asked, glancing at her before watching the traffic as they made their way across town to where the Pomroy's lived.

"I like that the house was off by itself, with some land around it." The realtor had said it was an acre and a half. That was a lot of grass to mow, but maybe there was a kid in the neighborhood who wanted to make some money.

"If it was the place on the corner, there were only a couple of small trees. That's not much privacy. It would be like living in a fish bowl."

She studied him. "Are you trying to talk me out of looking at the house?"

"No. Well, I just see you as more of an in-town dweller."

A laugh burst through her partially open lips. "In town? Seriously?"

He parked in the Pomroy driveway. "With as much time as you spend at the casino, it just seems like a small house or apartment in town makes more sense."

"Maybe to you, but I like my privacy. If the house doesn't need too much TLC, I'm buying it. It's better than what I've been seeing to rent, and if it's mine, I can do whatever I want to it." She slid out of the vehicle and landed harder on the prosthesis than the stub liked. The pain made her wonder if maybe Quinn wasn't right about her needing a small place that didn't require upkeep.

She hung back, grinding her teeth against the phantom pain that ran from her nonexistent toes to her hip.

Quinn stepped onto the porch and glanced back. "Do you want to be a part of this conversation?"

"Yeah." She moved slowly to not jar the leg again.

Quinn watched her, his eyes scanning the length of her and studying her leg. "I know you were discharged for medical reasons. Care to share?"

She shook her head.

He shrugged and rang the doorbell.

Making her way slowly up to the door, she'd scanned the closed garage door.

Quinn rang the bell again.

"I don't think she's home. The garage door was open the last time we were here." Dela stepped off the porch and walked around to the side of the house, peering in the windows. Everything was in its place. No sign of anyone in the house. She continued to the back. The backyard had a low cyclone fence. She swung the gate open and entered. A swing set and plastic child-sized car revealed the boy played in the yard.

She walked up to the back door and tried the knob. Locked. Might as well make a circle around the house. There wasn't a gate on the other side of the house. Rather than try to climb over the fence, with her leg aching, she retraced her steps and found Quinn standing by the open gate.

"Nothing," she said, walking by him and to the front of the house.

"It's Saturday. She doesn't work weekends."

"Maybe she's shopping. Want to wait for her to return?" Dela asked.

Quinn didn't answer.

She glanced over her shoulder at him. He was watching the house next door. Scanning the house, she spotted a curtain flutter.

"Let's go talk to that neighbor," Quinn said, striding by her.

She caught up to him as he climbed the three steps onto the porch of the two-story family home.

Quinn pressed the doorbell.

A dog barked and a child shouted, "Door!"

The scratching of dog nails on hardwood could be heard on the other side.

"Bop, no!" a frazzled female voice said as the door opened and a long-legged, shaggy dog pushed between Dela and Quinn, running down the stairs.

"Todd, go get him!" the woman at the door said, shoving a boy around eight out onto the porch.

When the boy had also squeezed between them, hurdling the steps and yelling, "Bop, here boy! Bop!", the woman smiled at them.

"Hello. We are Catholics." She started to shut the door.

Quinn put his foot in the way and showed his badge. "I'm Special Agent Pierce with the FBI and this is my associate." He motioned to Dela. "We'd like to ask you a few questions about your neighbors, the Pomroys."

"Oh, I thought you were a church group."

Dela glanced at the Casino logo on her polo shirt, wondering if this woman was observant enough to answer any questions about her neighbor.

"I heard from Cheryl next door an FBI man had been around asking questions. I was at work when you came by." She opened the door wider and waited for them to enter before glancing up and down the street and shutting the door.

"I'm sorry about the dog," Dela said.

The woman waved her hand. "Bop is always making a run for it. I've called the fencing company to put up a fence in my backyard like Paula's but they haven't had time to get to it, I guess." She walked into the living room. "Come in, have a seat. Would you like something to drink?"

"No, thank you, Mrs?" Quinn asked.

"Ms. Jennifer Gray."

"Ms. Gray, we have a couple of questions. Did you see Paula this morning?" Quinn asked, remaining standing.

Dela shifted all her weight to her good leg. She would have loved to sit down, but followed Quinn's lead in the questioning.

"I didn't talk to her, but I saw her putting Alfie in his car seat and a suitcase in the trunk of the car. I figured after what happened to Tristan she was going to her parents'."

"Where do her parents live?" Quinn asked.

"Portland, I think." She tapped on her chin with a perfectly manicured nail. "Well, not Portland, but one of the towns around it."

"Were you home Thursday night?" Quinn asked.

"Yes. I watched Alfie for Paula. She said some friends were staying at the casino and wondered if I could watch Alfie while she visited with them." The woman frowned. "She called me at eleven and said she was too drunk to drive did I mind keeping him overnight. I asked where Tristan was. She said he was on one of his wild goose chases. So I said as long as she was here to get Alfie before I had to go to work. She was here at seven."

Dela thought that was pretty self-centered of Paula to ask her neighbor to keep her child so she could fool around and possibly kill her husband. It also proved the woman had lied to them about thinking her husband was watching their child. "Did you understand what she meant by her husband going on one of his wild goose chases?"

The woman waved a hand and chuckled. "The whole neighborhood has heard about someone Tristan had seen on a crime fiction show. Once a week, he'd get all excited that he'd seen one of the FBI's Most Wanted fugitives here in Pendleton. We all would listen and nod then laugh about it when he'd leave."

The woman didn't even blush at her pronouncement of the whole neighborhood thinking Tristan Pomroy was crazy.

"What about last night or early this morning? Did she ask you to watch her son?" Quinn asked.

"No, I haven't talked to her since she picked up Alfie Friday morning." The woman glanced at Dela. "Did she have something to do with Tristan's death?"

"Why would you ask that?" Dela studied the woman.

"They had their share of quarrels. Paula complained he didn't let her spend money, and he complained to my husband that Paula thought money grew on trees."

"They argued about money?" Quinn asked.

Dela wondered why he asked that when the woman had just stated they did.

"All the time. Paula liked to go out and wear nice things. She said all Tristan wanted to do was sit in his den and watch true crime. When she asked for money to buy something she always had to bring him the receipts."

Now she understood why he'd asked. To get more information. Information that revealed, if Paula knew about Tristan's blackmail money hiding in an account in the Cayman's, she would want it. One way or the other.

"Thank you. Your answers have been helpful." Quinn headed to the door.

Dela followed, slower. "Did you happen to see any men or women visiting the Pomroy house when Tristan was at work?"

"Only the last couple of weeks. And then last night. There was a young woman who drove up to the house about dark. I noticed because I was coming back from walking Bop. She sat in her car for several minutes before walking up to the front door." The woman shrugged. "I didn't pay attention to when she left."

Quinn had spun around. "What kind of car was it?"

"A small compact. I'm not good with makes or anything. It was a dark color. Sorry, that's all I can remember."

"Thank you." Dela motioned for Quinn to open the door.

When they were seated in the SUV, Dela asked "What do you want to bet that young woman was Mattie?"

Chapter Sixteen

They left the Pomroy residence and drove to the house Mattie and her cousin rented. The small dark compact car sat in front of the house. Forensics had left and a deputy stood watch over the place.

"Deputy." Quinn flashed his badge and they walked over to the car.

"Forensics went over the car, too," the deputy said.

"Thanks. We're going to take a look anyway." Quinn sat in the driver's seat and started pushing and thumping on the inside of the car.

"Pop the trunk and the hood," Dela said.

He pulled on the levers.

She leaned into the trunk pulling back carpet and looking for hiding spots. When she'd been over every inch of the trunk, she backed away and slammed the lid down.

Quinn had moved to the back seat, digging his hands in between the cushions and tapping the door panels.

Dela raised the hood. A faint sliding sound caught her attention. There was a slit between the two sheets of metal that made the hood. "Quinn."

He appeared beside her.

"There's something in the hood." She put it down and raised the hood, again. This time there wasn't a sound. "It must be sitting down there." She pointed to the end of the hood nearest the windshield.

Quinn went over and talked to the deputy, then came back. "He's going to call someone to come out here and take the hood apart."

Dela's stomach rumbled. It was getting close to seven. The lunch her mom had made had worn off.

"You want to take my vehicle and grab some burgers?" Quinn asked, holding the keys in his hand.

She didn't like driving vehicles she didn't know. Her prosthetic right foot was hard to regulate the pressure on the accelerator. She knew the right pressure in her car to not go too fast.

"I'll wait." Her stomach rumbled again.

"I get it. You don't want to wreck a Federal vehicle. What do you want to eat?"

"A burger, fries, and iced tea, please." She was glad he hadn't pushed the point, but she hoped he hadn't thought she was such a bad driver she didn't want to take his vehicle.

"I'll be back before the other guy gets here."

As soon as Quinn pulled away, she opened the passenger door and sat in the car, with her feet and legs on the ground. She thought about moving to the back seat and pulling her body in to elevate her leg but decided that wasn't a good idea. There would be no way she could get out of the car quickly.

♠ ♣ ♥ ♦

Quinn returned before the wrecking yard truck, but by only five minutes. Dela was chowing down on the burger when the wrecking truck pulled in front of the house. Quinn set his food down and walked over to talk to the man.

Dela took another large bite and wrapped the rest of the burger up, setting it on her seat in the SUV, and joined Quinn and the newcomer at the front of the compact car.

"You think there's something in between the metal of the hood? And you want me to saw through?"

"Unless you have a better idea," Quinn said.

"I think we should take the hood off and shake it, see if there is anything in there before you ruin the hood."

Dela agreed. She and Quinn went back to eating while the man started up an air compressor and took the bolts out where the hood hinged.

The food was finished and they slurped the last of their tea when the man called for help. He, Quinn, and the deputy picked up the freed hood and tipped it to the front. The sliding sound moved from the back of the hood to the front, now sitting on the ground.

"See if you can shake whatever it is over toward the hole," Dela said, pointing to the opening she believed was used to insert the book.

Quinn and the deputy shook and moved the lid around like they were panning for gold.

"Stop!" Dela shouted when she saw the corner of the book at the hole. She slipped two fingers in on top of the corner and pulled it out. She grinned at the two law enforcement officers and gave the man who freed the hood a high-five.

"Thank you," she said to the deputy and wrecker driver as she carried the book back to Quinn's SUV.

Quinn slid behind the steering wheel and started the vehicle. "What does that book have that is so important?"

"You mean besides the amount he was blackmailing people?" Her gaze landed on a number that had to be the bank account in the Caymans. "I believe a number Paula would like to have. His bank account."

"Let's drop that off at the office. Then I'll get you back to the casino. I'd like to get information on Paula's parents and see if that's where she went." Quinn drove away from the car without a hood and onto the street.

"Why would she leave without this book and number if she knew about it?" After hearing how the woman liked money and knowing she knew about the book, it didn't make sense that she would just drive off without trying harder to find the bank number.

"Maybe she thought we were getting close and she wanted to distance herself from the two murders." Quinn turned onto the interstate.

Dela could understand the woman wanting to put space between her and the deaths. Especially if she did the killing.

She wanted to see her dog but didn't want to ask Quinn to make a detour. She'd check on things at the casino then drive to the clinic and check on him. Maybe tell him they might have a home when he was ready.

Her curiosity about what Paula had left on the door handle of room 834 was niggling at her. She'd go see

Teresa at the gift shop before she went to the security offices.

They didn't say much as Quinn drove to the casino. He pulled up in front of the entrance, leaving the vehicle running. "Call if you come up with anything new. I'll take this book to the office and see what they have come up with. Catch up to you in the morning?"

"I'll be here. Though technically, it is my day off. I don't plan on taking a day off until this is settled. I can't have Bernie Moon thinking I don't care about the casino's reputation." She pushed off the seat, remembering to put all her weight on her good foot when she landed on the ground.

Arthur greeted her inside the door. "Did you work all day and are back tonight?"

She smiled. "Yes. I'll be staying here until we find out who killed Tristan."

"I heard Jeff is missing." Arthur tipped his head toward the gaming table area.

"He was skimming from the casino." She wasn't surprised when the old man nodded his head. "You knew?"

"Didn't know for sure. That's why I didn't say anything. But the nights the casino was busy, he'd meet with a pretty woman when she'd arrive and before she left. Thought they were a couple, but I asked her one night when I got her car. She said they were just old friends."

Dela studied him. "Did she happen to say her name?"

"No. But here's her car's license plate number." He grinned and opened a small book he drew out of his breast pocket after moving a gray braid. Ripping out a page he handed it to her. "Something told me to write it down a couple weeks ago."

"Thank you. This might help us find Jeff." She walked toward the gift shop. The large windows facing the casino floor gave her a glimpse of Teresa working in the shop. Passing through the opening, her senses were awakened by the floral and herbal scents. Candles, potpourri, and colognes all battled for air space. There were many souvenirs and local artists' items for sale in the shop.

"Dela, what can I help you find?" Teresa asked, straightening from plucking items out of a box.

"Every time I come in here there are more wonderful things from the local artists." She scanned the wall with framed art. There was one painting of a horse and woman that if she bought the house, she would purchase for her bedroom wall.

"I have a question for you. Do you know Paula Pomroy?"

Teresa walked over to Dela. "Why does Pomroy sound familiar?"

"Her husband was killed on ten Wednesday night."

The woman snapped her fingers. "That's why. No. Why?"

"She was in here Wednesday and purchased something. She took it up and gave it to a man in room eight-thirty-four. Any chance you would remember?" That her friend would remember something purchased on Wednesday and not know the person who purchased it would be a miracle.

"Wednesday? I remember it was slow in here. Do you have a photo of her?"

Dela texted Quinn to send her a photo of Paula.

She chatted with Teresa about the painting and the artist until her phone dinged. Raising the phone up, she showed the photo of Paula.

"Oh, yeah, I remember her. Only because I had never seen her before and she walked straight in, over to those corkscrews, picked one up, and bought it without saying a word."

"A corkscrew?"

"Yeah. Not a cheap one either. It was one of the decorative ones, not the easy pump kind."

She followed Teresa over to the display. Not being a wine person, she hadn't known there were different kinds of corkscrews.

Teresa held up one with a beautiful, solid wood handle painted in a Native motif and a four-inch solid metal spiral with a wicked point on the end. "This is the one she bought."

Dela took a picture of the tool. "Thank you." As she walked out of the gift shop, she sent the photo to Quinn. *This is what Paula purchased. Could it be the murder weapon?*

I'll send the photo to forensics.

She also texted the car license plate number to him. *Arthur says this is the woman who helped Jeff Twigg steal from the casino.*

I thought you were going to take a night off.

Not until we find the murderer.

She headed across the casino floor to the door leading to the surveillance offices. Her leg and body were telling her to make it a night, but she wanted to catch up with Marty and find out what he might have uncovered on the surveillance videos.

The personnel watching the monitors all glanced

her way as she walked through the room.

"Shouldn't you be home, resting?" Lionel, the oldest member of security and surveillance since Godfrey was arrested, asked.

"I should, but with two murders now connected to the casino, I'm afraid, I won't be head of security much longer if I don't solve these."

"What can we do to help?" Lionel asked.

Dela smiled at the man. He could have been the assistant to the head of security when she was hired. In most places, a man in his position would have held a grudge, but he'd told her he didn't want to give more than his forty hours a week. He had a family that needed him at home. He went to work for the surveillance side of security instead.

She studied the night crew members that were present. Even though she trusted all of the surveillance and security personnel, she trusted the four at the monitors right now the most. "You are the group that are here helping out when the casino is the busiest. It's not easy, but what I want to know is have any of you seen a security member talking to Tristan Pomroy?"

"The dead guy?" Mick asked.

"Yes," Dela clarified.

They all said they had never seen him talking with anyone from security. She sighed heavily. "Okay. I know none of you were here Wednesday night when the murder occurred, but you have all been here long enough to know what to do if a camera goes down."

They all started telling her the protocol.

"Correct. So why do you think a member of surveillance didn't do that when their monitor went black?" She listened to each one. They all pretty much said, she either knew it was going down or had caused it.

"Whoa! You can make a camera go black? I thought you just watched them." She scanned the keyboards in front of them.

Mick waved her over. "Godfrey showed us the code to stop the filming of a camera when it had sensitive imagery."

She shoved her hands on her hips and glared at him. "What do you mean sensitive imagery?" Apparently, her former boss had been skimming from somewhere longer than he'd been working for the human trafficking ring.

Mick's face reddened. "When we started, and each time someone new comes along, we were told to teach this to them when some political officials go up to a room with someone other than their spouse."

Double frickin' shit! "You're telling me that you have all been covering sexual rendezvouses for local officials because Godfrey told you to?"

Lionel cleared his throat. "Not all of us. But there were times when Godfrey would see the person enter the casino and come stand behind us watching what they did and tell us when to black the camera."

The rage shaking her body made it hard for her to calm her voice. "From now on, that is not to happen. Do you hear me? And I want that passed along to every one of the security team. We are here to keep this casino clean and to be able to hand over any information law enforcement needs. We can't do that if we are helping the wrong people hide their acts of debauchery."

They all murmured and nodded. She shifted her

attention to Lionel. "I would like you to give me a list of the people Godfrey had you erasing on the surveillance cameras."

He nodded. A grin spread across his face. "This is why we will do whatever you ask to catch the killer and show the board you are the best person for head of security."

"Thank you all for your vote of confidence." She walked into Marty's office half ashamed that she hadn't caught on to her boss's greased palms earlier and elated that so many of security wanted her to remain as their boss.

Marty swung his chair around. "How goes the fight?"

"Slow and dirty," she replied, easing down into the chair next to him and propping her leg up. "Did you find out anything helpful?"

Chapter Seventeen

"I followed Tristan around for a month on the tapes. During working hours and off. This is the list of people he talked with." Marty handed her a paper.

Dela read the list. Jeff Twigg. No surprise there. Luke Saxton. Again, no surprise. Even Ronald Edmond, wasn't a surprise. Nor was Rosie. She was pretty sure it was in the deli where the woman would have been serving Tristan. But Mattie and Van Branson, those two she hadn't expected. She'd believed Mattie had never met Tristan and only saw Luke's name in the book after the man was dead. And the maintenance man who had been called to floor eight during the time of the murder had acted as if he didn't know the victim.

"This is interesting. Did you happen to flag the interaction between Mattie and Tristan and Van Branson and Tristan?" She asked.

"I did. I can put it all on a flash drive while you

sleep." Marty raised an eyebrow and crossed his arms.

"Sleep is for sissies," she said, crossing her arms.

"We need you fresh and alert to figure this out. Eight hours of sleep will only help you solve this faster. Go on. Go sleep. I'll have all the interactions between Tristan and the two you're interested in on a drive for you to watch in the morning."

Dela glared at him but she knew when she was beat—figuratively and literally. "Have that thumb drive, sweet rolls and coffee waiting at seven tomorrow morning," she said, pushing up off the chair.

Her phone rang. A glance at the name and guilt flogged her. She had run out of time to visit the vet clinic.

"Hey Molly, what's up?"

"Nothing. Just wanted to give you a report on Eats a Lot." The veterinarian chuckled after saying the name.

"I need to change that name. I don't like it either." Dela finger waved at Marty and walked out of his office, across the monitoring room, and out into the casino, while Molly told her how the dog's day went and how well he was responding to the surgery.

"He's young so it's no wonder he's healing quickly," Molly said.

"What are you doing tomorrow at one?" Dela asked. It couldn't hurt to have her friend's opinion of the property she was going to see.

"Not much. What do you have in mind?"

"I'm looking at property tomorrow in Tutuilla want to come along and give me your thoughts?" She was excited to look at the place but hadn't wanted to do it alone.

"Sure. Is it a rental?"

"No. If I like it, I'm going to purchase it. There's plenty of room for Eats a Lot. Ugh I hate that name." It made her see visions of her paycheck being eaten by the animal.

"Think about a name that ends with the same sound. That way he will learn it quicker. Do you want me to meet you there or…"

"How about you meet me at the casino parking lot at twelve-thirty. I wouldn't mind walking around the place a little before the realtor gets there. You know, so I can have questions ready to ask."

Molly sighed. "I know. We have to do reconnaissance before the enemy arrives."

Dela laughed. "It's not like that."

"It is completely like that. I'll see you at twelve-thirty. Get some rest."

"Yes, Mom." Dela ended the call standing in front of the elevators. She was glad her friend would go with her to look at the house. Now to get a good night's sleep so she could tackle the fact the dead woman and the maintenance man had been talking to their first victim.

♠ ♣ ♥ ♦

At 6:59 Dela walked into Marty's office. Two cups sat on his desk with steam swirling up. The scent of cinnamon and coffee rallied her still sleepy mind. The only thing dampening the moment was Quinn sitting in a chair, grinning at her.

"Good morning. Did you get a good night's sleep?" he asked.

Dela grunted at him and picked up the cup of coffee sitting closest to the box of sweet rolls. "As good as I could wondering if I should have brought Van in to interview last night."

"If he thought we were interested in him, he would have taken off by now." Quinn picked up the other cup and sipped.

"Where's Marty?" She pulled out the head of security's chair on wheels and sat in front of the keyboard.

"He said something about grabbing some sleep."

"He stayed up all night putting this together? There must have been more than one time that Tristan met up with Mattie and Van." She tapped the keyboard and the monitor came to life. The date and time were stamped in the bottom right-hand corner of the screen. It was dated a month earlier. "I wish we could hear what they are saying." She picked up a roll and watched the body language as Tristan talked with Mattie.

"It looks like she's threatening him," Quinn said, reaching for a sweet roll.

"Doesn't she know he could turn the tables on her boyfriend?" The two parted and a new image appeared. This time it was Tristan and Van. Tristan did all the talking and Van just stared at him with his arms crossed and his eyes on the other man.

"Looks like Van is bored," Quinn said.

"He doesn't look intimidated. I wonder what that conversation was about. Funny, Van acted like he didn't know the victim when we talked to him." Dela licked her fingers and wrote down the time of that encounter.

"How many times did Tristan converse with these two?" Quinn asked.

Dela fast forwarded. It appeared, Mattie had

challenged Tristan several times over the course of the month, but there was only the one meeting of him and Van.

"It's interesting that if Mattie knew Pomroy was blackmailing her boyfriend, why didn't she tell someone?" Quinn asked what Dela had been thinking.

"Do you think she was blackmailing him? And she didn't tell Luke. I'm starting to wonder if she really found that book in the laundry or if she was the one who killed him." Dela stared at the last video of her talking to the first murder victim. "Do you think they were in it together and someone else found out and killed them both?"

Quinn slurped the last of his coffee. "It's a good theory. But who would want them both dead?"

"The person who would gain the most." Dela turned off the monitor.

"Paula." Quin tossed his empty cup into the trash can and stood. "I had agents in Portland go out to Paula's parents' house. She's not there. And they checked out Ronald Edmond's place of business and apartment. She wasn't there either."

"We need to find out who her friends are and check to see if she is staying with one of them." Dela shoved to her feet, grabbed another roll in one hand and her coffee in the other.

"Where do you plan to find out who her friends are?" Quinn asked.

"We can start with where she works and then go ask more of the neighbors since we don't have a spouse to ask." She headed to the door and waited for him to open it since both her hands were full.

Walking through the room full of monitors, she

glanced up. A suspicious person hanging around near the security office doors caught her eye. She handed her coffee to Quinn and grabbed the mic clipped to her shirt. "Apprehend the person loitering by the security office door. Take him into the interview room. I'll be right there."

"Copy."

Two of the morning guards advanced toward the man. He started to run, but they were faster. She watched as they led him into the security offices.

"Good catch," Quinn said, handing her coffee cup back.

"You rarely see anyone standing near those doors." She glanced down at the woman watching the monitor. It was Verna. "Why didn't you alert security about the man hanging around the security office?"

Verna's wide eyes peered up at her. "I'm sorry. My mind is on other things this morning."

Dela studied the young woman. She had been nervous when they'd questioned her about not following protocol the other night, and now, she was being neglectful. "If you can't do this job then you need to hand in your resignation."

"No! I can. I don't want to lose this job. I'm just... It's family things."

Dela knew the importance of family, but not to the detriment of a job. "Maybe you need to take some sick leave and straighten out what's happening?" she offered.

The woman shook her head. "No. I can do my job."

Dela gave her one more up and down scan before saying, "Then do it. Or take a leave."

She heard the murmur of voices as she and Quinn

left the surveillance offices.

"You were a little rough on her," Quinn said.

She whipped around, nearly falling when her foot with the prosthesis didn't spin as well as her original foot. Quinn caught her, keeping her from falling on her face.

It was hard to make a point, when trying to emphasize by whipping around, nearly tossed her ass over her head.

"You need to get more sleep. You seem a bit dizzy and out of sorts." Quinn kept his hand on her shoulders as he peered into her face.

Dela wished she were a turtle so she could pull her head in and not let him see her frustration and embarrassment. "I'm fine, my shoe stuck to the carpet." She shoved away from him, splashing coffee on his jacket. "Sorry!" Things just kept getting more embarrassing. She walked over to the closest trash can and tossed the coffee and the roll before marching over to the security office door.

The two guards who hauled the loiterer in, stood outside the door to the small interview room.

"Thanks. Did he say anything?" Dela asked, walking over to the interview room door.

"Just to get our hands off him, he wasn't doing anything," Ross said.

She smiled. "Don't they all say that?"

The men both laughed.

Quinn walked into the security office.

Margie was the security officer on duty in the office. "Can I help you?" she asked.

Dela hid a grin as Quinn frowned. Margie was a new hire and had been off the last week due to a family emergency.

"He's with me," Dela said, not telling the woman he was FBI.

Quinn flashed his badge. "Special Agent Pierce. I'm here helping Dela with the homicide from Wednesday night."

"Oh. I've been gone. Pleased to meet you, and I'll remember you the next time you barge into the security office." The woman said it with a smile but her eyes said, you are no better than me.

Margie's words had a chuckle tickling Dela's throat. She cleared it and said, "Come on, let's see why Luke Saxton was trying to get into the security offices."

"That's who it was?" Quinn asked, walking up behind her as she opened the door.

Luke was pacing back and forth behind the table when they entered. He stopped and stared at them. "I know this looks bad."

"How bad?" Dela asked, motioning for him to sit as she took a seat across the table from him.

Once he pulled out a chair and sat, Quinn sat beside her.

"I just… I was hoping someone would let me in to get the things from Mattie's locker." His voice quivered.

"Why? What's in there that you want?" Dela asked.

"Her things. I know she had a photo of us. She'd told me about hanging it in her work locker." He shrugged. "You know. Things like that."

"You could have talked to one of her co-workers and asked them to get it. Or gone to the registration desk and asked for me. I would have assisted you in acquiring her effects." Dela studied him. Did he really want mementos or was there something else in there?

"Yeah. I haven't been thinking too good since… you know." He didn't look up from his hands, wringing in his lap.

Dela shoved to her feet. "Well, come on. I'll take you back to the lockers and you can clear Mattie's locker out."

Quinn put a hand on her arm. His eyes questioned her. She smiled and shook it off. One thing she'd learned as an M.P. in the army. That was when to call someone's bluff.

"Aren't the lockers locked?" Luke asked.

"Yeah. I figured you must have her key or combination if you were going to get into it." She worked hard at keeping a sincere expression.

He stared at her. "No. There wasn't any reason for me to have a key."

"Then how did you expect to get into the locker?" Quinn asked, glaring at Luke.

The man shrugged.

Dela sat back down. "What did you really come here for?"

"Answers." Luke stared at her. "Mattie was acting weird the past month. She said, I shouldn't come to the casino anymore. That it was too much of a distraction." He fisted his hands and slammed them on the table. "She was talking about going to California. That she was going to get lots of money and get out of this place." He glared at the wall between their heads. "She was going to leave me to become a model."

"Did she give you any indication of where she was getting the money?" Dela asked, pulling him back to the present.

"She laughed about some obnoxious little prick who was spying on people here. She said she knew what he was doing and he was going to pay her to keep quiet." He didn't look up from where he picked at a scab on his left hand with his right thumb.

"You knew she was talking about Tristan Pomroy. Because he was blackmailing you. Did you tell her about him?" Dela peered at his face, what she could see of it, staring down at his hands. His brow went from wrinkled concentration to ridges of anger. "You did tell her. Was that a month ago, when she told you to stay away from the casino?"

"Yeah. And you stayed away, didn't you?" Quinn picked up the questioning.

Luke raised his gaze to the special agent. "I thought if I stayed away, she'd see I was willing to do what she wanted to be with her."

"But she dumped you as soon as she had the book, didn't she?" Dela counterpunched.

"Yeah, she did! The night she brought the book over and waved it in my face. She said, the book was going to get her the money she needed to leave. I wasn't going to beg, but she didn't even give me enough time to think of a way to ask if she wanted me to come along. She said, 'I'm leaving and you are staying here. I don't need you ruining things for me.'" He slammed a fist down on the table. "She tossed me to the side once she had a way out of here."

"Did she say who she was going to get the money from?" Quinn asked.

He shook his head. "Another slam. She said I didn't need to know it didn't involve me." He placed both hands on the table and spread his fingers as if willing them not to curl into a fist. "Whoever got their hands on that book would be able to blackmail me. So, it did involve me." He glared at Dela. "She laughed when I mentioned that. 'I hope your next girlfriend likes eating at MacDonalds.' That was the last thing she said to me." He slapped his hands down on the table. "We've been dating for almost two years and she walked away laughing at my misfortune."

"Did you follow her? Maybe try to make her see the harm she was doing?" Dela asked.

"No." Luke shook his head. "I went to the fridge and started on the case of Bud I'd bought after work. I'd planned on having some of the guys over to play horse shoes on Saturday. I drank half a case and went to bed. Never invited anyone over. Couldn't get my last conversation with Mattie out of my head."

"Are you sure your temper didn't get the better of you and you went to her house to have one last talk with her?" Quinn asked.

Luke shook his head. "I didn't see her again after she left my house."

"Did you really think you'd find something in her work locker?" Dela asked, thinking it might not be a bad idea to check it out.

The man shrugged. "It's the only other place she hung out other than the place she shared with her cousin. Who, Mattie said, was a neat freak and got into everything when she cleaned."

That could have been the reason Mattie had hidden the book in the car. The one place her cousin wouldn't come across it. Dela stood. "Special Agent Pierce and I are going to go check her locker. If you really want the photo, stick around and I'll bring it to you. Otherwise, you may go."

The man glanced at Quinn as if he expected him to say differently.

"Go or stay for the photo. Your choice." Quinn stood and walked to the door.

Dela walked out into the security office. Ross had stayed behind to keep an eye on the room. "He can leave if he wants. We're going to check out Mattie's locker. He said there was a photo he wanted. If we find one, I'll bring it back to him. But if he leaves, don't stop him."

Ross nodded.

Margie also nodded.

Dela led the way out the back door of the security offices.

Chapter Eighteen

In the breakroom, Dela read the names on the lockers and found Mattie's. It had a key padlock on it. She pulled a pocket-sized lock pick set out of her slacks pocket and tickled the tumblers in the lock. It popped open and she swung the door wide.

"I'm glad you work on the side of law enforcement," Quinn said, as she slid the picks back in her pocket.

"These came in handy when we were looking for contraband in barracks." She pointed to the photo of Mattie and Luke taped to the inside of the door. "Think that's the photo he was talking about?"

"Guess we can ask him if he's still there when we get back." Quinn pulled the photo off the door.

Dela pulled out everything in the locker. There were lots of candy wrappers and scraps of paper. She placed it all on the table and sat down to go through it. The candy wrappers were trash. She put them in a pile.

The scraps of paper appeared to be random. Some had numbers, mostly from the configuration they appeared to be phone numbers. "Think these are people she knew?"

"I can have them run through the database and find out who they belong to." Quinn started writing down the numbers.

"Why would she have so many phone numbers on slips of paper?" She stared at Quinn. "And why keep them?"

"Maybe she found them in robe pockets in the laundry. Or she collected them from people she wanted to contact? It's hard to say. The only thing consistent about the woman is she wanted out of here and to go to California."

Dela nodded. "Let's go. There is nothing else in here of interest." She picked up the photo and carried it back to the security offices. It didn't surprise her that Luke had left. She wouldn't have wanted a photo that reminded her of a man who was going to leave without her.

"I'm going to send these numbers to Shaffer. You want me to go with you to check out that property?" Quinn asked.

"No. Molly is going with me." She noticed the flicker of dejection in his eyes before he grinned. "Good idea, she can tell you if it's a good fit for that moose of a dog."

"He's not a moose. But that would be a good name if it ended in an o t."

"What do you mean?"

She explained to Quinn about the name change being easier if it rhymed with the name he already had.

"What is his name?"

"Eats a Lot."

Quinn broke into a deep hearty belly laugh. When he caught his breath, he said, "That is the perfect name for him."

"No, it isn't. Don't you have numbers to send to Shaffer?"

He pulled out his phone and started inputting the phone numbers.

Dela glanced at her watch. She had a couple hours before she had to meet Molly. She really wanted to find out more about Paula's whereabouts. She was the perfect suspect for both murders. Her husband's death left her better off with his insurance claim and his little black book with the Cayman Islands account. And if Mattie was the woman who visited Paula the night before her death, then Paula more than likely killed her to get the book. For all they knew, she could be on her way to the Islands to collect the money and live out an unburdened life.

"What was the name of the place where Paula works?" Dela asked Quinn when he'd finished his message to the other special agent.

"Dobbs Western Wear. It's closed today." He glanced back at his phone. "Here's your answer about the corkscrew from forensics."

"What does it say?" She walked over to his side and stared at the phone in his hand.

"They said, the tearing of the skin and damage to the neck muscle corresponds to a wound made by a corkscrew." He glanced up. "I think it's time I wrote up a warrant to search Paula Pomroy's house."

"But she gave it as a gift to Ronald Edmond.

Shouldn't you also write up a warrant to search his house and business?" She had a feeling they would come up empty at both places. There was something about the first death that wasn't matching up with the second. "Have they had a chance to see if the wound on Mattie matches the one on Tristan?"

Quinn typed on his phone. The phone vibrated in his hand. "They're checking the photos."

Dela sat down. Her stub was still raw from being on it so long the last couple of days. She rubbed her thigh to ease the tension she felt building in her lower leg. Margie had seen her do this before. She hoped Quinn was too busy to see. More probing from him wasn't on her agenda today.

Marty and Godfrey had been the only two people in the casino that had ever seen her weep from the pain and frustration of her amputated leg. They had both walked in on her at the end of shift when she'd been in the little room they'd used for questioning. She'd had a busy night and had moved wrong twice, making her stub sit awkwardly in the sleeve of the prosthesis. But she hadn't had time to fix things. That morning she'd spent the last half hour of her shift, in the room, massaging and cursing her leg. Ike had been at the podium that night and must have called the two to tell them she was closed up in the room. After that time, she'd learned to make time to fix any abnormality that happened to her prosthesis.

"Forensics says that while they are both wounds with a serrated edge and trauma to the muscle, they can't be conclusive that it was the same weapon." Quinn glanced at her. "Which means, there could be two weapons or there could be two killers."

As soon as Quinn's head moved, Dela stopped massaging her leg. "But they both wanted their hands on the black book. Have you had anyone check it to see if there were more than the few people we saw being blackmailed? Or that maybe it held more answers?" She thought it took someone desperate to kill twice to get the book. But who would have known about the book? They were back to the names they'd found written in it.

"Did you ever figure out if the R.E. in the book was Ronald Edmond?" Dela pulled a paper out of a drawer and wrote down the initials and names they knew that corresponded. "After seeing the exchange between Tristan and Van Branson, I'm not sure he is the V.B. in the book." She looked up from writing and peered at Quinn. "Any thoughts?"

"We are working on a connection between Edmond and Pomroy besides the wife. I agree. Branson didn't seem threatened by Pomroy in the video. But, there must have been a reason the casino blackmailer was talking to him."

"Van will be in to work tonight. It's his Friday. I say we show him the video and see what he has to say." Dela liked having a plan rather than running around looking for answers. "I think we should talk to Edmond some more if he's still around."

"I can have him down here for questioning when you get back from looking at the house. About three?" Quinn asked, standing.

"That should be plenty of time. But I keep thinking that if Tristan was stashing money in an account in the Caymans, he would have had to have had a mark who paid more than the people working at this casino." She studied the names. "These people…" she tapped each name. "Would have little left over to pay a blackmailer after their living expenses."

"Unless V.B. has money and is the one paying the most." Quinn walked to the door. "In which case, that person would have the most to gain from Pomroy's death." He opened the door. "I'm getting something to eat, want to join me?"

If she didn't eat now who knew when she'd get the chance. "Yeah."

They walked in companionable silence over to the coffee shop.

Once seated in the booth and had ordered, Dela asked, "Don't you have other cases you need to split your time with?"

Quinn sipped his iced tea and grinned. "This is my priority. Shaffer will handle anything else that comes along. This is a normally quiet corner of Oregon. That's why I asked for this field office."

"You were looking to ease up on your workload?" she asked, picking up her glass of iced tea.

"Yeah. Between the special task force and then going into high profile cases in the FBI, I'm ready to relax in between cases, not rush from one to the next."

She laughed. "You aren't that old. What maybe a few years over forty?"

He studied her. "It's not old, but it is if a person is thinking about family life."

Dela stared at him. He was being sincere. He wanted a wife, kids, dog, and a house. He had the house. Was he planning on settling down in Pendleton? "I never thought of you as a family man. You were always so intense. Didn't seem like a good fit for a father."

He cringed. "Yeah. I had a lot of lives to keep safe when I was in Iraq. The information I gathered saved our troops."

"I understand, but I still don't forgive you." She peered into his eyes. She witnessed hurt quickly replaced with nonchalance. Her forgiveness meant something to him. Pondering that would only get her sucked in deeper. She wanted him to have a wonderful life. At one time, she had dreamed of being included in that life. Even though they had never dated or even had a moment, he was the one person in her adult life that she could see herself with. But not anymore. She knew to get close enough to a man to be intimate and marry, they'd have to accept she wasn't a whole woman. And she was still working on the acceptance herself.

The waitress arrived with their lunches.

They set to eating and didn't talk until Quinn was finished and she was picking at her fries.

"You want help naming your dog?" he asked.

Dela studied him. He was full of surprises today. "Have you come up with something that isn't dumb?"

"Mugshot."

Laughter burst out of her. When she caught her breath, Dela asked, "What made you think of that?"

"It has the same sound as lot and kind of fits your job. You may not be a cop, but what you do is a lot like what a cop does. And from the way you found him, he could have been a convict on the run." He winked. "He was running away for a reason."

"Mugshot." Dela thought about Quinn's reasoning and tumbled the word over in her mind a few times. "You know. I like it. Mugshot he is. Unless he doesn't like the name."

"You can't ask him if he likes the name," Quinn said, laughingly.

"No. But if he doesn't respond to it, when I call him, then he doesn't like it." She finished her iced tea and tossed her napkin on the plate. "I need to go meet Molly in the parking lot. I'll meet you at the security offices at three."

"I'll have Edmond there." Quinn rose when she did.

"I can take care of the bill on my way out," she said, wanting to take a step back to not have to tilt her head to look up at him and compromise her balance. But her legs didn't seem to want to move.

"I've got the bill. I invited you to lunch." Quinn grinned at her, showing a dimple, and headed to the register.

She inhaled and stilled her beating heart. She really needed to get over whatever it was he did to her. He wanted a family and she wasn't sure she could handle domestic life.

♠ ♣ ♥ ♦

On the drive to Tutuilla, Dela told Molly about the name she'd settled on for the dog.

"Mugshot? Really?" Molly laughed. "I guess it is better than Eats a Lot."

"It's growing on me the more I think about it." She didn't add so was the man who'd suggested the name.

She'd slid into Molly's car when the woman had pulled up to the casino entrance. Now she directed her friend to the house.

"This is a nice place. Your neighbors wouldn't be too close." Molly parked the car and they both exited the vehicle. "How do you plan to take care of one and a half acres?"

"I'm hoping there is a young person in the neighborhood who mows lawns."

"That much land is more than a lawn. It would need animals to keep the grass down."

"Really? You think I would need animals. I couldn't just landscape it and have someone mow?" Dela walked up to the front window and looked in. The place would need paint and some other work done to it before she could think about moving in. Did she have the time to fix it up?

They walked around to the back.

"Look! A nice big sliding door. That would make it easy for Mugshot to wander in and out without you having to get up and open the door for him." Molly cupped her hands on either side of her face and looked through the glass doors. "Oh man! This place is going to need a lot of work."

Dela stood beside her friend, cupping her hands and peering into the darkness of the house. A lump landed in her gut. Was she up for making over this house? And that wasn't the hard part. What about the large parcel of land?

She turned and stared at Cabbage Hill and the pine trees. The sight made her heart soar. She loved this view. Always had, even as a child. There was something comforting about seeing the edge of the Blue Mountains.

Tires crunched on the driveway on the other side of the house.

"Let's go see what the realtor has to say." Dela walked around the end of the house with Molly in tow. She caught her first glimpse of Cathryn Wright. The woman was tall and stout with reddish hair that was dyed, guessing from the steak of gray at the roots, and a sun-weathered complexion.

"Ms. Alvaro?" the woman questioned, holding out a hand.

Dela grasped the woman's hand and shook. "Dela, please. This is my friend Molly."

Cathryn smiled at Molly. "Aren't you the vet at Riverside?"

"Yes, I am."

"My son brought his dog to you last year. The Rottweiler who tangled with a porcupine?"

"Oh! I remember. Poor Max had a face full of quills. He was so good, I almost didn't have to sedate him. But after the first hour he wasn't looking forward to more plucking and I had to." Molly shook hands. "I hope Max is staying away from porcupines."

"He is." Cathryn held out papers for Dela. "This has been on the market for so long, the owner wants to sell. Let's take a look around and then you tell me what you are willing to spend."

Dela glanced over at Molly and grinned. If she could get it cheap enough, she could do a lot to fix it up.

Chapter Nineteen

Molly dropped Dela off at the casino parking lot. "Come by tonight and see Mugshot and stay for dinner. We'll celebrate you signing papers on your new place tomorrow."

"Sounds good. I could use a night off. And you can help me make a list of the first things to fix to make the house livable." She already knew where the painting from the gift shop would go. Instead of her bedroom, it would go in the living room.

"It's a deal. I'll also give you Travis to help with the remodeling."

"Thanks! See you later." Dela entered the casino smiling. There was a lot of work to do to the place, but she was getting it at half the market value for a house and acreage of that size.

She walked over to the deli and grabbed a cup of coffee before heading to the security offices. It was Rosie's day off. She wished the woman had been there. She had some questions for her about Tristan Pomroy,

Mattie, and Van Branson.

The door to the security office opened as she approached. Kenny exited. He stopped, closed the door, and waited for her. She could tell by his wrinkled forehead and the way his hand clenched and unclenched he wasn't happy.

"What's wrong?" she asked, stopping in front of him.

"First, why are you here on a Sunday? And second, why does that Fed have the run of the casino?"

Quinn must have pushed his FBI status around. She needed to have a talk with him if he wished to get help from the casino staff. Especially the Umatilla members.

"I can't take a day off until we find out who killed Tristan and Mattie. With you here doing the job of assistant head of security, I can work on finding the killer." She nodded toward the office door. "What did he do?"

"He took Benji off the floor to go up and insist a guest come down to the security office. He didn't go through me or tell me what was going on." Kenny narrowed his eyes. "I don't care if he is a Fed, he doesn't work here and doesn't have the right to tell us what to do."

"I'll have a talk with Special Agent Pierce." She patted the big man's arm. "I'm trying to get this solved and get him out of here."

"Thanks." Kenny's radio crackled and he headed off talking on his mic.

Dela had turned her radio off and left it in Molly's car while looking over the property. Now it was back on her person, but she'd not turned it on. No sense when she wasn't working the floor.

She opened the security door and walked in.

Margie nodded toward the interview room. "That full of himself FBI is in there with one of the guests."

"Thank you. I know. We both agreed the man needed to be questioned." She picked up the file she'd gathered on the two murders, walked across the room, and opened the door. Ronald and Quinn sat across the table from one another, glaring. Hopefully, this didn't turn into a pissing match.

"Mr. Edmond, thank you for coming down to talk to us," she said, taking a seat next to Quinn.

"I didn't have much of a choice." The man scowled at the FBI agent.

"I'm sorry to hear that. We just had a few more questions about your acquaintance with the Pomroys." Out of the corner of her eye, she saw Quinn pull out his notepad.

"Pomroys? I don't know anything about them." The man straightened and stared her square in the eyes.

"You had a discussion with Tristan in the deli the day of his death. And you met his wife in your guest room before the man was killed. You slipped out of your room before the time of death, and he was killed with the gift Paula gave you."

Ronald sputtered. "W-what do you mean the gift she gave me?"

Dela shared a glance with Quinn. Did she dare mention the corkscrew? "The little bag that was hanging on the door handle when you and Paula returned to the room after meeting in the bar."

His face turned as red as her mother's roses. "Unless he was strangled, I'm pretty sure the underwear she had in that bag weren't used to kill him."

She swung her face toward Quinn so fast her neck popped. "Who switched the contents in the bag?"

Quinn glared at the man. "Why did you slip out of the room without being seen that night?"

Ronald huffed. "I don't know what you're talking about. I walked out of that room at one-thirty after waiting for Paula to come back with ice. She didn't return so I left."

"The video camera in that hall didn't catch you leaving." Dela studied the man. "What was Paula wearing when she left the room?"

"A robe and that's all."

"Nothing underneath?" She glanced over at Quinn. She could have taken the robe off, killed her husband, washed the blood from her, the weapon, and the room, then put the robe on to go back out into the hall. If she had done all of that, she was one cold-blooded woman.

Someone in security had blanked out the camera on ten and she had a feeling had also blanked out the camera on eight. Which explained them not seeing Ronald leave the room or Paula returning. But if Paula killed her husband, why didn't she take the book? How had it ended up on the pile of laundry at the bottom of the chute and in the hands of the one person who would use it to get what she wanted? This conversation had brought up too many questions.

"She tossed on that robe and said she was going for ice. I waited until it seemed unlikely that's where she went. I dressed and left to look for her. Couldn't find her anywhere so I went down and gambled." He leaned back. "For all I know, she could have killed her husband and planned to pin it on me."

Quinn leaned forward. "What were you and Mr.

Pomroy talking about in the deli that afternoon?"

The man snapped his mouth shut like the lid of an ammo box. Apparently, his visit with Tristan was more incriminating than him bouncing the bed with the wife.

"I guess we'll just have to get some lip readers in here to watch the video," Quinn said. "You know only half the time they pick up the correct words. I bet there are lots of words that look like kill when you're lip reading."

Ronald flicked his gaze over to Quinn. "What we said had nothing to do with his death."

"How can you be sure?" Quinn asked.

The bounty hunter stared at both of them. "It had to do with my business."

Quinn leaned forward. "How?"

"I'd learned that Pomroy had sent in a sighting of a suspect on a wanted poster. Same guy I've been tracking. I suggested he tell me what he knew. He refused. Said he wasn't splitting the reward with anyone."

Dela thought that made sense given what they'd seen of the conversation. "Which fugitive were you both following?"

Ronald looked away.

"We need to know this. We have two homicides that we believe are linked." She opened the file and slid out the photo of the man wanted by the FBI for the show airing before Tristan started acting secretive and telling people he was going to come into some money.

Ronald stared at the photo.

"Is this who you were arguing about?" she asked.

"How did you know that?" Ronald leaned back, but his gaze remained on the photo.

"Process of elimination," Quinn said. "Is this man here? In the area?"

"What I'd uncovered said he was in NE Oregon. Then my friend, who keeps an eye on the incoming claims, saw Pomroy had called in. I discovered he lived in Pendleton. I did surveillance on his house, met his wife, and set up meeting her here to see what I could get out of her and her husband. He wasn't about to give up anything, and she didn't have a clue."

"Is there any way this person of interest could have known Pomroy had spotted him?" Quinn asked.

The man shook his head. "I don't know. I have ways of keeping tabs on the tips that come in on the people I'm after. This fugitive might have ways of knowing who sends in sightings."

Dela studied the man. The last couple of minutes seemed like the first honest words they'd obtained from the man. She turned to Quinn. "Is there a way to see if someone is getting into that information?"

"It would have to be someone in the FBI." Quinn stared at Ronald. "Do you have an informant in the FBI?"

"I'm not saying anything more." Ronald snapped his lips shut again and from the defiance in his eyes, Dela could tell Quinn wouldn't learn anything about his informant.

Quinn closed his notepad and stood. "Thank you for talking with us."

"That's it? You pulled me down here and now it's 'thank you, good-bye?'"

"Would you rather have us still think you are a suspect in the murders?" Dela asked, standing.

"Then I can leave here? The casino, go home?"

Ronald asked.

"It's fine by us." She stopped at the door. "But you might want to ask Detective Jones if it's okay with him." Dela walked out of the room with a grin on her face. She wondered how far Detective Dick was with the first murder? He probably didn't even know there was a second one connected.

Once Ronald had left the security offices, Dela sat and wrote all the questions that had popped into her head while they were talking with the bounty hunter.

"What are you doing?" Quinn asked, pulling a chair up beside her.

"Writing down what we don't know."

He started reading it off. "Where did the corkscrew go? I think that will be figured out when we find out who blanked out the hallway on eight as well as ten."

She tapped the comment she'd written about the camera down on eight.

"I agree, if Paula killed her husband, why didn't she take the book? That would have been her number one reason to kill him. To get her hands on the information that would make her rich."

She wrote the last one. Is there a fugitive working at the casino?

Quinn tapped the last question with his finger. "If so, he had a good reason to want Pomroy dead but what about Mattie?"

"That's what I can't figure out. Who would want them both dead? That brings us back to Paula." Dela glanced at her watch. "I promised Molly I'd come over for dinner. But I'll be back at ten to question Van."

Quinn leaned back in his chair. "Are you buying the place?"

She smiled. "I am." And walked out of the room without waiting for any comments.

Chapter Twenty

Driving back to the casino after the best evening she'd had in a long time, Dela couldn't stop smiling. Mugshot had licked her hand when she asked him if he liked the name. Then she'd scratched his ears and told him all about where they were going to live. Molly had remembered how much Dela liked fry bread and had made a batch to go with the stew. After the meal, the three of them, Dela, Molly, and Travis sat down and mapped out the list of things that had to be done for Dela and Mugshot to move into the house and the list of things to be done afterward. They had all decided the backyard fence was first and Travis said he and a couple friends would build it for half the price the local fencing installer would charge.

All that was left for her to do was go by the real estate office in the morning and sign the papers. After that, she would open an account at the local lumber store with Travis on the account.

It was nine o'clock as she parked and walked into the casino. Sunday night. Her favorite night to work. Everyone was moving slow, there were few people at the machines and even fewer at the gaming tables. Tonight and tomorrow were the lull before the wave of gamblers started filing in for Bingo on Wednesday and gambling the rest of the week.

It was rare she crossed the casino floor without checking everything out. Tonight was no exception. She'd learned in the army to always be on the alert for something that seemed off. Right now, she had a feeling something was wrong. Everything around her appeared normal but something… The speakers were buzzing not playing the canned music.

Hurrying to the security door, she had a near miss of the door as it flew open.

"Fisk, what's wrong?" Dela asked, grabbing the man around her age by the shoulders.

"Jerry can't stop the damn buzzing." He put his hands over his ears. Fisk, like her was a veteran. He suffered from PTSD, but up until now, hadn't had a problem as a security guard.

"Go to the surveillance room. There shouldn't be any buzzing in there." She shoved him along the wall toward surveillance and hurried into the security office.

Oliver was at the podium. "Fisk can't do his job with the buzzing."

Dela glanced over at the man who worked the podium in the office on Sunday, Monday, and Tuesday nights. He'd retired and did this to supplement. "Who is looking into the speakers?"

"Someone from tech. Don't know his name." Oliver pushed the button on the mic. "Who is working on the sound system?"

"Poppy," came the voice over the radio.

Dela spoke into her mic. "What's her location?"

"Sound room."

"If Special Agent Pierce arrives, tell him I'll be right back." Dela walked to the back of the security offices and out the door. She followed the hall to the room behind the tech department. In the small room that housed the speaker system for the casino, she found Poppy, Marty, and one of the swing shift maintenance people crammed in the small room.

"Can you just turn the whole thing off?" she asked, causing them all to swing around.

"I'm trying, but it looks like the only way to do that is to cut the power." Poppy pointed a thumb at the maintenance person. "He's trying to figure out if it will cut power to anything else."

Dela nodded for Marty to follow her out into the hallway. When the head of security did, she asked in a low voice. "Does this feel like a hiccup in the system or something premeditated?'

He stared at her. "You think someone did this on purpose?"

She shrugged. "Lately, I'm suspicious of everything that goes on here."

"And with good reason. I'll go check video of the sound room and see who might have entered it and messed with things." He glanced at the room. "I'm no help in there. Only taking up space."

"Thanks." Dela entered the room as Poppy did a happy dance. "Did you get it turned off?"

"Yeah. We went around the main and turned off the power to the speakers." The woman smiled.

"Good. That sound was annoying." Dela peered at Poppy and the maintenance guy. "Now can you see what caused the problem?"

"We'll get right on it," the man said, pulling out a device with small prods and wires.

"Thank you." Dela walked back to the security office.

Quinn walked through the opposite door as she walked in the back door. "How come there's no music playing?" he asked.

"Glitch in the sound system." Dela stood with the door open. "You want to go get Van or have him brought to us?"

"Let's go see him. He'll feel more comfortable in his own environment." Quinn crossed the room and followed her out into the back hallway. "Does the sound system go down often?"

"Never since I've worked here." She wondered if he thought it suspicious as well.

"There seem to be a lot of different things happening here lately."

She spun on her good foot and faced him. "That was my thought as well. But why would someone mess with the sound system?"

Her radio crackled. "Dela?"

"Copy. This is Dela."

"Hey, it's Poppy. From what we can figure there is something somewhere in the system that is shorting things. Ray suggests he and his crew check out all the speakers. I can disconnect the sound so they are all getting juice and they can test them."

"Then that's what needs to be done." Dela dropped her hand from her mic. "What could cause a short?"

"Something interfering with the electrical connection." Quinn walked by her. "We need to talk to Van before he gets pulled out to check the speakers."

She hurried after him to the maintenance department. They stepped into the room at the same time.

Everyone was putting on tool belts and grabbing ladders.

Dela scanned the room. She didn't see Van. But she did see the shift supervisor. "Sam, do you know what time Van Branson usually gets here for his shift?"

The man in his fifties walked over and stood in front of her. "He shows up about fifteen minutes early." He glanced at his watch. "So should be here any time."

"Thanks." She faced Quinn. "Wait here?"

"No. We'll just be in the way. Let's go back to security."

They walked down the hall and her phone rang. She glanced at the name. Why would Marty call on the phone?

"Hey Marty, why didn't you use the radio?" she answered.

"I found something interesting. And too many people listen to the radio."

This intrigued and angered her. She'd had an inkling someone in security or surveillance had been helping whoever killed Tristan but this made her sure of it.

"We'll be right there." She tucked her phone in her pocket and picked up the pace. "Marty has something."

They didn't say anymore as they walked through the security offices, out to the casino floor, and over to the surveillance door.

Walking through the room full of monitors, she took in who was working. They crossed to Marty's office and walked in.

"What did you discover?" Dela asked, pulling up a chair beside the head of surveillance and propping her prosthetic on the box under his table.

"I'm getting tired of finding blank video when I want to look at an area that has suspicious activity." He had the view of the hallway outside the sound room on a monitor. She watched and saw a slight flicker, then the time stamp jumped ahead half an hour.

"You and me both." Frustration bubbled deep in her gut. She held down the growl that wanted to crawl up her throat.

"What are you both talking about?" Quinn stared at the video while Marty explained someone tampered with the sound system.

Dela's mind was racing. "What about the camera in the other hall? How did they get to that area?"

Marty started tapping keys. The four monitors above his table came to life with video from all the directions a person could have used to get to the sound room. There wasn't a skip in time on any of them. And it didn't show anyone going toward the area.

"I don't understand? If no one went to that area, why is there a skip in the time on the video outside the door?" Dela glanced at Marty and then Quinn.

"Who had access to this video feed?" Quinn asked.

Marty typed on the keyboard and up popped gibberish to Dela.

"It looks like Verna Pyle." Marty's forehead wrinkled. "Every video you've asked me to look up about this murder, she's been the person whose monitored the cameras."

Dela exchanged a glance with Quinn.

"Is she still here?" Dela asked.

"No, she went home right after the buzzing started. She said the sound was triggering a migraine." Marty said the last with skepticism.

"I'll have Shaffer go pick her up and take her to the office in Pendleton." Quinn pulled out his phone and walked over to the corner.

"Have you seen Verna and Tristan ever conversing?" Dela asked.

Marty shook his head. "She never went down to the deli or any other place to eat during her shifts. She always stayed up here, eating food from home." He stared at the gibberish on the main monitor. "I was training her to take over for me. Do you really think she could have murdered someone?"

"From what she's shown us, I would have told you no. But considering what we are finding out, that timid mouse persona may only be that." Dela thought of how torture had been used on Mattie. Could the woman she'd talked with, who nervously wrung her hands, have tortured a woman close to her same age? It didn't make sense.

Quinn returned to the conversation. "Shaffer will pick her up and call us. He also said that the blood samples found in the supply room were too compromised to tell if it was the victim's blood."

"Paula could have slipped out of the robe, killed Tristan, shoved him in the chute, then washed off, and walked back to eight-thirty-four and put her clothes on, leaving, again, before the camera started working." Dela snapped her fingers. "Did you ever get Paula's phone records? She would have had to call whoever was manning the cameras to tell them when to turn them off and back on."

"Unless they had made it to where they went off when she left the room and came back on when she appeared dressed in another part of the casino." Quinn knocked a hole in what Dela thought was a good way to connect Paula with her accomplice.

"I can pull up video of Paula that night and see where she showed up on the camera that was being watched by Verna. She had to have turned the camera off after Paula walked out of the room." Marty began typing on the keyboard. "If the camera came back on when Verna saw Paula in one of the other cameras, then we know they were working together."

"It's after ten, let's go have our chat with Van. By then Marty will have answers and we can go talk to Verna." Quinn walked over to the door.

Dela couldn't shake the feeling either Verna was a cold-blooded killer who was a good actress, or she had been set up.

Chapter Twenty-one

Van was checking out the speakers around the casino floor feature when Dela and Quinn approached. The waterfall fountain that splashed water down around the feet of the bronze horses in the scene covered the sound of their footsteps. Van crouched with his back to the floor, looking at something behind a fake rock.

"Van, can we speak with you?" Dela asked as she and Quinn stopped at the railing at the edge of the scene.

The man shot to his feet. When he turned to them, he held what looked like a corkscrew in his hand.

"Where did you get that?" Quinn asked.

Van held it out. "Behind here. I think it's what shorted out the speakers."

"Could you bring it to us?" Dela asked, watching the man. He seemed as surprised to find it as they were at seeing him holding what could be the murder weapon.

The maintenance man nodded, walking toward, them watching his step as he crossed the high spots to keep from getting his feet wet.

Quinn pulled a latex glove out of his pocket and tugged it on. When Van stood on the other side of the railing, the special agent reached across and took hold of the corkscrew.

"Could you step over and answer some questions for us?" Dela asked, watching the man. He seemed stunned to find the bottle opening device in the display. She studied the corkscrew as Van climbed over the railing. It looked like a replica of the device Teresa had shown her as the one Paula had bought.

"I'll be right back," Quinn said, heading for the casino entrance.

She had a feeling he was going to put the item in an evidence bag. Dela turned her attention to Van. "How did you come to be checking out these speakers?"

"When I came on shift, Harry told me what they'd been doing and that he'd checked all the speakers on this end of the floor except the ones in the feature area." Van waved his hand. "I take over whatever tasks Harry hasn't finished when I come on shift. Everyone has someone they take over for."

Dela nodded. It seemed a bit of a coincidence one of their suspects found the corkscrew. But he'd look frightened when he'd turned around. As far as she knew, no one outside of law enforcement knew Tristan had been killed by a corkscrew.

"The reason Special Agent Pierce and I wanted to talk to you is because we came across a video that shows you and the murder victim, Tristan Pomroy, having a discussion about a week before he died. When we asked you if you knew him, you said you didn't." She pulled out her phone and found the video of the two men.

Van stared at it. "That's the guy who was killed?"

"Yes, Tristan Pomroy."

He stared at the exchange.

"What were you…or I guess I should say, what was he talking to you about?" Dela continued to watch Van's face. It had gone as blank and unseeing as the expression he'd worn during the conversation with Tristan.

"I don't remember. Something about he wanted me to spy on someone in the maintenance department." Van shrugged and peered down at her. "He thought someone was purchasing items to then sell elsewhere."

"What did you tell him?" She studied his eyes. They looked familiar.

"To go find another snitch. I wasn't going to help him." He crossed his arms as he had during the conversation with the victim.

Quinn returned. He glanced from Dela to Van and back to Dela. "What's going on?"

Dela told him what she'd learned.

Van confirmed with a nod of his head. "Can I fix the frayed speaker wire?"

"Did you ask him all your questions?" Quinn asked.

"Yeah. You can go back to work." Dela led Quinn away from the feature. "Did you see how scared he looked when he'd turned around? Do you think he knew about the corkscrew and was trying to get rid of it?"

"I don't know. You questioned him without me present so I can't make any assumptions on what is hearsay." His eyes narrowed.

"It felt awkward standing there saying nothing." She headed to the security office. "What did you do with the corkscrew?"

"I locked it in the glovebox of my vehicle. I'll run it to the OSP forensic lab and see if it has blood on it." Quinn put a hand on her arm, stopping her. "We need to see if we can find a link between Verna, Paula, and possibly Van."

"I'll ask Wallace to check into Verna and Van in the morning. You'll have to check on Paula on your side." Dela continued to the security office.

"Where are you going? We need to go to the field office and question Verna. Unless you want me to do it."

She faced Quinn. "You and Verna can both wait for me to finish up asking questions here. I'm going to see if Poppy thinks that corkscrew could have messed up the speakers, and then I'm going to ask Marty to see if he can find any instances where Paula met up with Verna or Van, and leave a note for Wallace." Dela took a deep breath and said, "You can wait for me or I will catch up to you at the field office in thirty to forty minutes."

"That will be close to midnight. We can wait and interview Verna in the morning," Quinn said.

"How? Are you going to let her loose and say come back in the morning? You had Shaffer haul her in. She's going to know we are adding up the evidence against her. She's not going to come back tomorrow."

"I can question her. This is your day off. Let me do

the questioning and you go get some sleep." Quinn started to put a hand on her arm.

Dela took a step back. "I'm not a child who needs to be told when to go to bed. I will go to bed when I have exhausted all I can do for the night."

"I'm not saying you're a child. I'm saying you put everyone else first and hurt yourself." Quinn pivoted and marched off toward the casino entrance.

Damn the man. Every time she started putting some space between her and her feelings for the guy he did or said something that made her wonder 'what if.'

♠ ♣ ♥ ♦

Parking the car in the spot closest to the FBI field office door, Dela turned off the ignition and drew in a long breath. She'd nearly dozed off on the fifteen-minute drive to the office from the casino. But she'd discovered from Poppy the corkscrew had been in a trickle of water. She figured the corkscrew had been tossed behind the rock and the vibration from the speaker had shifted the bottle opener to slide and touch the metal where the wire entered the speaker, thereby shorting out the system.

The door opened and Quinn walked out of the building.

She exited the car and walked up to him. Her leg had started bothering her as she'd talked to Marty about linking Paula, Verna, and Van in any videos.

"I saw you pull up on the surveillance cameras. Thought I'd escort you to our office on the second floor." He smiled and held the door for her.

The first thing that popped into her head was hoping they had an elevator. However, it was doubtful given the building only had two stories.

Thankfully, Quinn walked over to a narrow elevator door and punched a button. The door slid open and she entered. The building wasn't very old and the front half of the first floor was a church. It seemed like an odd combination.

The elevator dinged and the door swished open. Quinn motioned for her to exit first. She spotted a door with Federal Bureau of Investigation printed on the frosted window and walked that direction.

Quinn reached the door ahead of her and opened it.

She studied him as she walked by. Why was he being so gentlemanly? "Have you already questioned Verna?"

"No. I've been waiting for you." He motioned to the shorter man with the same haircut and a suit that had brought Mattie's cousin to the house. He stood by a door. "You haven't been formally introduced. This is Special Agent Shaffer. Shaffer this is Dela Alvaro, Head of Security at the casino." Quinn nodded to the door behind Shaffer. "He brought Ms. Pyle in about forty-five minutes ago. We've left her sitting by herself until now."

"Did she ask you why you wanted her to come to the FBI office?" Dela asked Special Agent Shaffer.

"She said she didn't understand why the FBI wanted to talk to her. And looked pretty shook up." Shaffer grasped the door handle and opened the door.

Verna sat at the table, tears ran down her cheeks, and her hands shook. This is what Dela had expected to see, given the other times they had questioned Verna at the casino. She still didn't see her as a murderer. But what if she had been coerced into helping?

"Verna, sorry you were brought here. But we have

many questions for you." Dela took the chair across from the surveillance employee.

Quinn sat down beside her and pressed a button on a recording device. "Could you state your name and why you think we brought you here?"

Verna glanced at Dela. She nodded for the younger woman to go ahead.

"I am Verna Ruth Pyle. I'm not sure why you brought me here. I know I made a mistake the other night by not following protocol. I thought the casino would deal with it, not the FBI." She flicked her gaze to Quinn then right back to Dela.

"Verna, we've found that you were watching the monitors for several other instances when the cameras were turned off. If it had been the one incident, I would have said, yes you were being overzealous to show us you could be second in the surveillance team. But with it happening again and again… Now I'm thinking you were helping someone cover up a murder."

The woman's eyes widened. "I wouldn't do something like that! I want to work in surveillance. I wouldn't jeopardize my career."

"Then how do you account for all of these instances?" Dela wanted the woman to be innocent but she also had to keep an unbiased frame of mind.

"When were they?"

Quinn laid a paper on the table in front of Verna. "These are the days, times, and location that the cameras were turned off and then back on."

She read the information and shook her head. "I didn't black anything out. I don't know how."

Dela starred at her. "I just found out through this investigation that everyone who works surveillance was taught how to turn off the camera when a local official takes a woman up to a hotel room."

Quinn made a sound in his throat. She ignored him.

"I know you were shown how to do it when you started working. Lionel told me it was by order of Godfrey Friday, the last head of security." She zeroed her gaze on the special agent so he knew she wasn't pleased with what she'd found out.

"I may have been shown but I never did it." Verna stared at the paper in front of her. "Before I noticed the camera feed was down, I had used the restroom." She moved her finger down. "And this time, Robin asked me if I had something for a headache. I had to go to my purse in the lockers and get it."

Dela stared at her. "You left your station for ten to fifteen minutes and didn't get anyone to watch it for you?"

"Robin said she would keep an eye on things." Verna stared at her. "She sits beside me. And this one, today. I wasn't feeling well. I asked her to watch my monitors while I got a pill for my migraine and laid down for a while till the pill kicked in. Then the speakers started buzzing and it became worse, so I asked to leave."

"What's Robin's last name?" Quinn asked.

"Everly."

"R.E." Dela and Quinn said, locking gazes.

It hadn't been Ronald Edmond that Tristan had been blackmailing. But what did the accountant have on the surveillance employee that got him killed?

Chapter Twenty-two

The ringing of the bedside phone woke Dela.

"Yeah?" she croaked into the phone and tried to read the clock through blurry eyes. 6:45, possibly?

"You weren't answering your cell phone so I had them put me through on this phone," Wallace's soft voice held a tremor of excitement.

"I turned off my cell phone so my mom wouldn't wake me up early." She knew the techie wouldn't get her sarcasm. But it felt good to say it.

"You left a note wanting me to look into Verna Pyle and Van Branson. Verna started working here two months after Van. They both gave previous employers that are fake."

She sat up in bed. "Why didn't that get caught when they applied and were interviewed?"

"You'll have to ask HR. Not my department."

"What else did you discover?" She remained in bed, but pulled a notepad and pen out of the bedside table.

"There isn't any record of Van before three years ago."

"I know that. He said it was because he was born at Big Muddy during the Rajneesh era." She had been wondering if his not having personal identification because of that was true. "Do you know anything about that culture and if they registered the children?"

"I'll look into it. But Verna also has nothing before she attended college. And they both live in the same apartment building." Wallace said it as if he thought the two were living together.

"He's twice her age." The image of Verna as they'd questioned her popped into Dela's head. The young woman had the same eyes as Van. "Check and see if you can find any marriage records for Van and try to find a birth certificate for Verna." She jotted these questions down on her notepad. If they were related, why were they keeping it quiet?

"I'll check on it." The line went dead.

Dela stretched and slipped her foot over the end of the bed. She'd been so tired when they'd finished with Verna last night, Quinn had insisted on driving her back to the casino. He said Shaffer could bring her car back in the morning and Quinn could give him a ride back to town. That kind of thoughtfulness was beginning to wear on her notion she didn't need someone in her live making things easier.

Using her crutches, she stood, and swung her way over to the bathroom. A quick shower and she'd be ready to tackle the videos Marty found and interview Robin Everly. It was the surveillance member's day off, but she'd have Marty call the woman in for something.

Quinn planned on being here around nine because she needed her car to get to the realty office to sign the papers on her new place at ten.

After her shower, she sat in her underwear going through the steps of putting her prosthesis on when there was a knock on the door. Only a handful of people knew she was staying in the room and she'd told housekeeping not to bother cleaning until she was gone.

Using her crutches, she swung over to the door and looked out the peephole. A groan slithered up her throat. "Quinn, what are you doing here so early?" she asked through the door.

"Let me in, I brought sweet rolls and coffee."

"I'm not dressed." And I only have one leg.

"I'll wait here while you get dressed."

He didn't know about her prosthesis and how long it took her to get dressed, considering she had several layers of liners and a sleeve and the leg to put on before she could actually put her pants on.

"Go down to the security office. I'll get there as soon as I can."

"Am I interrupting something?" His judgmental tone threw her off.

"What do you mean by that?" she snarled back. How dare he insinuate she didn't want him in the room because she had a man over. It was none of his business if she had or hadn't.

"Exactly what it sounds like."

"That you think I don't deserve happiness?" She smacked her head against the door. What was she doing making these comments through a door where more than Quinn would hear them? "Just, please, go to the office. I'll be down in twenty minutes."

She hobbled back to the bed and continued putting on the items that kept her stub protected and the prosthesis on her leg. Before the interaction with Quinn, she'd been intrigued by what Wallace discovered about Van and Verna and ready to jump into finding out what she could about Robin Everly. Now she wasn't looking forward to dealing with Quinn.

♠ ♣ ♥ ♦

Thirty minutes later she walked into the security office.

Margie motioned to the interview room. "There's a grumpy FBI man in there. You might want to deal with him after about a gallon of coffee."

"Thanks for the warning." Dela grasped the handle and walked in.

Quinn sat with his back to the door. The pale blue, short-sleeved shirt he wore stretched across his broad back as he studied papers on the table in front of him.

She wondered if this act of back to the door was his way of telling her he didn't care if she showed up or not. His accusation still rang in her mind. Was he jealous? She'd tossed that around as she'd dressed.

"What did you have besides coffee and sweet rolls to show me?" she asked, walking around the table and sitting across from him.

The special agent studied her. "You look rested for as late as I brought you back to the casino."

"I learned how to function with little sleep in the army. Did Shaffer bring my car over?"

"He'll get it here later. He had something personal come up." Quinn opened the folder sitting under the paper he'd been reading.

"I need the car before ten. I have to sign the papers

at the realty then." She watched him slide the folder toward her.

"I can take you."

"I'll call my mom. I'm sure she'd like to know what I'm buying." As much as she really didn't need her mom saying it was too much work, she did want her approval, even though there was no way mom would talk her out of buying the place.

"I thought your mom was against you moving out?" He raised an eyebrow.

"She is. But I'm an adult and she might be happier with it, if I include her in fixing up the place." Dela glanced down at the folder. "Wow! She made a beeline for the Caymans. How did she get out of the country without the FBI grabbing her? And how did she get the information on the bank account there?" Paula Pomroy had purchased a small house in the islands. It appeared she planned to stay, thinking they couldn't extradite her to the U.S. on murder charges. However, Dela had looked it up. The U.S. had an extradition treaty with the Caymans. Paula would be arrested and sent back if they could conclusively link her to Tristan's murder.

"She must have used a fake passport. Which means she'd been planning this for a while." Quinn shoved the paper he'd been reading at her.

It was forensics on the corkscrew. It had been the murder weapon of Tristan. But it was inconclusive if it had killed Mattie. Her gaze collided with Quinn's. "Two killers, or one killer and two murder weapons?"

"We'll know shortly. Marty told me you had him call in Robin Everly. She should be here around nine." Quinn picked up the coffee cup sitting by his left elbow.

Dela scanned the table. "Where's my coffee and rolls you'd offered earlier?"

"Figured you were eating while you dressed for it to take you thirty minutes to get ready."

Double Frickin' shit! This guy acted like her keeping something from him was illegal. Her life was her life and if she didn't want him to know about her half a leg, he could just go screw himself. She glanced at her watch. 8:05.

"I'm going to go grab a cup of coffee and some breakfast. Text me when Robin shows up, unless you want to hear what Wallace told me about Van and Verna. In which case, I'll be at the coffee shop." She stood and walked out of the room.

Once she was seated in the coffee shop, she texted Marty. *Let me know when Robin shows up. I'll come to you.*

Copy.

She looked up from texting and watched Quinn walk across the coffee shop and up to her booth.

"What did you learn about…" he stopped as the waitress arrived.

"I'll have coffee, a cheese omelet, and toast. No hash browns," Dela ordered.

"I'll have the same," Quinn said.

When the waitress was out of earshot, he began again. "What did you learn about Van and Verna?"

Dela told him what Wallace had told her.

"They both have missing backgrounds and are living in the same apartment building, yet no one here has ever seen them together?" Quinn pulled out his phone. "I'll see what I can dig up on them."

The waitress arrived with their coffee. As she

walked away, Quinn put his phone in his pocket. "What do you think this Robin Everly has to do with the murder besides possibly blanking out the cameras?"

"I'm not sure. Do you have the copy of the page with the money Tristan was collecting from people?"

Quinn dug in his folder and pulled out a paper.

Dela studied it, particularly the sums next to R.E. "He blackmailed different sums for each person. But R.E. and Jeff Twigg have the same amount listed."

"Do you think she is the woman who helped Jeff cheat the house?" Dela thought out loud. If so, she really wanted to get her hands on the woman.

"We'll know when we see her," Quinn said, leaning back as their breakfast arrived.

"Possibly. If she wore a wig or disguise, it might not be as easy for someone to recognize her. I would have thought when we were watching the video of Jeff and the woman, Marty would have said something." Dela began eating, wondering what they would learn from Robin. And if Paula was as greedy as she seemed, they might be able to get her back to the states to collect the life insurance on Tristan. At least a letter could be sent stating Paula needed to sign papers at the insurance office to get the money and see if that would bring her back.

"Did you ever run the license plate of the woman who helped Jeff?" That would connect Robin if she was the one helping him.

Quinn glanced up from his plate of food. "I did turn it in, but now that you mention it, I never heard back." He pulled out his phone and started texting.

Dela finished off her breakfast and sipped her second cup of coffee, watching Quinn glare at his phone.

Her phone buzzed.

Robin is here. Marty texted.

"She's here," Dela said, sliding out of the booth and shoving money under her plate.

"They're having trouble finding the license plate. It appears it is off of a car that was totaled several years ago." He stood, leaving money by his plate.

"Wouldn't a car like that get pulled over if it didn't have stickers?" She knew when she returned home and pulled her car out of her mom's garage the plate had stickers from the last time she'd been home on leave, four years prior. She'd prayed all the way to DMV that a cop didn't pull her over.

"Not if they were stealing tags and putting them on. As long as they didn't do anything illegal there would be no reason for a cop to check out the plate." Quinn walked beside her across the casino floor and up to the hidden surveillance door.

She held her ID in front of the lock and the door popped open. They entered and she scanned the four people on duty. They were all long-time employees. Dela walked over to Marty's office and walked in.

He was sitting on his chair with his back to the monitors. Robin sat across the small room from him. Her gaze landed on Dela and then Quinn. She started to stand.

"Stay where you are," Dela said, pulling up a chair beside Marty. She tried to remember what the woman looked like that had been helping Jeff steal from the casino. She couldn't conjure up the face. "Marty, could you pull up the video of Jeff, please."

The head of surveillance swung his chair around

and started tapping the keys.

"Robin, it has come to our attention that every time Verna was away from her bank of monitors, cameras were turned off in areas that benefited a killer." Dela studied the woman.

"I don't know what Verna told you, but she isn't an angel." Robin crossed her arms.

"Here you go," Marty said.

Dela shifted so she could see the monitor and keep an eye on the woman. The view of Jeff dealing and then the woman waving money at him and the exchange of chips rolled across the monitor. Robin stiffened when Marty stopped the video with the woman's face in full view.

"That looks like you only with a long brunette wig." Dela said. "You and Jeff were skimming money from the casino. Tristan Pomroy found out and blackmailed you. Did you and Jeff decide you didn't like paying him and plan to murder him?"

"No! We didn't kill him. Honest. The little twit was taking more than we were even skimming from the casino. We wanted out. Woman to woman, I went to Mrs. Pomroy. I asked her if she could get her husband off our backs." Her lips tipped into a crooked grin. "She hadn't even known he was blackmailing people. I told her about the little book and asked if she could find a way to stop him."

"When was this?" Quinn asked.

"About three months ago. She said, she'd see what she could do. Then a month ago, she came to me and said she knew I worked in surveillance and could I black out cameras. I told her I could. She contacted me a week later with the date, time, and cameras that were to be blacked out." Robin held up her hands. "I didn't have any idea she was going to kill her husband. I thought she was going to do something we could use against him to keep him from taking all of our money."

"Yet, when you knew he had been killed you didn't come forward, did you?" Dela glared at the woman.

"You would have thought I had something to do with it." The woman stared at her.

"You did. You gave the woman a reason to kill her husband and helped her hide it." Quinn said. "What cameras did she want you to black out and when?"

As the woman mumbled the times, dates, and cameras to Quinn, Dela stared at the stilled video. How would they pin this on the wife when she was out of the country? They could take down Jeff and Robin's statements and hope they came up with DNA proof or something that would prove Paula killed her husband, but unless they found that or got a confession from her, Robin would be the only one being held accountable for Tristan's death. Something still bugged her. Why would the woman blatantly walk in and purchase a corkscrew and then use it to kill her husband? That would be the most incriminating evidence against her. And it didn't make sense. Why hadn't she asked for the gift shop camera to be blacked out too?

"Did she say anything about blacking out the gift shop that night?" Dela asked.

Quinn studied her.

Robin shook her head. "No."

"We still don't know why Tristan went up to the housekeeping supply room on ten." Dela leveled her gaze on Quinn. "Did you ever compare the phone records of the husband and wife? Did she call him to meet her there?"

Quinn pulled out his phone and started texting.

Dela stood. "I'm going to see what else Wallace pulled up on Tristan's computer." She stopped at the door. "Tribal police need to arrest Jeff Twigg for stealing from the casino and Robin needs to be taken in custody for accessory to that and murder."

Quinn and Marty nodded and she walked out of the surveillance offices.

Chapter Twenty-three

Dela sat beside her mom as they drove to the realty office in Pendleton.

"I can't believe you are actually buying a house. One I haven't even seen," Mom had been talking nonstop since she pulled up to the casino entrance and Dela slid in the passenger seat. After talking to Wallace and asking him to pull up all of Tristan's emails and anything else where he would have received a message, she'd called the realtor to let her know she was running late, and then called her mom.

"Molly went with me. She agrees it is a great buy."

"But an acre and a half? How will you take care of it?" Mom glanced over at her.

"Molly and Travis are helping me figure it out. Travis will do all the remodeling for half the cost of a licensed carpenter and he'll do a better job because he is a friend." She loved that her friend's son was excited to help her.

"It sounds like your mind is made up," Mom

parked the car in front of the realty.

"It is. Come on. You'll like Cathryn." Dela exited her mom's car and walked up to the door of the building. Mom joined her and they walked in together.

"I'm here to sign papers with Cathryn," Dela said, to the receptionist.

"Right this way."

They followed the young woman down a short hall and into a conference room. Papers were spread out across the table. Cathryn sat at the long side away from the door.

"Come in, Dela. And who did you bring with you?" Cathryn stood and reached out a hand across the table.

"This is my mom, Debra Bolden." Dela made introductions.

The two did hit it off talking about everything as Dela browsed the contracts and signed.

"My bank should have sent the check for the amount to you this morning," she told Cathryn. "Did it arrive, or do I have to wait until then to get the keys?"

"Your check arrived about five minutes before you did. You'll find the keys in here." Cathryn handed her an envelope. "The envelope also has the name of the contractor who built the house, the information about the parcel, and how to get the utilities turned on."

"Thank you. That's all good to know. I'll send you photos when we get it fixed up." She shook hands and motioned for her mom to head to the door.

Out in the car, she stared at the envelope.

"Are you sorry you bought the house?" her mom asked.

"No. I'm just thinking of all the possibilities." She

smiled. "I need to set up an account at the lumber store. Would you please take me there, then I'll buy you lunch and we can go see my new home."

Mom smiled. "It does my heart good to see you happy. Maybe getting your own place and something to look after is a good idea."

"Thanks. Oh, and we need to swing by Molly's and I'll introduce you to Mugshot."

"Mugshot?"

♠ ♣ ♥ ♦

By the time Dela returned to the casino, her car stood in a parking slot and Quinn had returned and stood just inside the entrance waiting for her.

"Did your mom approve of your new project?" he asked, falling in step beside her.

"As a matter of fact, she did. Thinks it's a good idea I have a project outside of work. What did you find in the phone records?" She continued across the casino floor, past the water feature, and into the security office.

"I know you said you weren't leaving until you caught the killer but you really need to get a life," Kenny said, standing up from a desk in the security office.

"I did. I bought a house this morning. Now I need to talk to Wallace." She motioned for Quinn to follow her. She kind of liked him following her orders. It had been the complete opposite in Iraq.

Dela, with Quinn on her heels, left the security office and entered the hallway leading to all the internal casino offices. She stepped into the tech offices.

Wallace glanced up, then motioned them over. "You said you wanted to see all the messages he received or sent. Here is a list of his emails for a week before his death. He also belonged to a Facebook group for people who kept an eye out for 'Most Wanted' fugitives. That is full of weirdos." The tech supervisor raised his eyebrows and twirled a finger beside his head.

Dela took the pages of messages. Some were between Tristan and his boss. Nothing unusual with them. Someone with the email address of blondebetty97 suggested he meet her at their usual spot at midnight. Dela glanced up at Quinn. "He had been rendezvousing with someone named blonde Betty ninety-seven. What do you want to bet it was on the tenth floor?"

She pulled out her phone and dialed Marty.

"Yo," he answered.

"Can you pull up video of the tenth floor on the evenings that Tristan was in the casino?" She knew it was a huge task. "We need to see if he was meeting a blonde on ten."

"I'll see what I can do."

"Thanks." She handed the pages she'd read to Quinn and continued down the next page. And found another email from blondebetty97. It read, *What do I have to do to keep you from turning my father in*?

Dela read the man's response. Her blood boiled. "That little perverted weasel."

Quinn grabbed the paper from her hand and Wallace nodded.

"He had sex with a young woman in payment for not turning her father in? That is low. And we have another suspect." Anger hardened Quinn's face.

"*If* we don't think Paula killed her husband." Dela scanned the next page. Blondebetty97 wasn't sending or receiving any more emails. She waved the papers in her hand toward the computer. "Can you figure out who blonde Betty ninety-seven is?"

"I'm working on it. I have to go through servers and link up with other servers but I should have it by the end of the day." Wallace sat back down at his computer.

Dela motioned for Quinn to exit the room. Out in the hall she faced him. "What did you find in the phone records?"

"The couple, Paula and Pomroy, texted back and forth about eleven that night. Paula said something about I know what you've been doing. Let's meet up and make things right. She suggested the tenth floor, room ten-ten right by the fire stairs." Quinn looked up from his notes.

"She took the stairs when she left eight-thirty-four. But why pretend to have sex with Ronald and then go meet her husband naked in room ten-ten unless she'd planned on killing him?" Dela wasn't getting anywhere with what they knew. "And how did she get his body from ten-ten into the laundry room and shoved in the chute without leaving a mess?"

"I know it's been days, but has anyone check on that room?" Quinn shoved his notepad in the inside pocket of his suitcoat and walked toward the service elevator.

"I'll see if anyone has stayed in that room since last Wednesday." She pulled out her phone and dialed the main desk.

"Faith speaking."

"Hi Faith, it's Dela. Can you check and see if anyone has stayed in room ten-ten since last Wednesday?"

"Sure. This have anything to do with what happened?" She tapped keys as she talked.

"Maybe. Won't know until we check it out." The elevator they'd rode up in stopped on the tenth floor. Dela stepped out and headed down the hall following the exit signs. She found room 1010 right next to the fire escape stairs.

"It doesn't look like it's been used for a month. That's a room that is saved for overflow because people complain about smoke seeping in the hallway from employees smoking in the stairway."

"We might need to do something about that. Thanks." Dela ended the call and faced Quinn. "It hasn't been used in a month." She pulled out the master keycard that was part of her head of security tools and opened the door.

The room had the stale air of an unused room. There was an indention on the end of the bed closest to the door as if someone had sat there. She checked the bathroom as Quinn looked under the beds and around the room.

"I can't find anything that might tie anyone to the murder." She leaned against the wall by the bathroom. "Maybe Tristan never made it to this room? Paula sat here waiting and when he didn't show, she left."

"Who else would have known he'd be up here?" Quinn crossed his arms and stared at her.

"Someone could have seen him getting in the elevator and when he came out on the tenth floor…" Dela shook her head. "But who would they call who could be up here quick enough to kill him and stuff him in the chute? Especially if they didn't know about Paula having the cameras blacked?"

She exited the room and glanced down the hall. "The supply room is down the hall behind the elevators. Someone coming up in the service elevator would have gotten off inside the supply room. Would they have walked out into the hall, lured Tristan into the room, and then killed him?"

"How did they get the corkscrew?" Quinn asked.

"Maybe Paula dropped it on the stairs? But then who picked it up? Was it random or on purpose?" Dela put her hands on her hips. "This doesn't make any sense."

"We know Van was on the stairs when Paula was also on the stairs. What if he didn't walk down two flights, instead went up two flights? And maybe she handed him the corkscrew when she told him the toilet wasn't plugged?" Quinn looked pleased with himself.

"Plausible. Guess we better take another look at that video." Dela walked down the hall glancing at the floor and walls for any signs of blood.

Standing at the elevator, Dela said, "The killer could have been waiting for Tristan when he stepped out of the elevator. Either grabbed him and dragged him to the supply room or lured him there."

"It would have been within the time frame the camera was blacked out." Quinn's phone buzzed. He glanced at the screen. His forehead wrinkled as his eyes scanned the device.

"What's wrong?" Dela didn't want to move closer to him but was curious what had him confused.

"The corkscrew that killed Tristan didn't kill Mattie, but they believe it was another corkscrew with a shorter shaft or a different person, not as strong, plunged it into her neck."

"That means it could be two different people." Dela stepped into the elevator when the doors opened.

Quinn followed. "That or the same person didn't have the same anger against Mattie as they had against Tristan."

"Like Paula. She was mad and upset with her husband, but Mattie was just someone trying to get hold of her money," Dela said as the elevator settled and the doors opened. She stopped after taking three steps and faced Quinn. "And if she knew about blonde Betty ninety-seven, there was even more incentive for her to bury that corkscrew in her husband's neck." Yes, she was liking Paula for the murders more and more.

"But how do we prove it?" Quinn asked, walking beside her to the surveillance door.

She held her ID up to the lock and the door swung open. "By carefully piecing together her movements that we can see and that of the other suspects." They walked through the monitor room and into Marty's office.

"Didn't expect to see you back here so soon," Marty said, leaning back in his chair, watching surveillance footage of Van Branson.

"Have you seen any video where he and Paula Pomroy talk?" Dela asked, taking a seat next to Marty.

"Not so far. I'm going backwards. I didn't find any footage of Verna and Van together for the last two months." Marty took a bite of sandwich and tapped a couple keys.

Dela's phone rang. It was Wallace.

"What have you learned?" she asked.

"You must be the right person for head of security," he said.

She chuckled. "Why do you say that?"

"Van Branson is Verna's father. Her mother and Van weren't married so she has her mother's last name."

"Were they ever at Big Muddy?" she asked.

"It's hard to find records of who was there if they hadn't signed up as a voter."

She could hear keys tapping. "What else are you digging up?"

"His real name isn't Van Branson. That's an alias he's used off and on over the years. If you shave his face and head, he looks a lot like the guy Tristan called the Feds about a week before he was killed. Vladimer Chernoff."

Dela stared at the video playing on the monitor. She'd known the person in the sketch had looked familiar. It was the eyes. "Thanks. If you come up with anything else let me know."

She motioned for Marty to stop the video. Then she repeated everything that Wallace had told her.

Marty whistled and Quinn pulled out his phone.

"We may have just found our murderer," Dela said, wondering how they could connect him and Paula. Because somewhere along the way, she had to have given the corkscrew to him to kill her husband.

Chapter Twenty-four

Still huddled in Marty's office, Dela and Quinn were discussing how to get the information they needed to prove what they now believed about Van being the murderer.

"What if Verna told him about questioning her last night?" Dela didn't want the two getting away.

"Knowing he is a wanted man, I texted Shaffer and told him to pull in agents from Portland and grab Branson. Once we have him in custody, we can question him all we want." Quinn nodded toward the video monitor. "Can we speed up this process by having each one of us watch different days?"

"Yeah, I can get you each set up with a monitor to watch." Marty started tapping keys.

Dela's stomach had been gurgling and gnawing on itself for thirty minutes. "I need to grab something to eat. I'll be back in twenty." She stood to leave and Quinn stood.

"I can get something to eat on my own. I've been doing it for a long time." Something about the way he didn't let her out of his sight was starting to really annoy her.

"I need dinner, too. Remember, we had breakfast at the same time this morning."

Marty's eyebrows raised, but Dela ignored his stare.

"Only because you followed me into the café." She marched out of Marty's office, across the monitor room, and out onto the casino floor. The coffee shop didn't appeal to her. She didn't want as much as the bar and grill would serve, so she headed to the deli. She usually avoided it when Rosie wasn't working. It was the woman's presence that made it inviting.

"You really want a hot dog or a sandwich?" Quinn asked, following her to the deli.

"Yeah, I need a change." She walked up to the counter and ordered a turkey sandwich with chips and an iced tea. The teenager behind the counter smiled and handed over her change. "Auntie Rosie said you are a woman to look up to."

Dela smiled at the girl. "I think the same of your aunt."

The young person smiled. "She talks about the people who work here as if they are family. Having worked here the last two weekends, I agree."

"The board of trustees would be happy to hear you say that." Which reminded her, she had to give Bernie an update soon. She moved to the side as the girl put her order up and filled a cup with iced tea. Once Dela had her tea, she walked over to a table at the back of the deli seating area.

She was staring at her phone when Quinn sat down across from her.

"Did you get a message?" he asked, raising his cup to take a sip.

"No. Contemplating whether to call Bernie Moon or wait until we know more."

"I say wait. We know Branson is a fugitive but we don't have hard evidence against him that he killed Pomroy."

The teenager arrived with their sandwiches. "Is there anything else I can get you?"

"I think we're good. Thanks." Dela smiled and watched the girl walk back to the counter. "Do you think Verna is blonde Betty ninety-seven?"

Quinn put the sandwich down he'd been about to bite. "She is blonde, but Betty? Where would that come from?"

"She left the message about her father. We know Van is her dad." Her gut wasn't hungry all of a sudden. The woman had seemed scared and nervous every time they questioned her. Was it because she feared for her father or because of what she'd done to keep her father safe?

"Verna said she'd used the restroom right before Robin turned off the cameras. But she would have known to check for that and could have turned the camera back on."

"With Robin next to her, probably monitoring if the camera remained off?" Quinn bit into his sandwich.

Dela picked hers up and squeezed it. "I wonder if you can record and keep the camera black?" She put the food down and picked up her phone. *Can a camera be black and still record what is happening*? She texted to

Marty.

This time she bit into her sandwich, chewed, and swallowed. Her stomach accepted the nourishment. Halfway through the sandwich her phone buzzed.

It can be done if it is set up ahead of time and the person knows how to program the camera. Why?

Would Verna know how to program the camera? Yes.

Thanks. What about Robin Everly. Would she know?

Not as certain there.

Do you know how to find the footage from the time period during the murder from the cameras that were blacked out?

If I can find where it was hidden. He sent her a smiley emoji. *You know I love a challenge.*

She sent him a thumbs up. "We'll have an answer to whether or not it can be found soon." Dela finished off her sandwich and slowly munched on her chips.

"When are you going to start working on your house?" Quinn asked.

"Tomorrow. Travis is going to hire some friends to help him build a fence and dog house for Mugshot. Then we'll get started on the inside." She smiled thinking about how it would look when they finished.

"How soon will you be able to move in?" Quinn crumpled up the chip bag and the paper that had been around his sandwich.

"I'm thinking this fall. There is some major work that needs to be done to make it work for me."

He stared at her. "What do you mean by that? Do you have a hobby that requires something special?"

She'd flapped her gums too much. There was no

way she would tell him they needed to put handicapped bars in the master bath and widen a couple of doors so her crutches would fit through them easily. "There is just a lot of work that needs to be done. The house has sat empty for several years and it was built in the eighties. So, there are some updates I want done."

"Eighties. At least you missed the era of the green shag carpet and avocado green bathroom sink, toilet, and tub."

She studied him. "Is that what's in your house?"

"Yeah. As soon as I get the leaky parlor fixed, the bathroom is being gutted."

"Sounds like you have things all figured out." She stood, grabbed her trash, and threw it in the garbage can. "Time to go stare at videos, unless Marty has worked miracles already."

♠ ♣ ♥ ♦

Several hours later, Dela stood and stretched. They, she and Quinn, had been watching video from the last six months looking for connections between any of the people on their suspect list. As well as the victims. So far, all they had found were meetings they already knew about from Marty's previous scans.

The head of surveillance was still working on finding the feed that was hidden by a blacked-out camera.

"I'm surprised you haven't heard anything from Shaffer about picking up Van," Dela said, walking toward the door. "I'm going to get a cup of coffee, anyone else want anything?"

Quinn pulled his phone out of his suitcoat. "I'm surprised too. I'll see what Shaffer has to say. Bring me back an iced tea, please."

"Marty, you want anything?" she asked.

"A large cola slurpy, please." He glanced up long enough to grin and then was back tapping at the keyboard.

She walked out of Marty's office and crossed the room with all the monitors. Lionel sat at the one on the end again. They weren't having any luck finding what they needed to prove anything. All they had were suspicions. They couldn't get a warrant for anyone's arrest with that.

"Would you look at that?" Lionel pointed to the middle monitor on the top row of the section he watched. "You'd think someone who sits here all day and night watching other people do stupid things would have better sense than to prance around in here with someone other than her husband."

Dela took a peek. One of the night surveillance team was squeezed up against a man Dela knew wasn't her husband. And they were headed to the elevators connected to the rooms.

Hmmm. That would mean anyone who wanted to commit a murder and worked surveillance would never meet up with the intended victim here.

"Thanks, Lionel!" Dela headed back into the office.

"That was quick," Marty said.

Quinn was scowling as he listened to his phone.

"If Van or Verna had anything to do with the murder of Tristan, they would make sure they were never caught on video here at the casino. And the one time that we do have Van and Tristan, we only have Van's word for what they'd talked about."

Dela texted Wallace. *I need the addresses of Van,*

Jeff Twigg, and Robin Everly.

Quinn ended his call and turned a dark, pinched face her direction. "Shaffer said Van and Verna's apartments are cleaned out. They must have taken off right after we questioned her."

"Send your Fed buddies after them. We have neighbors to talk to." She opened the door. "Marty, I'll send that slurpy in with a guard. Come on Quinn. We have a lot of people to talk to."

She stopped long enough on the casino floor to ask Ross to get a slurpy for Marty. Then she headed to the casino entrance. Dela didn't look back to see if Quinn followed. She could hear his footsteps behind her. Once they were out in the parking lot, she slowed her pace. "Your car or mine?"

"Want to tell me what this is about? We spent hours staring at video and now you want to go talk to neighbors?" Quinn walked toward his SUV.

Dela grinned. She'd figured he'd want to drive. "With so many of our suspects knowledgeable about the surveillance cameras at the casino they aren't going to have a meeting with Tristan or Paula where it would be caught on video. My thoughts are they met at either their homes or the Pomroy's. We need to speak to the neighbors and see if any of the neighbors have cameras that might have caught who came and went at Van, Verna, Robin, and Paula's. Possibly Jeff Twigg's house, too. I'm not ruling him out. He was the first to run when Tristan's blackmailing all came out."

They were seated in the SUV and Quinn was headed toward Pendleton on the freeway. "Where do you suggest first?"

"Paula is at the center of all of this. Let's go visit

with her other neighbors and the one we already questioned." Dela had a feeling that whoever had visited the Pomroys the most would be the killer. The person had to have been blackmailed and then pulled into Paula's scheme to get rid of her husband. But who would have been desperate enough?

Quinn parked in the Pomroy's driveway. It looked as quiet and empty as it had the last time they were here.

"You know interrupting people's dinner is not a good way to get them to cooperate," Quinn said as they remained seated in the vehicle.

"I forgot what time it was." She studied the houses on either side and across the street. There were more cars in driveways and the street, proving there were people home at all of the residences. "Let's start with the neighbor we visited before. Chances are we can get her to call the others over to her house at seven-thirty. That would give them time to eat, and we could do a quick look at Van and Verna's apartments." Dela exited the SUV feeling confident this plan would work.

They walked up to the door and rang the doorbell.

The dog barked, children hollered, and a man cursed.

"I don't think it will be that easy," Quinn said under his breath as the door opened and a man in slacks and a button-down shirt scowled at them.

Dela hoped this was an omen. She stepped forward and held out her hand. "Sergeant Lockland, I didn't expect to see you here."

The man shook hands, his face contorting as he worked to figure out how he knew her.

"Lockland." Quinn held out his hand to shake with

the Pendleton City Sergeant.

"Quinn, you I recognize. What are you doing coming by at dinner time?" Lockland didn't even flit his gaze back at Dela.

He'd decided she was an FBI peon. Anger built in her chest as she listened to Quinn explain how they had been by and talked to his wife earlier and wondered if the couple would help them round up the neighbors around the Pomroy house later this evening.

"Sure, anything to help the FBI. So you're the one looking into the murder at the casino. Terrible thing to happen to Tristan." Lockland made as if he cared for the man.

Before Dela could say, she was looking into the murder, Quinn cut her off by placing a hand on her shoulder.

"This is Dela Alvaro, head of security at the casino. She and I are working on the murder. In fact, her observations and interrogations have been more helpful than my FBI connections."

She wanted to give him a smile, but he was spreading too much flattery into his words for the lieutenant to take the comment seriously.

"We'll get the neighbors over here, around seven-thirty, you say?"

"Dinner's getting cold!" Ms. Gray called from somewhere down the hall.

"We'll be back. Thank you." Quinn nudged her to step away from the door.

"Think you poured it on a little too thick," she said, stomping back to the vehicle.

"He was ignoring you and showing disrespect. I wanted him to see you are an asset to your job." Quinn started the vehicle and backed out of the driveway.

"You could have just said, I had been influential in digging up evidence, not all that sappy 'her observations and interrogations have been more helpful than my FBI connections.'" She slumped back in her seat and rubbed her leg above the socket.

The silence in the vehicle, drew her gaze from the street ahead to the man sitting beside her. He stared at her hands, kneading her leg. She instantly pulled her hands away and stared out the side window.

"What are you trying to hide from me?" he asked. "I know you left the army on a medical discharge after you and your team had an IED blow up under your jeep. But I can't find any other information. Your mother made a comment about she didn't want you living alone because you could be lying on the floor for days before anyone found you. When I pressed her with questions, she changed the subject." He pulled over and twisted his whole body to look at her.

Dela shrank away from his inquisitive gaze. She hadn't planned to have anyone other than her mom, Molly, and several close friends ever find out she wasn't whole. Marty knew. That's why he kept the box under his table for her to prop her foot up on.

"You know, I can dig deeper if I want to. But I'd prefer to hear the truth from you." He reached out toward her and pulled his hand back. "Had you fallen this morning and that's why you didn't want to let me in, or couldn't let me in?"

That sparked her anger. "I thought you had the impression I was with someone I didn't want you to see?"

He shook his head and grinned. "I knew that would

get you talking. At first, I did. What else did you think would have pop in my mind, that you wouldn't want me to come in?"

She shook her head. "Typical male. I say I'm not dressed and you think, no matter, I can come in anyway. Then I say, no, and you think it's because I'm entertaining. No means No, nothing else."

He tipped his chin down and dropped his gaze to her leg. "What happened?"

"I'm not ready to tell you. Let's get to Van and Verna's apartment building. We want to get back to the Lockland's on time." She stared forward and clenched her hands together on her lap to keep from rubbing the ache in her thigh and down her non-existent leg.

Chapter Twenty-five

The feds were still hanging around the apartments. Dela slipped around the man guarding Verna's apartment as Quinn asked him questions.

Inside the rooms were neat and tidy. The only sign of a quick getaway were the still open empty drawers on the dresser and a couple of hangers on the floor of the closet. She'd cleaned out her clothes and toiletries. From the cords draped across the bedside table, she had a computer and cellphone. Why hadn't she taken the time to grab the computer charger? There wasn't a photograph in the place. All that remained were items that looked as if they had been purchased at thrift stores.

Dela wondered how many times Van and Verna had moved trying to stay ahead of the FBI. If her father were still alive and she'd discovered he was wanted by the FBI would she have helped him escape capture? She shook her head. Tough call to make. Having never had a father, she didn't know anything about that bond. If her mother had committed a crime, she would do all she could to see that she got the lightest sentence, but help her run…Truth was too firmly ingrained in her to help her mother hide.

"See anything helpful?" Quinn asked, standing in the doorway of the bedroom.

"Not really. It's been stripped clean. Kind of what we'd expected." She walked to the doorway and waited for him to move out of the way. "Any chance we can talk to the neighbors?"

"There are agents already doing that," Quinn said, walking into the living room.

"Any surveillance cameras set up outside?" She hoped there were and they could catch Tristan or one of the suspects visiting the duo.

"There are. I'm having Shaffer send it to my phone." Quinn stepped out of the apartment and nearly tripped.

Dela looked down and saw a calico cat streak along the hallway. "Any idea if that's Verna's cat?"

A woman in her seventies stepped out of the apartment next door to Verna's. "Did you see my Callie? She slipped out when that nice young man was talking to me."

"Is Callie a calico cat?" Dela asked, smiling at the woman.

"Yes. She is quite the escape artist. Verna always helped me find her when she'd get loose."

"You knew Verna well?" Dela asked.

"As well as she'd let me. I could tell she had a secret. I thought it was because she spent a lot of time over at Van's apartment. Not overnight or anything like that. They just seemed to click."

"What else can you tell me about the two?" Dela asked, leaning against the hallway wall next to the woman's door. She shifted all her weight to her good leg.

"They had a fight about two weeks ago. Van was in her apartment then. I heard him stomp up to the door, pound on it, and Verna let him in. He started shouting, but it didn't sound like him. If I hadn't seen him go by my window and then heard him pound on her door, I would have thought someone else was in there yelling."

"Why do you say that?" Dela found this interesting.

"Because he was yelling with an accent. I think it was Russian. I'm not good at accents, but that's what it sounded like." The woman nodded her head.

"What was he yelling about?" Dela noticed Quinn stood back a yard or more, writing in his notepad.

"She didn't have to sleep with anyone to save him. He'd been doing fine on his own and didn't need her ruining her life for him." The woman mopped at a tear that appeared at the corner of her eye. "It was breaking my heart to hear him pleading with her to let him go." She shook her head. "I don't have any idea what he meant by that. Then last night I heard noise and looked out. The two of them were carrying suitcases out to her car. But he didn't get in with her. He left on his motorcycle."

"Thank you. You are very observant. Did Verna ever have any other visitors besides Van?" This was what they really wanted to know. Had Verna and Van been in cahoots with Paula or someone else to get rid of Tristan?

"There was a young man came by twice. The first time he and Verna left, like they were going on a date. The second time, she pulled him into the apartment as if she didn't want anyone to see."

"By young man, what age do you think he was?" Dela knew as people aged their idea of young and hers was different.

"In his thirties, maybe, not forty yet."

Quinn stepped forward. "Is this the man?" He showed her a photo of Tristan.

"No, that wasn't him. He had some size. Not as big as Van but not a wimp."

Quinn showed her another photo. It was Jeff Twigg.

The woman smiled. "That was him. I thought what beautiful hair he had. My Albert was bald as a bowling ball most of his adult life."

Dela wondered what Jeff Twigg would be doing dating Verna. Most likely they were setting up a crime. "Thank you. I hope you find Callie soon."

"Thank you, dear. You have a good evening."

As they walked out to the car, Quinn said, "Nice job of getting the woman to talk."

"You just have to give someone like her the nudge to talk and they will."

"I wonder what Twigg and Verna had to talk about," Quinn said, starting his SUV.

"Either he was dating her, or he was trying to talk her into blacking out the camera. When she refused, Robin did it." She thought on that a minute. "But why ask Verna first when your partner in crime worked in the same area?"

"It doesn't make sense. Unless all of the people in

the victim's book decided to work together to kill the man blackmailing them." Quinn drove away from the apartment building and back across town to the Pomroy's neighborhood.

It was early but there were people being let into the Lockland residence. Quinn parked and Dela followed him up to the front door.

When Sergeant Lockland answered the door, Quinn said, "Thank you for allowing us to use your home to gather information about a homicide."

"I'm curious to see how you conduct this questioning. And I have learned that the death of Mattie Collier is involved with your case." The man studied Quinn and when he didn't comment, his gaze moved to Dela.

She smiled and whisked by him into the house.

"So good to see you again," Ms. Gray said, taking Dela by the hand and leading her into the living room. "We have all the neighbors on this side of the street and across the street here."

Dela was impressed with all the people sitting in the living room either in the usual furniture or dining room chairs.

"Aaron doesn't bring his work home with him. This is a fun way to be a part of some criminal activity."

"Ms. Gray—"

"Jennifer, please."

"Jennifer, and all of you present. This isn't a game. We are looking for a murderer and anything you say here, needs to stay here. If the person we are looking for knows you have any knowledge that could get them caught you could become a target."

"I agree," both Quinn and Lockland said at the same time.

Dela grinned inwardly that the two "real" cops agreed with her.

"We need to know if you have seen anyone hanging around the Pomroy house or if you've seen a particular person visiting the house often the last few months." Quinn pulled out his notepad. When someone raised a hand, he'd asked their name and where they lived. Then he let them talk.

Dela listened and one thing kept being brought up. Tristan and Paula rarely went anywhere together. But she had several people who came by during the day. One was a man in his thirties.

Quinn handed his phone to Dela. "Bring up Twigg's photo."

She found it and walked around the room, showing it to everyone present.

"Is that the man you saw visiting Paula?" Quinn asked.

"Yes. One time he came with a young woman. She was petite, dark hair," A woman sitting alone offered.

Dela scrolled through Quinn's photos and found a picture of Robin. "Whis woman?"

The woman smiled. "Yes, that's the one. She drove up in a compact dark colored car. The man got out from the passenger side."

"Did you see how Paula received them?" Quinn asked.

"She didn't look happy to see them. But she let them in and they stayed about an hour."

They now had an eye witness to Paula talking with the woman who had blacked out the surveillance cameras that allowed a man to be murdered.

Dela faced Jennifer. "The night after Tristan's death, you said you saw a young woman sitting in a car in the Pomroy driveway."

"Yes, she was in a small dark car. Do you think it was the woman who had visited Paula before?" Sergeant Lockland's wife was getting into the whole questioning.

"I'm not sure. Did you happen to notice if Paula went out later that night?" If Mattie had tried to extort money from Paula for the book, the woman could have followed her home or sent someone to deal with Mattie.

"I'm not sure. I went to bed early." Jennifer glanced at her husband. "Isn't that the night you came home late?"

Lockland nodded. "But the garage door was down. I don't know if her car was inside or if she was gone."

"What about lights? Were any on?" Dela asked.

The sergeant closed his eyes. "On. There were several lights on, including the front door light. I thought maybe with Tristan gone she had the lights on for comfort."

Dela wondered if the front door light was because she was waiting for the person to arrive who she planned to pay to kill Mattie.

"Thank you for your cooperation," Quinn said, closing his notepad and motioning for Dela to go with him.

She smiled at Jennifer. "You wouldn't happen to be the neighbor who has Paula's extra house key, would you?"

"I do have her key. Sometimes when she goes to her folk's she has me water her plants." The woman stood and strode out of the room.

"Do you have a warrant to search the Pomroy house?" Sergeant Lockland asked.

"We do. My associate Special Agent Shaffer is bringing it." Quinn smiled. "Would you like to help us do the search?"

The sergeant's eyes lit up. "I wouldn't mind helping out."

Dela held back her smile. She understood Quinn was drawing the man in to get more information out of him.

The neighbors were all filing out of the door, when Jennifer returned with the key. "Here you go. Just bring it back, in case Paula calls and needs me to take care of anything."

"I'll bring it back. I'm going to help them do the search." Lockland took the key from his wife.

Dela asked, "She didn't ask you to water her plants before she left? Or called since and asked the favor?"

"No. Which is strange. She usually does say, hey, I'm going to be gone, could you check on the plants." Jennifer's brow wrinkled. "Did you talk to her at her parents'?"

"She's not there." Quinn herded Dela out of the house. Sergeant Lockland walked ahead of them across the lawn and over to the Pomroy residence.

"Where's your associate with the warrant?" Lockland asked.

At that moment headlights turned the corner.

"That's him there." They all stood on the porch waiting for Shaffer to park, exit his vehicle, and walk up to the porch. He showed the papers to Lockland, who then placed the key in the lock.

"Think we'll find any evidence?" Dela asked as the door opened.

"I hope so. If not, it's going to be pretty hard to get her convicted." Quinn walked through behind her.

The house appeared the same as the last time they'd visited. Everything in its place. The play pen sat in the same spot in front of the window.

"Lockland, you take the kitchen. We're looking for a corkscrew or anything that connects her to this list of people." Quinn showed the sergeant a page in his notepad. The man headed to the kitchen.

Shaffer started searching the living room.

"Let's check the den." Quinn led the way to the room they'd searched after Tristan's death.

Dela walked over to the desk that she'd looked through on their earlier visit. Items were out of place on the top. The drawers had been rummaged through. Papers and things not neat and tidy like the first time. "Either Paula was looking for something or someone else was."

Quinn picked up the phone and hit the redial button. He listened and hung up. "The last person she dialed was Edmond. That was his voicemail."

"Can you find out when she made that call?" Dela had a feeling the two had been working together. To what end, she wasn't sure.

Quinn walked out of the den talking on his phone.

Dela checked out the dining room, laundry and half-bath. She climbed the stairs using the railing. Upstairs she found the child's room. It looked as if a tornado had passed through. Toys and clothes strewn about. The next room was a guest room, judging from the still new scent of wood and paint and lack of clothing or personal items in the room. The bathroom was next. Again, must have been the guest bath. Nothing personal. The master bedroom and bathroom looked much like the child's room. Clothing thrown about, items missing from the bathroom. All the products a male would use were still in the cabinet and in the shower. A small notepad sat on a bedside table. Dela picked it up and studied the blank page. There appeared to have been writing on the page before.

She dug around and found a pencil. Lightly shading the indented area, she brought up what looked like a flight number. "Quinn!"

The special agent appeared in the door. "Yeah?"

"This needs bagged, and the number looked up to see if it is a flight to the Cayman Islands." She pointed to the notepad.

He pulled out his phone, texting the information before he pulled an evidence bag out of his inside pocket and picked the notepad up by the corner, dropping it into the bag. "We need more evidence."

Dela wandered out of the bedroom and down the hall to one more door. She opened it and found a desk, chair, and pamphlets about the Cayman Islands. Some pamphlets were tossed in the trash can and three others were on the desk. There were several different photos of her, just the right size to fit on a passport. Someone had made a fake passport for her. They'd already figured this out, believing Paula was in the Cayman Islands.

She grabbed the pamphlets in the trash and then dumped the rest of the contents on the desk. A square photo lay on top of the small mound. A photo of Ronald Edmond. Paula would need a man with Tristan's ID to go into the bank and withdraw or transfer the money. Or even keep it in the account but be able to use it.

Quinn walked into the room. "Anything else?"

"We need to find Ronald Edmond." She held up the photo of the man.

Chapter Twenty-six

Dela sat in her car staring at the vet clinic. She had come to visit with Mugshot, but her mind kept circling back to how could they find the evidence they needed to charge Paula and Ronald with Tristan's murder and possibly Mattie's.

"Hey, are you coming in?" Travis called from the door of the building.

She waved and exited the vehicle. It was after hours. She'd called ahead to see if she could visit the dog. After she and Quinn left the Pomroy's, they'd gone back to the casino. Wallace and Marty were still working on the things they'd asked of them, so she'd called Molly to see about a visitation.

Inside the air-conditioned office, Dela slowed her pace and walked back to the kennel that housed Mugshot.

"Hi boy. How are you doing?" She opened the door and pet his large head, scratching behind his ears.

The animal peered at her with recognition.

"He's been healing well," Molly said, entering the room. She and Travis lived in the back half of the building.

"That's good to hear. When can he get up and try to walk?" Dela continued to pet his head and watch him.

"He was up today. We took him outside for the first time. He was weak, but he adjusted to three legs pretty fast. By the time you take him home, he'll be getting around just fine."

She peered up at Molly. "He has to be able to do everything himself because I can't hold his weight with one good foot."

"He'll be able to hold you up if you need him. I believe he's German Shepard and Malamute. Both very loyal. Both breeds are also dogs who are intelligent and will protect you." Molly smiled. "I think the best dog you could have has found you."

That made Dela feel better. She scratched Mugshot some more and used the kennel to stand. "I set up an account at the lumber yard today and gave them Travis's name to be one to sign for lumber. When he is ready to start on the yard and dog house, he can go in and order the lumber he needs."

"I'll let him know. He's recruited two of his friends to help. I agreed with his pick. They should make a good working crew for you." Molly nodded to the back of the building. "Do you have time for some ice cream?"

Dela smiled. "I can always make time for ice cream with a friend."

Once they were seated, Molly asked, "Have you

made any progress on the murder?"

A deep, weary sigh escaped Dela. "Yes and no. Quinn and I think we know who did it, but we are having difficulties finding the proof." She glanced at her friend who stirred her ice cream more than usual. "Why are you asking?"

"Bernie and another board of trustees were having a discussion at the market. Travis overheard what they were talking about."

"Let me guess. They didn't like the fact I hadn't caught the murderer yet." She shoved the ice cream to the center of the table. "I wish I could call him up and tell him what we do know. But I can't trust Bernie to keep the information to himself. He used the excuse of the papers hounding him when he tried to learn what was happening a couple days ago."

Molly pushed the bowl back toward her. "Eat. When you and Quinn find the evidence you need, then everyone will know who killed the man at the casino."

"And the young woman in Pendleton."

Molly stared at her. "The death of Mattie Collier is connected to the casino murder?"

"Yeah. But you didn't hear it from me." She cleaned up the ice cream. "I need to go. We hope to have everything pulled together tomorrow so we can arrest the persons involved."

Dela stood. It had been another long day and tomorrow didn't look any better. "When this is over, I want us to go to my house and finalize the remodel plans."

"I would love to help. What about your mom?" Molly raised an eyebrow.

"She's going to help with the painting and tiling.

She has become adept at both over the years remodeling her house."

Her friend put a hand on Dela's forehead. "Are you feeling okay? You said that as if you meant it."

Dela laughed. "I did. Mom went with me to sign the papers and afterwards I took her to look at the house. She thought it was a wreck but also thought it was good for me to have something to look forward to and keep me busy other than work."

"A win, win then." Molly walked Dela to the door out the back of the living quarters. "Watch your step through the yard. We had a dog here a while back that liked to dig holes. We filled them in but some have sunk."

"Thank you for the ice cream and conversation." Dela walked out of the light streaming through the open door toward the parking lot where her car sat.

She managed the uneven yard and slipped into the driver's seat of her car. Her phone jingled. She'd left it in the car while visiting Mugshot.

It was Wallace.

"Hello," she answered.

"I texted you fifteen minutes ago and you didn't answer," the man's voice had rose an octave.

"What's up?" she asked, worrying another person had been harmed at the casino.

"I found out where the blonde Betty ninety-seven came from." His excitement now trickled into his voice.

"And?"

"Here at the casino. Someone was using our server to send their email. I have a friend that can hack Yahoo who is looking into the name for me."

"Ummm, don't tell Special Agent Pierce you have

someone hacking anything." She was law abiding, but this was a matter of catching a killer. And the hacking was merely a means to find out who had sent the message.

"Yeah, that's why I called you." Wallace still sounded excited.

"What else have you learned?" She started up her car and headed toward the casino.

"Van was lying about growing up on the Big Muddy. He was born in Russia. His family moved here when he was in his teens. He ran with a Russian gang until Verna was born. Then he moved around a lot and was part of a bank hold up where two people were shot. That's why the FBI is after him. Verna didn't know he was her father until she turned eighteen and did her own research. As far as I can tell, neither one has been in trouble with the law since the bank heist." He paused, drew in a deep breath, "But what I gathered from a couple of conversations I joined online, some say Van/Vladimer got away with a quarter of a million dollars. What I don't understand is if he had that much money, why is he working as a maintenance man in a casino?"

"Good question." Dela pulled into the casino parking lot. "Let's pick this conversation up again in the morning."

"See you then."

She ended the call and stared at Quinn's vehicle parked in the slot next to where she always parked. What was he doing still here?

All she wanted to do was take the elevator up to her room, soak her leg, and go to bed. But curiosity had her pulling out her phone and texting Quinn. *Where are you?*

Surveillance with Marty.

Dela entered the building and headed across the casino floor. It was quiet for a Monday night. She spotted Geri, one of the security guards, wandering through the slot machines.

"It looks quiet tonight," she said.

"Yeah. Usually is on Monday. We had a couple of drunks that we tossed out, but that's been about it." Geri nodded toward the deli. "I'm going to get a cup of coffee. This is going to be a long night."

"Is Harvey around?" Dela didn't see the late shift assistant head of security.

"He was wandering around here a minute ago." Geri walked away.

Harvey worked the quiet nights. He was ready for retirement and knew the casino inside and out. But lately he'd been saying off the wall things that had Dela wondering if he should see a doctor.

She held her ID up to the surveillance door lock and it swung open. A new shift watched the monitors. She tapped Sunny on the shoulder. "Keep an eye on Harvey, please."

The young woman nodded as if she understood what Dela meant. It wouldn't surprise her if the group watching the monitors hadn't come to the same conclusion as Dela about the man's mental state.

She walked into Marty's office and pulled out a chair. "What are we watching?"

Quinn glanced at her. "You need to get some sleep."

She glared at him. "This is as much my case as it is yours."

Marty pointed to a video. "This is what I could piece together that was hidden from the blacked-out cameras."

Dela stared at the three monitors that came to life. "Can we watch them one at a time?"

"Yeah." Marty tapped the keyboard and the view outside the room on the eighth floor fast forwarded, showing Ronald leaving the room within ten minutes of the start of the video. The man was dressed and didn't look the least bit upset. Forty-five minutes later a disheveled Paula returned to the room.

"Stop." Dela said, staring at the woman.

Marty tapped keys and the video stopped with the woman opening the door.

"Look at her pocket. There are wet spots." She pointed. "Can you zoom in on the pocket?"

The head of surveillance did his thing and the monitor was filled with the robe pocket. The wet stains looked a lot like a T. The shape of a corkscrew.

"I think she has the corkscrew in her pocket." Dela glanced over at Quinn.

He had a grin on his face. "That's what it looks like to me."

"Keep it moving," Dela said, staring at the video until after the woman disappeared behind the door and through thirty minutes of fast forward when Paula walked out of the room and down the hall to the elevator.

"Let's see the camera on ten near the stairs." Dela moved her attention to the monitor on the left.

It came to life, fast forwarding until the door opened. Marty slowed the video and Paula appeared. She glanced around and knocked on the door of 1010.

The camera didn't show who let her in.

"That's interesting," Dela said. "Someone with access to a master key or who worked the desk and made a key for that room had to be involved." She glanced at Quinn and then Marty. "Can you bring up the camera on this door before the time on the blacked-out camera?"

"Give me a second." Marty tapped the keyboard and she continued watching the video of room 1010.

They continued watching room 1010. At 2 am Paula ran out of the room naked with her husband chasing her. She ran down the hall and ducked into the supply room. Tristan followed. Fifteen minutes later, a naked Paula and Ronald Edmond in sweat pants and a T-shirt walked back to room 1010. She stepped out five minutes later wearing the robe and headed to the stairs. Ronald came out wearing the same clothes and walked to the elevator.

"What do you want to bet, Ronald was standing behind the door naked, waiting for the two to run in?" Dela shivered. It had been a well thought out crime. Except that Verna must have learned about it and made sure there would be evidence. But why hadn't she told Marty or her about the wife attempting to murder her husband?

"I don't understand why they didn't take the book?" Quinn said, staring at the blank monitor. "They had to know about it. Why else would they kill Tristan if not to get their hands on the money in the Cayman Island bank?"

Dela sat up straight and stared at Quinn. "Because they didn't know about that money until Mattie showed up with the book in her hand asking for money to hand it over. What does Ronald do for a living?" She didn't wait. "He is a bounty hunter. He said he was following a lead when he came here. He was following Van Branson. Maybe he wasn't completely sure Van was Vladimer, but he needed to get Tristan out of the way so when he did prove it, he could collect the reward. Only he made friends with Paula, who probably told him how much she would get in insurance if her husband died. Ronald added up that and what he could get turning Van in and they made a plan."

"They couldn't have had fake passports made in the length of time they met and worked this all out." Quinn stood and paced. "We need to find Jeff Twigg and Robin Everly. They are somehow mixed up in this."

Dela leaned back in the chair. "Yes. And why did Paula toss the corkscrew in the water feature? She could have walked out of the casino with it in her purse and no one would have known."

Quinn answered his phone. "Pierce. Yeah? Good. Can you hold him there until I can talk to him?" He nodded his head. "I'll be there by noon tomorrow." He motioned to the monitors. "This is enough for tonight. Get some rest, we're headed to Seattle in the morning. I'll pick you up at seven."

"Why are we going to Seattle?" Dela didn't mind calling it a night but wanted to know why he was dragging her along.

"They have Van and Verna in custody. They were trying to catch a boat to Alaska."

Chapter Twenty-seven

Two hours after Quinn picked her up and a couple cups of coffee to wake her up, Dela began asking questions. She'd been glad Quinn hadn't been talkative to this point either.

"What do you think you'll learn from Van or Verna?" she asked.

"Maybe nothing. But Verna had the sense to make sure the cameras were capturing what went on. There had to be a reason. And you saw Van's face when he held that corkscrew. He'd seen it before."

"You know they didn't kill Tristan. The evidence against Paula and Ronald is pretty damaging." While getting ready for bed the night before, she'd thought about the video they'd watched. There wasn't a jury in the world who wouldn't be able to figure out what had happened in that room if they saw the footage.

"But they may shed some light on the things we don't have answers to. They could also give us more evidence that will enable us to get Paula and Edmond both extradited to the U.S."

"Do you really think you need more? I mean…what we watched last night can't be denied by either of them." She shivered at how playful Paula had looked luring her husband to his death.

"When it comes to convicting murderers, you can never have enough evidence." Quinn picked up his paper cup and wiggled it. "Empty. I'm ready for a pit stop, how about you?"

"Sure. All these coffee stops you're taking are going to make us late." Even as she gave him a hard time, Dela needed to get out and move around. The knee above her stub easily became enflamed and stiff if she sat too much.

Quinn pulled off the freeway and down into Yakima, Washington. He found a small coffee shop and parked.

Dela eased out onto her feet, waiting for Quinn to enter the building. She held onto the vehicle and swung her prosthetic leg back and forth, working the knee. After about ten swings, she backed up, closed the door, and headed into the coffee shop.

Quinn was exiting the restroom when she walked in the door. He veered her direction. "Everything alright?"

"Yeah, just stretching. I'll take a large black coffee." She scanned the bakery case. "And a blueberry scone." Without another word or glance his direction, she headed to the restroom.

When she returned, Dela was surprised to see Quinn sitting at a small table eating what looked like a quiche.

"Don't we need to hit the road?" she said, lowering onto the chair opposite him.

"We have time to relax a few minutes. Van and Verna aren't going anywhere."

She sipped the coffee. Dark and robust, just the way she liked it. The brew was also very hot. She set the cup down and picked at the scone.

"How's Mugshot doing?" he asked.

She would have groaned out loud except she didn't want him to know this was exactly what she had feared. Small talk wasn't something she wanted to do with this man. "He's good. He walked outside yesterday. Molly said he is healing quickly and will be the perfect dog for me." She smiled and warmth hummed through her body. While she could have had a dog while growing up, she'd always played with Grandfather Thunder's dogs. He'd been the best neighbor, allowing her to spend time in his yard and listening to her complaints about her mom and life in general. He'd become her surrogate grandfather. That was probably why he was so helpful in learning about the dog's owner. He knew she needed a dog.

"I'd think the best dog would be one that can sit on your lap and not eat more than you do." The frown on Quinn's forehead made her chuckle.

"Haven't you ever had a dog?" she asked. Better to turn the attention on him than her.

"I've thought about it. But I'm not home enough to give a dog a good life." He glanced up from the quiche he was pushing around with the plastic fork. "Guess I'll have to stop by once in a while and pet Mugshot."

The intensity in his eyes shook her. What was he really asking? She swallowed and said, "Yeah, I don't see why you can't stop by if you feel the need to pet Mugshot. But you need to call first to make sure I'm home." She shoved the rest of the scone in her mouth, picked up her coffee, and stood. After chewing and swallowing the sweet bread down with coffee, she said, "Let's go."

Quinn grinned, tossed his paper plate and fork in the trash, and picked up his coffee.

The next awkward thirty minutes, Dela tried to close her eyes and pretend sleep but every bump and sway of the vehicle her eyes popped open. She was wired from all the coffee and didn't know what to do. She didn't want to talk about her or him and they'd talked the case to death.

"We have another two hours to go. How about you tell me why you have a medical discharge?" Quinn's soft tone drew her gaze to him. He sat with his face pointed forward. But she could see by the white knuckles gripping the steering wheel, he wanted her to tell him.

She sighed. He'd been right when he'd mentioned he could look it all up. Better to tell him and not let him make his own assumptions.

"As you know, my team was hit by an IED. We lost two members and the rest of us came out with something missing. I was one of the lucky ones. I'm just missing half a leg." She said it sarcastically but did know how lucky she was. "Mick can't remember who he is from one day to the next. Gary lost an arm and half of his face. Amy is missing her left arm and part of a leg. Tex is paralyzed from the waist down."

Quinn's hands squeezed the steering wheel. He slowly turned his head and stared at her. "That is what I was trying to avoid when I took your prisoner. He was the person who told us when insurgents were going to attack our patrols."

"I guess saving one guilty man didn't save everyone." She snapped her mouth shut and stared forward the rest of the ride.

♠ ♣ ♥ ♦

Dela didn't see any signage that said what business was in the building they were parking under. "This is the FBI building?"

"Not really. But it is for now. All the rioters in large cities along the west coast have targeted federal buildings. To get our work done and not have to deal with them, we've moved our headquarters to unmarked buildings."

Dela stepped out of the SUV noticing there were a dozen similar vehicles in the parking area. "They don't figure it out when they see all of these vehicles?"

"We make enough of a presence at the real FBI headquarters that they don't know we've moved." He walked over to an elevator.

She followed and stepped in beside him. His allowing her to be a part of his questioning of Van and Verna was not protocol. She knew that and appreciated his letting her tag along.

The elevator stopped and the doors opened. The bustle that met her shocked Dela. The noise and bodies moving about as if their work had urgency was almost too much for her senses. It brought back getting ready for missions in the army.

Quinn took hold of her arm when she didn't move. "Come on."

She allowed him to lead her through the chaos and

over to an office.

He knocked on the door and walked in.

"Special Agent Pierce, about time you showed up. We can't keep fugitives and their family tied up in this facility for too long." The woman sitting behind the desk appeared too petite and fashionable to be an FBI agent. Her narrowed eyes betrayed the tiniest bit of a smile on her lips.

"I know. We arrived as quickly as we could." Quinn motioned to Dela. "Dela Alvaro this is HQ Supervisor Jin Prescott."

"Ms. Alvaro are you with law enforcement?" The woman's small Asian face shifted to her, while the woman's gaze scrutinized her.

"I'm Head of Security at the Spotted Pony Casino on the Confederated Tribes of the Umatilla reservation." While she wasn't considered "real" law enforcement, she had the training and the knowledge to be if not for her leg.

The woman smiled but her eyes didn't convey any warmth. "I'd like to have a word with Special Agent Pierce. In private."

Dela glanced at Quinn, he nodded toward the door. She walked over to the door and let herself out. Unsure what to do while she waited, she wandered over to a low wall/room divider and leaned against it.

"Whoa! Don't put too much weight on that or you'll end up on my desk."

Dela glanced down at the woman sitting at the desk behind the barrier. "Sorry! I'm waiting and didn't mean to interrupt."

"Hey, I'm just working on some analytics, a break now and then is good." She stood and held out her hand. "Special Agent Talia Bernstein. What division do you work in?" Her gray gaze flashed to Dela's chest where she was void of ID.

"I'm a guest here with Special Agent Pierce. We've been working a case together and two witnesses were brought in here last night." She wanted the woman to not have someone throw her out while Quinn and HQ Supervisor Prescott were arguing over whether she could stay or even watch the questioning.

At that moment, Quinn strode out of the HQ Supervisor's office and scanned the room. He zeroed in on her and walked that direction.

"Gotta go. Good meeting you," she barely managed to say before Quinn motioned for her to follow him.

"That meeting didn't go too well?" she asked, when they were striding down a hallway. She worked hard to keep up with him, given his legs were longer and they both worked normally.

"She didn't like that I brought you along. I told her I thought the young woman would confide in you better than me." He slowed down as they approached an elevator. "They're in holding two floors down."

"I'm actually going to sit in when you question the two?" This was one of her favorite parts when she was an M.P. There was nothing more exhilarating to her as getting the truth out of a person.

"You will question Verna. She's not a fugitive and other than being with Van when he was picked up, the FBI has no reason to hold her. I'll question Van, but you'll be able to watch. As I will watch you talk with Verna."

The doors opened, and they stepped out into a

reception area much like a lobby of a police station.

Quinn flashed his ID at the man behind a desk. "We're here to question Vladimer Chernoff. But first my associate would like to visit with the woman that was brought in with him."

The agent looked her up and down. "Where's her ID?"

"She's not FBI, but HQ Supervisor Prescott okayed her participation." Quinn nodded toward the phone at the man's elbow. "You can call her if you like. We'll wait."

The man stared at the phone for less than a second. "No. No sense disturbing her. The woman is in room six. When you're finished, I'll have them bring Chernoff into the interview room at the end of the hall."

Quinn nodded and walked down the hall to a room with the number six on the door.

He eased the door open. Inside, a woman sat on a chair by the door.

Verna watched them with wary eyes.

"Hi. I'm here to see if I can help everyone understand what your involvement is and to get some answers about what happened at the casino." Dela walked up to the table and took the seat across from the woman.

"Can I get you anything to drink?" Quinn asked.

"I'll take coffee. Verna, do want anything?" Dela felt for the woman. She didn't believe she had committed murder but she had been a party to the cover up.

The woman nodded. "Water please."

Quinn nodded and left the room.

Dela wished the woman at the door would leave,

but figured it was FBI rules or something.

"Verna, we found the video you took under the blackout Robin had placed on the cameras."

Sad brown eyes gazed at her across the table. "I couldn't let them get away with killing that man even if he planned to turn my father in to the FBI."

"I know. You are law-abiding. I don't understand why you didn't tell someone if you knew about it far enough beforehand to override the camera's blackout."

The young woman glanced toward the woman at the door before leaning forward and whispering. "I only heard them talking soon enough to code the camera. I didn't realize it wasn't them actually doing the killing until I saw Jeff at his table the whole time. Then I knew they were working with someone else. Afterwards, when I talked with father, he said the man who killed Tristan was blackmailing him. He wanted the money missing from the bank robbery to keep his mouth shut about who Father really was." She sat up. "Father never saw a cent of that money. He believes the other man involved in the robbery, the one who did the killing, took all of the money. Father never saw any of it. He went into hiding, knowing the cops would be looking for all of them. Without money it was harder for him to hide. He's pretty sure that the man with the money and who killed people is in another country. He has been trying to find the man to prove his innocence."

"Why did the two of you run?" Dela asked, believing the woman spoke the truth. She could see Van being pulled into a scheme to make money but she didn't see the man killing anyone.

"Father's identity had been compromised. Tristan had discovered who he was and the man who killed him also knew. And Tristan's wife. She knew. She made a comment to him when they passed on the stairs that night."

Ah-ha! Van *had* run into someone on the stairs. Someone who knew he was a fugitive.

"Can you tell me more about Jeff and Robin's part in the murder? Did they have anything to do with Mattie's murder?"

Verna shrugged. "I don't know what their part was other than blacking out the cameras. They must have had a reason to help."

It was obvious the woman didn't know the victim had been blackmailing Jeff and Robin. "If what you say is true, maybe your father can work out a deal with the FBI to help find the other men who robbed the bank." She wanted to give the woman hope. If, as she said, her father didn't kill anyone, then he would only have armed robbery charges that may or may not be dropped if they caught the man who actually killed the employees.

Verna sat up straighter. "Do you think they will believe him?"

"He can try. I'll suggest it to Special Agent Pierce. Is there anything else you can tell me that might help?"

The young woman sat back in the chair. "The only thing I can think of is Robin was more into Jeff than he was into her. She would have done anything for him."

Dela thought about that. Could Jeff have dragged Robin into the whole scheme? He'd already talked her into helping him skim money from the casino. It wouldn't have been that much of a stretch to have him ask her for a little favor. But why? Why would Paula drag Jeff into her scheme to kill her husband?

"Thank you, Verna. I'm pretty sure you are free to go, but I'll ask to make sure."

The woman picked at her hands. "It doesn't matter. As long as Father is here, I'll be here."

Dela pulled a piece of paper out of her small cross-body purse and wrote her phone number on it. "If you need anything, even just to talk, call."

"Thank you." Tears rolled down Verna's cheeks.

Dela left the room. She stood in the hall breathing deep and wondering what was going to happen to the talented woman.

Quinn joined her. "Nice job. Sincerity gets more answers than bullying."

She stared at the special agent. "There isn't any other way to talk to a person whose only crime is loving their father."

The skin of his neck and face grew redder. "You're correct. I'm sorry. Do you want to listen to my interview with Vladimer?"

"Yeah. You heard what his daughter said? He didn't kill anyone at the robbery. If you can offer him a lesser sentence, I bet he'd help you find the real killer."

"I have to run that by legal first."

She crossed her arms and stared at him.

"Ah, you mean right now before I question him."

"You would probably get better results. And let him know his daughter is fine. I'm sure he is worried about her." Dela knew if it was her mother in Van's place, she'd be more likely to cooperate if she knew her daughter was fine.

"I'll go down to legal and talk to them." He walked along the hall and found an empty room. "You wait here."

She walked through the door and faced him. "You never brought me that coffee. And I could use some lunch."

Chapter Twenty-eight

With a full belly and a cup of coffee in her hand, Dela sat at a monitor watching and listening to Quinn interview Van. The maintenance man had been shut down, until Quinn told him his daughter was free to go and he'd pulled strings to get the charges of murder dropped from his convictions if he could help them catch the man who had shot the bank employees.

After Van had told Quinn all he knew about the two men he'd helped with the bank robbery, Quinn started asking the questions they needed answered for the casino murder investigation.

"You ran into Paula Pomroy on the stairs that night, didn't you?" Quinn asked.

"I didn't know who she was until she made a comment about if I wanted to stay out of jail to keep my mouth shut." Van ran a hand over his beard. "I couldn't think of any other reason she would know I didn't want trouble with the law unless she knew my past."

"Did you see the corkscrew in the stairway?" Quinn asked.

Van nodded. "The woman shoved the door open fast and charged onto the landing like the place was on fire. She ran into me. The corkscrew dropped. I snatched it up and handed it to her. Then she made the threat. When I saw the same one in the water feature, I wondered if she was trying to frame me for her husband's death."

"You can place the corkscrew in her hands before the murder took place?" Quinn asked.

"I don't know if it was before or after."

Quinn stared at him. "Which floor were you on when she came out of the door?"

"Ten."

"Then it was after." Quinn studied him some more. "How did you pick up the corkscrew?"

"By the handle." The man's face dropped. "They're going to find my prints on there aren't they?"

"If they do, you can be ruled out as the person who found the corkscrew in the water feature but it is pretty clear, she hoped to incriminate you by tossing the weapon where she hoped it would be found by a cleaning crew."

Van ran a hand over his face. "I can't believe my bad luck. First the bank robbery and now this."

"Is there anything else you need to tell us about either Tristan or Paula Pomroy? Or perhaps Ronald Edmond?"

Dela sat in the booth. "Or Jeff Twigg." She knew Quinn couldn't hear her but she hoped he'd think to ask that question.

"Edmond said if I gave him the money from the

bank heist, he'd forget he saw me. I told him, if I had the money, I wouldn't be working as a maintenance man."

"How did he take that?" Quinn asked.

"He didn't believe me. Said I had until noon the next day to get him the money. I didn't have it and figured he'd turn me in so I told Verna she could stay here, she really liked her job, or she could be ready to head somewhere else. Then after you pulled her in again for questioning, she decided to go with me."

"This was after the murder?"

"Yeah. A couple days after." Van snapped his fingers. "The day I found the corkscrew. It was like, damn he knows I'm wanted and now I've touched something you thought was important."

Quinn looked at the camera. Dela felt as if he were searching for her to add some enlightenment. He stood. "I'll be right back."

Within a minute of exiting the room he showed up where Dela sat.

"What do you make of Edmond still being here after Paula disappeared?" Quinn asked.

"Either he killed for her and then she cut him out or he killed for her, then was planning to make a little more money and stayed behind to collect." She studied Van. "But why didn't he come back to collect?"

"That's what I'm wondering. He told us he was going back to Portland. I need to make some calls." Quinn pulled out his phone.

Dela stared at the man on the monitor. She believed he was a good man. She'd felt a good aura about him. He was running rather than hurting people.

But what about Paula, little Alfie, and Ronald?

Were they all going to live the good life in the Cayman Islands?

♠ ♣ ♥ ♦

Dela stood, wondering if she should go look for Quinn. He'd been gone over fifteen minutes and there was only so much she could do sitting in a room alone watching a man in a room alone.

Her phone buzzed. It was Travis texting to ask questions about the fence he was installing. She replied as Quinn walked in.

"Edmond is running. None of his colleagues or neighbors have heard or seen from him since he left for Pendleton last week."

"Can you stop him from leaving the country?" Dela asked, shoving her phone into her purse.

"We have his name and photo at all the places to get out of the country." He shook his head. "More information came in on the bank account in Tristan's name. It was emptied Friday morning by a man with Tristan's ID."

Dela stared at Quinn. "Then the male accomplice can't be Ronald. We know he was still in Pendelton then."

"There is one person who has been missing since we first interviewed him. And he'd been seen at the Pomroy house."

"Jeff Twigg. He is a little bigger build than Tristan, but if his photo is on all of Tristan's ID and Paula would know the answers to all the questions…" Dela growled. "Why didn't someone catch onto his stealing sooner?"

"He is good at it, and since Robin was his accomplice, I'm sure she figured out the angles to make sure the people watching the monitors didn't see her do the same thing twice to keep from being seen. You just have good eyes." He smiled at her. "Let's head back to Pendleton and see if Robin knows she's been played."

Dela followed him to the door. "Do you think Ronald figured it out and that's why he disappeared? We know he had to have killed Tristan. The video is hard to deny. When Paula ran off leaving him here, to take the fall for the murder, he had to have panicked."

"We'll catch him." Quinn poked the button to the elevator as HQ Supervisor Prescott walked down the hall.

"You can't leave. You have to write up a report about your interview with Vladimer Chernoff." The woman stopped in front of Quinn and crossed her arms. The top of her head came to his shoulder but she looked tough as a warrior.

"I can make phones calls if you need to finish up here before we head back," Dela said, showing the woman she wasn't the reason he was taking off without finishing his paperwork.

"Chernoff's interview was taped. You can hand him over to legal. They are cutting him a deal to help them capture who really killed the bank employees." Quinn stuck a hand out when the elevator doors that had opened during the conversation started to close. "Come on, Dela."

She shrugged and entered the elevator behind Quinn.

When the door shut, the noncompliant special agent blew out a breath as he rubbed a hand over his face while staring at the decreasing numbers above the door.

"It appears you and HQ Supervisor Prescott have history," Dela said, remaining behind him in the elevator.

"You could say that."

The elevator stopped and the door opened. Quinn stepped out and she followed. After all, he was her ride home.

When they were in the SUV and headed out of Seattle, Dela asked, "Do you have history with every woman who crosses your path?"

He glanced at her and grimaced. "Low blow, Alvaro."

She shrugged. Not that she was heartless but it was nice having him feeling uncomfortable rather than her. "Any chance we can grab snacks and do a non-stop back to Pendleton?"

"Sure."

Quinn pulled in line at a fast food restaurant and within fifteen minutes they were back on the road.

After they'd finished off the burgers and fries, Dela said, "We know Ronald and Paula killed Tristan. What do we do to bring them to justice?"

"I asked legal to draw up extradition papers on Paula to get her back over here to face the charges of manslaughter. I also put into action a warrant for the arrest of Ronald Edmond. The video we have is enough proof to bring charges against both of them. That and the fact Paula was seen after the murder with the corkscrew."

"Okay, that takes care of Tristan's death. What about Mattie's?"

"I'm hoping a visit with Robin Everly will reveal more about her, and Jeff's, part in the whole scheme."

He glanced over at Dela. "I asked Shaffer to keep an eye on Robin so we know where she is when we get back to Pendleton and can talk to her."

"Good idea. The people we need to talk to keep disappearing." Dela leaned her head back and replayed all that they knew through her mind. "When I talked to Verna, she didn't seem to like Robin. I wonder if Verna had caught her doing shady things?"

Quinn slipped his phone out of his pocket and handed it to her. "Look into the document Shaffer sent me on Robin. See if anything sends up a red flag."

Dela slid her finger across the screen. "I need your print to access."

She held it to him and he placed his pointer finger on the screen. The phone came to life and she entered his email and found the document.

"When you asked me about how would I know what it felt like to learn my wife was having an affair…I came home a day early from an assignment and found Jin, my wife, in bed with someone I'd respected." He didn't take his gaze off the road ahead. "It's like catching a fist the size of Hulk in your gut. You can't breathe and you want to vomit."

That was his history with the woman. And yet, she was the one who fooled around and acted like he had done her wrong.

"I see. Does it also bother you that she is farther up the ladder than you?" Dela asked, wondering if that didn't also eat at him.

"You've heard of sleeping your way to the top. The man she was in bed with made sure she moved up and I stayed down." The anger and disgust in his voice, drew her gaze to him.

The corner of his mouth tipped down, his eyes were dull, and his jaw twitched. She wasn't sure if he wanted her sympathy or scorn for the woman he'd married. They weren't really friends, just colleagues. And yet, the pain on his face and in his voice as he spoke, bonded them in a way.

"Not all women climb the ladder by bed hopping. And not all women trounce on a man's heart and ego to get what they want." That was all she had. Nothing profound or personal.

He glanced over at her. "Always one for the direct reply." The corner of his lips raised a little. "That's what I've always liked about you. A person knows where they stand with you and what you stand for."

She took that as a compliment and went back to reading the longer than she'd expected document on Robin Everly. When she finished, she pulled her phone out of her purse and dialed Kenny.

"Hey, Dela. I heard you and the special agent went on a road trip today." The mirth in his tone made her realize everyone at the casino would know and think she and Special Agent Pierce were doing more than finding a murderer.

"We were talking to potential suspects and are headed back right now." She knew that wouldn't even be heard, considering the man had his mind in the gutter. She'd been in the army long enough to know exactly how most men thought. "Do me a favor and pull up all the information Robin Everly gave HR and Marty about her credentials and past, and email them to me."

"Is she a suspect?" This had tugged his mind out of the gutter.

"An accomplice at this time. Thanks." She ended the call.

"What did you see in the documents?" Quinn asked.

"Red flags that should have prevented her from getting a job with the surveillance team. She must have lied on her resume. I want to check before we talk to her."

She leaned her head back on the head rest. "If I fall asleep, will you stay awake?"

"Take a nap. I'll be fine."

Not contemplating that he'd had about as much or less sleep than her since the first murder, she dropped off, knowing he would stay awake.

Chapter Twenty-nine

Dela stepped out of the SUV and wished she'd stayed awake and asked Quinn to stop once. Her stiff knee wouldn't straighten and her whole leg, the real and the imagined was throbbing.

Quinn stood beside the vehicle watching her. "Are you going to be okay?" He came around the front.

"I'm good. Just give me a few minutes." She swung her leg, lubricating the knee that felt like a soccer ball. "You can go on. I'll be right behind you."

He shook his head. "We need to confront her at the same time." Quinn slipped an arm around her right arm and led her away from the car, shoving the door shut. "We'll walked around the block."

She'd never walked arm and arm with a boy or a man. At least not outside of rehab. There had been a couple of male therapy assistants who had helped her just like Quinn was doing, in the first months of her learning how to balance on the prosthesis.

As her leg moved more freely, she slowly pulled away from him.

Back at the vehicle, she said, "Thanks. The knee gets stiff if I don't move it enough."

"No problem. All you have to do is tell me what you need and I'll do my best to help."

She glanced up into his eyes and there was that intense gaze she'd witnessed before. What was he trying to convey?

"Where do we find Robin." She scanned the block of houses.

"Shaffer said she was at home. Guess who she lives with?" Quinn raised an eyebrow.

"Jeff?"

"That's right. Let's see if he's been home since Wednesday." Quinn led the way up to a small house with a green roof and shutters. He knocked and they waited.

"Are you sure she's here?" Dela asked.

"Shaffer said, he saw her go in and not come out."

Dela glanced up and down the street. "He can see both the front and back doors?" She tried to cover the skepticism but it slipped out.

Quinn grinned. "He isn't doing it alone." He knocked again.

"I don't think she's here. She gave him the slip."

Quinn pulled out his phone. "Shaffer, have whoever is watching the back move in and try the door. We're not getting a result from knocking." He stayed on the phone, listening. "Copy."

He shoved the phone in his pocket and watched the street.

Shaffer approached. He handed a paper to Quinn

and opened the door with a key.

Dela stared at Quinn.

"This is a rental. Shaffer got the key from the landlord with this warrant to search the premises. It is the home of a suspect that we believe is using the victim's identity."

Shaffer turned the knob and shoved the door open. "FBI. We have a warrant to search the premises."

Dela waited until Shaffer and Quinn gave the all clear before she stepped into the building.

"You're sure you saw her come in and not go out?" Quinn was questioning the other agent.

"She didn't come out." Shaffer said, staring at the empty living room.

Dela wandered to the bedroom. It had been inhabited by both a male and a female. Their occupying the house had been as a couple. How did that make Robin feel knowing Jeff and Paula were in the Cayman Islands together?

She wandered into the kitchen and stopped. "Quinn!"

The special agent ran into the kitchen. "Yeah?"

"Look on the drain board."

Three children's size spoons and a bowl with cartoon characters were in the dish drainer.

"Did you see any other kid things?" he asked.

She shook her head. "Do you think Paula went to the Caymans and left her son here?" She hadn't thought the woman was that heartless but she did watch her husband being killed or killed him herself. They still didn't know which.

Shaffer nodded to the back door. "There's a cellar door out back."

Dela let Quinn and Shaffer lead the way. The door was unlocked. Again, they entered first and she followed behind.

Paula was tied up with a gag in her mouth. Little Alfie played in a large cardboard box beside her. There wasn't any sign of Robin.

♠ ♣ ♥ ♦

The house became full of police and EMTs. Besides Quinn and Shaffer there were city police and state police. The state police were collecting evidence, the city police talking to neighbors, and the EMTs were checking out Paula and Alfie.

As soon as the EMTs gave the all clear, Quinn motioned for Dela to take a seat in the living room chair in front of the one where Paula sat holding her son on her lap. Quinn carried in a chair from the kitchen and sat down beside Dela.

"What can you tell us about being tied up?" he asked.

Paula shook her head. "I had put Alfie in the car seat and was placing my bags in the trunk of my car when I was hit and shoved in the trunk. When I came to, this woman was calling me names and saying I'd ruined her life. I have no idea who she was."

Paula was lying. She stared at the top of her son's head not making eye contact.

"That's interesting. Because this is Jeff Twigg and Robin Everly's house." Quinn studied her.

"We happen to know that they both visited you at your home on several occasions," Dela said. She glanced at Quinn to see if she should say anything about the videos. He was studying his phone.

Paula sputtered, "I don't know what you're talking

about."

"Several of your neighbors picked out both Jeff and Robin as people they saw visiting with you. You can't deny it. As well as you can't deny you are an accessory to your husband's murder."

Paula's head snapped up and she glared at Dela. "I am not an accessory."

"Then you killed your husband." Quinn held up his phone, showing a naked Paula and Ronald in sweats coming out of the supply room. "We have the video of you and Ronald Edmond returning from that room after your husband chased you in there."

"That bitch! She was supposed to black it out. No wonder she just kept smiling at me and not saying anything when I asked why she had me tied up. When I get my hands on her."

The woman must have been squeezing her child. He began to cry and that seemed to calm her down. Between clenched teeth she said, "I'm not going down for this alone. Ronald was the one waiting for him and stabbed him in the neck."

"We're looking for him. Do you know why there was a photo of him in your home office that looked like it would go on a passport or photo ID?" Quinn asked.

"I'm not saying anything more." Paula clapped her lips together.

Quinn motioned for Dela to follow him to the door as a State Trooper put handcuffs on Paula. A state worker had arrived and took Alfie.

Dela didn't condone what the woman had done, but she sympathized for her watching as a stranger carried her son away. Paula should have thought about her son when she made the plan to kill his father.

"Where do you think Robin is?" Dela asked.

"I imagine she and Jeff had some place other than the Cayman Islands they planned to retire on the money Tristan blackmailed from them and others."

"Will you be able to find them and get them back here?" Dela didn't like anyone getting away with a crime.

"They'll be looked for but not as hard as if they killed someone. They just used information to bilk a killer out of her ill-gotten gains." Quinn continued to his vehicle. "I'll take you back to the casino and then come back and finish tying things up."

Dela climbed into the SUV. "What about Mattie?"

"I'll have to try and get Paula to say something with her lawyer present. We need to find out if she sent Edmond to kill Mattie or if Paula did it herself."

"You know, Paula never mentioned the book or blackmail. Do you think someone else quieted Mattie?" Dela twisted in her seat. "We need to ask Paula if Mattie came to her with the black book. I've been thinking about this. According to Mattie's cousin, Mattie had the book with her when she left the house. Why didn't she give it to Paula that night? I would think a woman who had just killed her husband would have had some cash stashed to help her get away. She could have paid Mattie off, had the book in hand, and then sent someone to kill Mattie and take the cash back."

Quinn nodded. "She'll be taken to the Umatilla County Jail here in Pendleton until she goes to custody of the US Marshal in Portland for Federal Indictment."

"Do you think the county will let us talk to her?" Dela asked.

"I'll be on record as one of the arresting agents. They should let me talk to her." Quinn made a U-turn. "I'll figure out a way to get you in to talk to her as well."

Chapter Thirty

By the time Dela and Quinn arrived at the Umatilla County Jail it was the swing shift. The woman officer at the lobby buzzed them back once Quinn showed his badge.

The deputy on duty was helpful after a glimpse of Quinn's badge and finding his name on the arrest record.

The deputy showed them to a room. "I'll bring her right in."

Dela was surprised the deputy never asked to see an ID from her. But she was also pleased. It made it less awkward to explain her presence.

As soon as Paula saw them, she hurried into the room. Her gaze sought Dela's. "What did you do with Alfie? Where is my son?"

"He'll be a ward of the state since you killed his father. Unless you have a family member who would take care of him," Quinn said without a bit of remorse.

Dela was glad he said it. She would have had a hard time spitting it out. The rage, fear, and sorrow on the woman's face made her look ten years older. "Paula, we need to know if Mattie Collier brought Tristan's little black book to you."

"Who is Mattie Collier?" Paula's brow furrowed.

"A young woman who worked in the laundry room. She found the little book and realized your husband was blackmailing people. She came to your house on Friday night. Witnesses saw her. What did you tell her?" Dela studied the woman's features.

Paula's eyes widened. "I don't know if anyone came to the house. That bitch Robin was watching Alfie while Jeff and I were putting his fake ID together in my office."

Dela stared at Quinn. That meant Mattie had talked to Robin. Either thinking she was Paula, or asking her to give Paula a message.

"Thank you." Dela stared at the woman. "Did you know about your husband's blackmail scheme and account in a Cayman Island bank?"

"Jeff told me about it one night at the casino. I was waiting for Tristan and sat down at Jeff's table to play cards. He took a break and motioned for me to follow him."

"How long ago was this?" Quinn asked.

"Six months, maybe more."

"What did Jeff tell you?" Dela asked.

"That Tristan had been getting lots of money out of him and others. He wanted me to find out what he did with the money and we'd split it. I couldn't find anything about it at home and figured it was here at work. Jeff said he was working on a way to get into

Tristan's work computer. Then Ronald showed up saying he'd split the bounty on a man Tristan had found. That's when I decided, I didn't want half, I wanted it all." She sniffed. "I lost my boy because I trusted Jeff. When he figured out where the money was, he said if I helped him make an ID with all of Tristan's information and his photo, he'd get the money out of the account for a hundred thousand." She cursed. "I knew if I didn't get rid of Tristan, I'd never see any of it, even with Jeff's help because he would come after us. He might have been a small man but he was vindictive as hell, and strong."

"Thank you for the truth. Keep telling the truth and you could see your son sooner rather than later." Dela studied the woman. She and Edmond had killed her husband, but she hadn't had anything to do with Mattie's death.

Quinn nodded and the deputy took Paula out of the room. They left the jail and walked outside.

Once they were in the SUV, Quinn said. "Either Robin or Jeff killed Mattie."

"We won't know until we catch one of them." Dela hoped that would happen soon. But at least she had something to tell Bernie Moon.

♠ ♣ ♥ ♦

A week after Dela and Quinn had found Paula and Alfie, Quinn stopped by the casino.

"What are you doing here?" Dela asked, as she walked out of the security office heading to the deli for a cup of coffee.

"Edmonds was found trying to cross into Canada. He'll stand trial with Paula for Tristan's murder. And we have Robin and Jeff in custody."

She spun toward Quinn. His hands on her arms stopped her forward momentum.

"Thanks. I'm glad Ronald was caught. Can't have a bounty hunter getting away with murder." Her cheeks heated as his hands remained on her arms. "Which one killed Mattie? Jeff or Robin?"

"Jeff. Robin told him about Mattie having the book. He went to find the book, taking a corkscrew from their house, knowing it was the weapon Paula had used on her husband. Mattie was home, refused to give him the book and he killed her. Hoping it would be pinned on Paula. He had no plans of sharing anything with her. Or Robin for that matter. Once she learned that, she called the local police and told them everything."

Dela eased out of his grasped. "Hell hath no fury like a woman scorned."

"Will you ever forgive me for taking your prisoner?" Quinn asked in a quiet voice.

She headed to the deli. "Stop by my place at six tonight to visit Mugshot and I'll see if I can conjure up some forgiveness."

Quinn stood in the middle of the casino staring as she smiled and walked over to the deli.

"That handsome special agent is standing by the water feature looking like he's catching flies," Rosie said, when Dela walked up to the counter.

"He'd never do well in a poker game, he can't hide his emotions."

Thank you for reading book one in my new Spotted Pony Casino Mystery series. If you want to know more about how Dela was promoted to Head of Security, check out *Stolen Butterfly*, book 7 in the Gabriel Hawke Novels. Proceeds from the sale of that book go towards the MMIW (Missing and Murdered Indigenous Women) movement.

Dela's next book is titled, *House Edge*, look for that toward the end of the year to see how she and Mugshot are getting along, and if Special Agent Quinn Pierce will be involved.

Paty

About the Author

Paty Jager grew up in Wallowa County in NE Oregon and has always been amazed by its beauty, history, and ruralness. She has always had an interest in the Indigenous people and their culture and enjoys learning more every time she writes a book.

Paty is an award-winning author of 51 novels of murder mystery and western romance. All her work has Western or Native American elements in them along with hints of humor and engaging characters. She and her husband raise alfalfa hay in rural eastern Oregon. Riding horses and battling rattlesnakes, she not only writes the western lifestyle, she lives it.

By following her at one of these places you will always know when the next book is releasing and if she is having any giveaways:

Website: http://www.patyjager.net
Blog: https://writingintothesunset.net/
FB Page: https://www.facebook.com/PatyJagerAuthor/
Pinterest: https://www.pinterest.com/patyjag/
Twitter: https://twitter.com/patyjag
Goodreads:
http://www.goodreads.com/author/show/1005334.Paty_
Jager
Newsletter- Mystery: https://bit.ly/2IhmWcm
Bookbub - https://www.bookbub.com/authors/paty-
jager

Thank you for purchasing this Windtree Press
publication. For other books of the heart, please visit
our website at www.windtreepress.com.

For questions or more information contact us
at info@windtreepress.com.

Windtree Press
www.windtreepress.com